The Lady and the Tiger

by Sam Starbuck

The text of this book is set in Garamond.

This novel is the twelfth volume published by
Extribulum Independent Press
extribulum.wordpress.com
Printer's Row, Chicago, IL

Nameless – 2009
Other People Can Smell You – 2009, Revised 2010
Charitable Getting – 2010
Dr. King's Lucky Book – 2011
Trace – 2011
By The Days – 2011
The Dead Isle – 2012
Six Harvests in Lea, Texas – 2020
The Found Fortune Deck – 2022
Fête for a King – 2022
Infinite Jes – 2022
The Lady and the Tiger – 2022

ISBN 979-8-9859604-4-0

This book contains some material which may be triggering or upsetting, although generally brief. For a full list of content warnings and spoilers, please turn to the last page of the book.

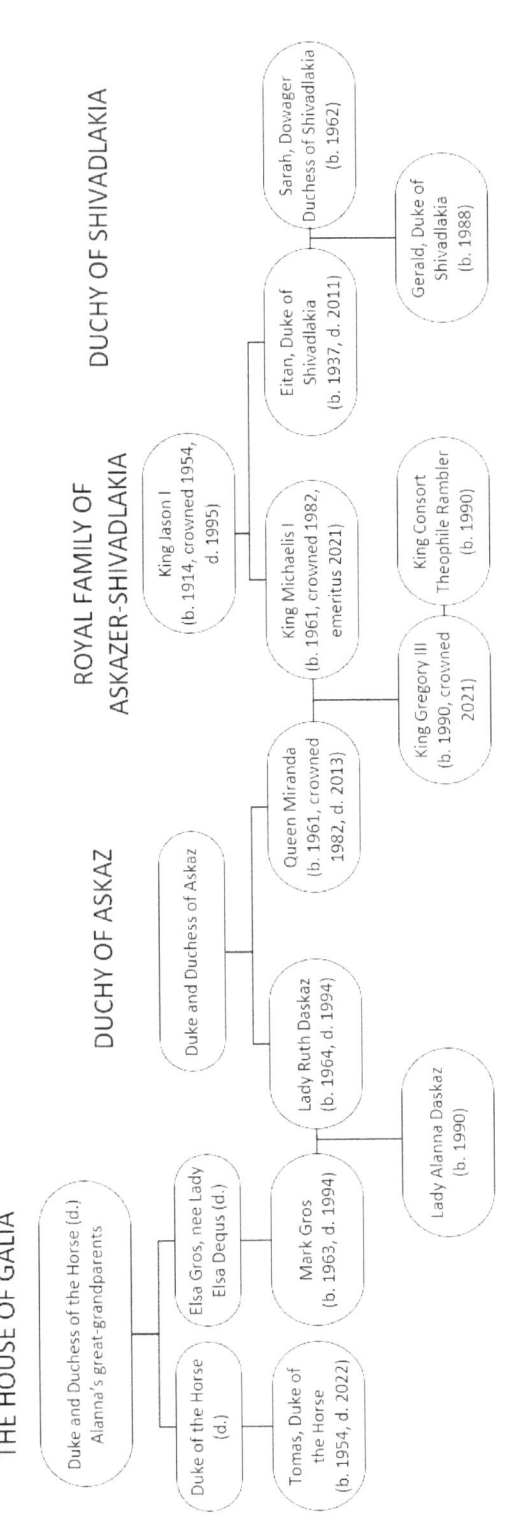

DUCHY OF THE HORSE OF THE HOUSE OF GALIA

Duke and Duchess of the Horse (d.)
Alanna's great-grandparents

Duke of the Horse (d.)

Elsa Gros, nee Lady Elsa Dequs (d.)

Tomas, Duke of the Horse (b. 1954, d. 2022)

Mark Gros (b. 1963, d. 1994)

DUCHY OF ASKAZ

Duke and Duchess of Askaz

Lady Ruth Daskaz (b. 1964, d. 1994)

Lady Alanna Daskaz (b. 1990)

Queen Miranda (b. 1961, crowned 1982, d. 2013)

ROYAL FAMILY OF ASKAZER-SHIVADLAKIA

King Jason I (b. 1914, crowned 1954, d. 1995)

King Michaelis I (b. 1961, crowned 1982, emeritus 2021)

King Consort Theophile Rambler (b. 1990)

King Gregory III (b. 1990, crowned 2021)

DUCHY OF SHIVADLAKIA

Sarah, Dowager Duchess of Shivadlakia (b. 1962)

Eitan, Duke of Shivadlakia (b. 1937, d. 2011)

Gerald, Duke of Shivadlakia (b. 1988)

CHAPTER ONE

LADY ALANNA DASKAZ – Al to her friends and colleagues, the Lady Alanna on the rare occasions she made it into the press – often thought that palace breakfast was the highlight of her day. She loved her work, of course, serving as right hand and head of Royal Operations for the king; sometimes she even worked during breakfast. But just the act of being in the royal dining room was a pleasure.

When she was a child, her mother brought her to palace breakfast several times a week, mainly because Lady Ruth loved to visit with her sister Miranda, the queen of Askazer-Shivadlakia. Alanna had made friends with her cousin Gregory, now the king, while sitting under the dining table and earnestly discussing dinosaurs.

She and Gregory were sometimes mistakenly labeled in foreign press as siblings, even as adults. They both favored their mothers, the Askaz side of the family, slightly built with olive skin and dark hair, though Gregory's was curlier, more like his father's, and Alanna's hair lightened to a pale brown as she grew older.

After her parents passed, her grandmother still brought her at least once a week, often leaving her there for the day for Aunt Miranda and King Michaelis to look after. Once she was old enough she'd traipse down to the palace on her own, to make mischief with Gregory and his cousin Gerald. Most often, they eavesdropped on Michaelis's meetings with important ministers of Parliament. In hindsight, he had probably known and allowed it, as much to train them early in palace business as because he was indulgent of his only son, his wife's niece, and his brother's rambunctious boy.

As an adult, working in the palace after Gregory's election to king, Alanna found breakfast a useful time to bring things to Gregory's attention, get the occasional opinion from Michaelis, and tweak Jerry, who had never left the mischief-making phase. Saturday brunch at the palace was less useful, since business was largely banned from the table, but it was by far the best breakfast of the week.

It was particularly boisterous that Saturday morning. Michaelis's partner Jes and Jes's teenage son Noah had come to breakfast, and Noah's curiosity about pretty much everything in the world meant that his primary source of entertainment, Gregory's fiancé Eddie, was excitedly explaining something to him. Jes, who never met an opinion they weren't prepared to express in strong terms, was bickering with Gregory about taxes. Jerry, who used to show up to Saturday brunch hungover and occasionally still drunk, looked like he'd had a full night of sleep, hazel eyes sharp as he contentedly grazed on fruit and cracked jokes. And there was Michaelis, presiding over the table as patriarch, offering commentary on every conversation regardless of his previous participation in it.

Nobody else paid any mind when her phone beeped softly, but Alanna looked down at it immediately. She got enough notifications throughout the day that she'd taken to setting the Do Not Disturb function to run all weekend long. Notifications that got through her complex Do Not Disturb filter were few and far between – it usually meant either her grandparents or someone important on the palace staff was trying to get in touch.

This time, it was the palace communications team; the on-call public relations officer had messaged her. She opened the text curiously.

Sorry to interrupt your Saturday, but I thought you'd want to see this sooner rather than later, the message read, attached to a news service link. When she saw the headline, she said, "Gregory?" with enough alarm in her voice that even Eddie fell silent.

"Something wrong, Al?" Gregory asked, following her gaze to her phone screen.

"The Duke of the Horse of the House of Galia is dead," she said. "News is just getting out now. Looks like he passed late last night from a stroke."

"Good fucking riddance," Michaelis said, and every head immediately turned from Alanna to him. "Pardon my language," he added, a little sheepishly.

"I don't know who the Duke of the House Horse is but it sounds like you have something to share," Eddie said to Michaelis.

"Isn't that the fellow…?" Gregory asked, and Michaelis nodded. "Well. Good riddance indeed. Can I see?" he asked Alanna, who passed her phone to him.

"Who is he?" Noah asked, looking amongst the adults in the room.

"He's the king of Galia, functionally," Jes said. "They haven't had an actual king in what, a couple of centuries?" they asked Michaelis.

"Something like that. The royal line died out, so whoever was Duke of the Horse at that point took over. Probably because he had command of the biggest portion of their military – the 'horse' in the title refers to the cavalry forces the dukes led, back when they kept a standing army. Throne's been in the ducal family line since. The current duke had no children, either, which means the throne may go vacant. If I were you, Gregory, I'd invade," Michaelis said with a grin.

"Mm, don't know what I'd do with Galia," Gregory said absently, scrolling through the story. "But of course we will extend our deepest condolences and offer any aid we can provide in this time of uncertainty."

"I'll get people started on the draft letter to their government and a press release," Alanna said, taking her phone back from Gregory and adding it to her previously blank to-do list for the day.

"Don't let it interrupt your meal, at least," Gregory said.

"Indeed, Alanna. I doubt anyone else is mourning him very deeply," Michaelis added.

"Relatively young, though," Gregory continued thoughtfully. "He was only a few years older than you, Dad."

"He's not family, is he?" Jerry asked, brow furrowing. "Don't we traditionally just…not deal with Galia?"

"Not family, no," Michaelis said. "Well, I should say, not on the royal side. Possibly distantly through your mother, Gerald. Have to look that up, but most of the old nobility around here are related somehow."

"Who is this dude anyway, beyond the whole House Horse thing?" Eddie asked.

"I am loving that you're just calling him the House Horse guy," Jerry said.

"The Duke of the Horse of the House of Galia," Michaelis said, with a sharp look at them both, "is, or rather was, named Tomas, and if you don't want to speak ill of the dead there's really nothing to be said about him at all."

"Babe, you're a historian. You love speaking ill of the dead. It's literally your second career," Jes said.

"They've got you there, Dad," Gregory said. "Besides, it's not like you spoke well of him while he was alive. We've technically been in a cold war with Galia since Dad punched him in the face before I was born," he told Eddie.

"You did *what*," Eddie said gleefully.

"You have a cold war?" Noah asked, face lighting up. "Do you have spies?"

"It's not a cold war, and there are no spies," Michaelis declared. "We have had what the newspapers refer to as 'frosty diplomatic relations' since my last state visit to Galia, which was before most of you were born. It's not public knowledge that I assaulted a fellow head of state, Noah, so that is not to go beyond this room. If I'd known Gregory was going to announce it at brunch, I wouldn't even have briefed him on it."

"Yes, I announced it to my father who did it, his partner, their child, two of my closest advisors, and my future husband. Clearly I'm a menace to national security," Gregory replied tartly.

"Okay, but can I at least know why?" Noah persisted. Gregory just looked at Michaelis, who scowled and made a gesture of surrender.

"First, I didn't like how he spoke to my wife, and neither did she," Michaelis said. "On the rare occasions we visited, we had to arrange to bring only male staff, and make sure one of them always escorted Miranda if I couldn't be there. That was irritating, but not enough to warrant a diplomatic incident." He paused, considering, and then added, "I'm also going to preface this by saying that I was very young — younger than you are now, Gregory — and while it is an extenuating circumstance, it's no excuse for either one of us."

"Just tell the story. I promise not to use you as precedent," Gregory replied.

"I think the Duke of the Horse had some misguided image of me and he was trying to befriend that image rather than actually interact with me. We were having drinks in a very small party, and he was playing what in retrospect was a peculiar game of masculine one-upmanship," Michaelis said. "Started with talk of sport and hunting, which I didn't mind at all, but then he steered it towards women in a way I did not like. When I didn't play along, he thought I would perhaps appreciate his low opinion on Shivadh attitudes towards sexuality, and Shivadh culture more generally."

"Oh," Noah said, and then echoed Michaelis and Gregory. "Good riddance."

"Indeed. In any case, between what he'd already said and his mounting criticism of my country, I unfortunately escalated to violence at a certain point, and the next morning we were politely escorted to the border by his personal guard."

"Officers of the House Horse," Eddie said sagely.

"Guard of the Horse," Michaelis corrected.

"Is it really," Eddie replied, amused.

"Duke Tomas didn't want to admit he'd been sucker-punched by a fellow royal, and I certainly didn't want my poor behavior getting out, so nobody said anything about it at the time, or thereafter. And that's the last we spoke. About thirty-two, thirty-three years ago now," Michaelis said. "Except for the occasional back-door diplomacy lower down in the administration, but even then."

"There were a few Galian diplomats at the coronation," Gregory said. "Officially-unofficial. Nobody from the administration directly."

"It hasn't generally mattered," Michaelis continued. "Galia hasn't really got anything we want other than money, which we have enough of, and they don't want to spend their money on what we have to offer, other than the prodigious amount of seafood that Galian restaurants buy from the fishing fleet. So it hasn't been a huge loss on either side. I wonder who takes over if the seat is fully vacant," he added. "They might even decide to try democracy."

Gregory's phone interrupted with a ring, and both he and Alanna looked at it. Much like her notifications, his phone had a lot of filters to get through. He checked the caller ID, raised his eyebrows, and answered.

"Gregory ben Michaelis," he said, and then smiled. "Milo, hi. I saw your name come up but I didn't know if it was actually going to be you. I understand condolences are in order. Ah…yes, I can see how that would be the case. My father certainly has strong emotions he wishes to convey," he added. Michaelis looked extremely curious. "No, it's no bother, I'm just at brunch." There was a longer pause, and then he said, "I see. Give me one moment, would you?"

He took his phone from his ear and muted the microphone. "Galia wants to send a diplomatic team to the palace. Today. They'd be here by evening."

"They're going to make you king of Galia!" Jerry said. "Askazer-Shivadh-Galia, here we come!"

"No problem," Alanna said, giving Jerry a quelling look. "Get the number of people coming and ETA and I'll make sure the palace is ready. I can probably get some of our law team back in the office for tomorrow if need be."

Gregory nodded at her and unmuted the phone; she began to take notes as he repeated details to her. "Thanks, Milo, just had to check with my staff. When would they be arriving? Early evening, okay. How many? Including staff. Five, got it. Oh, it'll be nice to see you."

Alanna raised her eyebrows, intrigued.

"You might as well stay through Monday if you can. Yes, of course," Gregory continued. "Listen, between you and me and the satellites, do you have any idea what this is about? I mean, reopening diplomatic relations, political upheaval…succession. Say no more. If you need anything, the same number will get you through. Okay. Ciao."

He ended the call and set the phone down.

"You seem on very good terms with whoever that was in Galia," Michaelis observed.

"Yes – fortunate, but entirely by coincidence. He was at school with us. Did you know Milo Ansevali is the Secretary of the Duchy of Galia now?" he asked Alanna.

Alanna tried to place the name and came up with only a vague sense of familiarity. "I'm not sure I know who he is," she said.

"You remember Milo. He was a year below us, but in our classes half the time," Gregory said.

"The little guy, right?" Jerry asked. "Wasn't in any of my classes, but he was on the rifle team, I remember him."

"I have zero memory of this," Alanna said.

"I suppose you might not have noticed him. He was quiet, and you were in the girls' dorm. Anyway, he's done all right for himself. He's going to be here this evening to discuss succession. Which does in fact sound like they might ask me to take the throne," Gregory said, looking worried by this. "I do not love the idea of ruling Galia."

"Can't recommend it," Michaelis agreed. "A leader ought to be elected, even if he is king. Basis of our whole system of government."

"I'm going to go ahead and scratch that formal letter of condolence off my list and add about fifteen items pertaining to figuring out how to gracefully refuse a throne," Alanna said, making a list of people she needed to send carefully non-panicked texts to.

"If he doesn't want it, I'll take it," Jerry said.

"You'd be better than the old duke was," Michaelis said. "Alanna, you may wish to include that as a genuine option in your various contingency plans."

"Putting Jerry at the head of a country?" Gregory asked thoughtfully.

"I've lived my whole life preparing to become a puppet governor," Jerry announced.

Jes put their arm around Noah's shoulders. "I need you to understand," they told him, "that you're seeing history being made in this room right now, and 99% of all history is exactly as absurd-sounding in real time as this conversation is."

"I know I said this shouldn't interrupt brunch, Al, but I think it's now going to have to interrupt brunch," Gregory told her, and Alanna nodded. "What do you need from me?"

"Carte blanche on the entertainment budget and permission to forge your signature?" Alanna said.

"Granted."

"Overtime on staff? Five people means guest suites need to be aired out and prepped, and I'm going to have to bribe Simon not to take his usual day off tomorrow."

"Yes – and get some personal staff on standby in case anyone's fancy enough to need a valet," Gregory said.

"Got it. I should get to my office. I'll let you know when things are in motion," Alanna said, standing. "Anything else?"

"Yes," Gregory said. "This is a formal apology for your ruined

Saturday and a promise to make it up to you."

Alanna smiled at him. "I'll slip a few trinkets for myself into the entertainment budget. You'll never know."

"You are my favorite embezzler," he told her. "Okay. Go on."

"I'm going to have a word with Simon about the food," Eddie said, rising to follow her out. "Everyone else, listen sharp. I want all other gossip involving His Grace punching people."

"You punch one duke, one time," Michaelis grumbled as they left. Eddie caught up to Alanna in the hallway and bumped her with his shoulder affectionately.

"Hey, leave the kitchen stuff to me. Staff, food, begging Simon to come in on his day off, I got that part covered," he said.

"You don't have to, Eddie. It's not in your job description."

"Not in the palace communications sense, but in the King Consort sense – this is stuff the spouse of the king would handle, right?"

"I suppose. In a weird, archaic, gendered way," Alanna said.

"And it'd help you, and I know what I'm doing, so let me handle it. Gotta learn this trade sometime. Also, if this Duke Tomas is any indication and Galia is full of homophobes, then when they show up to a reception catered by the king's boyfriend, it'll be just..." He made a chef's kiss.

"Eddie, I'm not only saying this because Gregory loves you," Alanna said, stopping in front of the kitchen doorway. "You should be proud of yourself, because you've just demonstrated a truly Shivadh fucked-up sense of humor."

"I take it as a great compliment," Eddie said. "Okay, this is my stop. Message me if you think of anything I should cover. Simon!" he called, walking into the kitchen. "I'm gonna give you five minutes of all the swearing your heart can handle and then we have places to be. Get ready for some really stupid news!"

Alanna laughed as she headed for her office, a small and cozy room across the hall from Gregory's. Her phone beeped again, a message from Jerry; it was captioned *Milo's the one in the headlock* and featured a grainy pixelated photograph, clearly taken by an early digital camera, probably pulled off someone's social media.

The boys were all in the uniform of Institut Alpin, the boarding school she, Gregory, and Jerry had attended; most of them looked to be thirteen or fourteen. She could pick out Gregory in the middle, and two boys she recognized vaguely on his right. On his left, Jerry – already a head taller than everyone else in the picture, with the same broad shoulders and sharp angular features as his father, Michaelis's brother Eitan – was beaming at the camera. Jerry had a small sandy-haired boy in a loose, affectionate headlock; the younger boy looked thrilled to be there, a huge grin on his face, green eyes alight with laughter.

Looking at the photo, she thought she remembered him in the back of a math or a history class, but she'd never really paid much attention to most of the boys at Institut Alpin until her last few years at school. And then she'd really only paid attention to the tall ones (well, hormones were shallow). By the time Milo was old enough to interest her she'd probably been working through her crush on Jerry, actually.

Am I a bad person that I still don't remember him? she texted back.

Society will judge you, I cannot, Jerry replied. *Want me to bring you lunch when you inevitably forget to eat?*

Snack around two would be great, she replied.

I attend! Jerry said. *I'll see if I can remember any tall tales from school days in the meantime.*

It was probably to Gregory's credit that calling the staff back in on a Saturday went pretty smoothly. Most of them understood that emergencies sometimes happened and seemed fine with a few hours of overtime, especially paid and catered overtime. By late afternoon, all of the rooms were prepared, Simon had stopped swearing, and the weekend PR officer had a series of templates ready for whatever Galia might get up to while visiting Askazer-Shivadlakia semi-officially for the first time in decades. Michaelis had made himself tactfully scarce but told Alanna he'd keep his phone nearby. Helpfully, Milo had sent them a guest list, so they weren't wholly unprepared.

Milo Ansevali, secretary of the duchy, was not a member of the peerage but must have been well-connected to have been educated at Institut Alpin; he was now in charge of general staff operations under the Duke of the Horse, a high office for a relatively young man. But then, Alanna supposed, he was more or less her counterpart, doing a job that was demanding but not particularly overwhelming, and he seemed well-qualified.

His older sister, Ofelia Ansevali, was also in the delegation. She was a lawyer somewhere in the diplomatic office, and she was bringing two assistants, one a paralegal. Alanna wasn't sure how much legal business they were going to be doing, but Galia was certainly coming prepared. The notes Gregory sent along said she'd been educated in Galia, so at least Alanna wouldn't be expected to remember her as well. The image palace comms had found of her showed the same striking green eyes and sandy blonde hair as Milo's, but with a solemnity Milo's photos didn't have.

The last member of the party was the royal historian, Bruno Sheff, and Alanna knew enough history to recognize Sheff as a Galian corruption of Shivadh – probably the descendant of someone who'd moved across the highlands back in the day and taken up residence in Galia. He'd only been in the job two years, and the shine hadn't yet worn off his doctorate, which he'd earned from a prestigious university in Italy. His faculty photo from his teaching days showed a square-jawed man with an unkempt shock of black hair and eyes almost as dark.

By evening, they were as ready as they were going to be, and Gregory had gone out to wait in the reception yard of the Shivadh palace, where the kings traditionally met incoming guests. Alanna and Jerry had settled into an upper window overlooking the yard, which they'd used for spying since they were children, so they had a fantastic view when the Galians arrived.

"Mm, handshakes all round and Italian cheek-kisses for Gregory from both Ansevalis. If they are homophobes they're doing a good job of hiding it," Jerry said, watching Gregory greet Milo with a smile.

"I don't think it's out of the question that an entirely new generation might be a little more liberal in their thinking than the duke was thirty years ago," Alanna said. "Also, I thought you said Ansevali was a little guy. He's as tall as Eddie."

"Haven't seen the man since school, Alanna. You didn't remember him at all," Jerry reminded her.

"Gonna remember him now. Very cute," Alanna pronounced.

"I am offended and delighted that you are rating the hotness of the guy who's probably about to offer Gregory a kingdom," Jerry said.

"Whenever I delight you I know I've done something worrying," she told him, watching the Ansevalis, Bruno Sheff, and the support staff follow Gregory inside. She caught Gregory glancing up at them briefly, well aware they were spying. So did Milo, who followed Gregory's look and met her eyes for a split second. His eyebrows raised; she didn't even have time to duck back before he looked away and stepped inside.

"Oooh, spotted by the cutie," Jerry said. Alanna crossed the hallway to the staircase, where she'd be able to hear them from above as they passed through.

"...dinner ready soon if you're hungry, or we can hold dinner if you'd like to settle into your rooms first," Gregory was saying, voice echoing upwards.

"A quick refresh, perhaps," someone replied, with a light Italian accent. A woman's voice, so probably Ofelia Ansevali. "Half an hour or so should suffice."

"Staff will show you to your rooms. I'll have them check in to bring you to the dining room when you're ready," Gregory said.

"Thank you. Will your family be joining us for dinner?"

"My father has an unfortunate prior engagement," Gregory lied. Alanna supposed Michaelis probably did consider "toasting the duke's death over a cookout dinner at the fishing lodge" a prior engagement. "The Lady Alanna Daskaz and Gerald, Duke of Shivadlakia, will be joining us – Milo, you remember them from school?"

"Certainly. A pleasure to see them again."

"And my fiancé, of course, Eddie Rambler," Gregory added.

"Ah, I'm glad to hear it!" said another voice.

"Bruno's a fan," Milo said. "I'm sure we'll be delighted."

"I'll see you for dinner, in that case. This is where I leave you; if you need anything, staff will be nearby."

Gregory came bounding up the stairs as if he had someplace to be, quietly skidding to a stop at the top in front of Jerry and Alanna. All three listened for the fading footsteps of the envoy below.

"Milo saw us spying," Jerry said. "Also, Alanna thinks he's hot."

"I said cute, not hot," Alanna replied.

"I'm going to allow us to consider him hot," Gregory said.

"Sister's very attractive too, speaking as the only one who'd appreciate that here," Jerry added.

"Much as I'd love to continue this conversation, it's not the most relevant, and I'm on a schedule," Gregory said. "Eddie's dressing for dinner. We'll be in the dining room pretty much from now until whenever they show up. Do you want to be there early before our guests show up, or fashionably late?"

"Early," Alanna said, at the same time Jerry said, "Late."

"Perfect," Gregory said with a grin. "Do either of you need outfit approval?"

"I'm good," Jerry said. "I promise nothing too loud."

"I'll be in the usual Lady Daskaz getup," Alanna sighed. "Conservative jewel-tone sheath dress number eighty, here I come."

"Love you in pearls," Gregory told her, kissing her cheek. He kissed Jerry's too and then headed off towards his apartments, presumably to fetch Eddie.

"Feels like old times," Jerry said, as they strolled in the other direction, towards the little suite they sometimes used as a dressing room before state events. "Getting up to trouble with you and Greg. If this is going to be our life all the time, now that he's king, I can't say I mind."

"Do you honestly think they're going to offer him Galia?" Alanna asked.

"I don't know if I'd bet on it, but you heard Gregory say it, they're here to talk succession. If they aren't here for him, then they clearly need some kind of advice or guidance. They might be here to ask him to help them install a democratic monarchy, like old Gregory II did for Askazer-Shivadlakia."

"Best possible outcome, I suppose, but kind of a big ask to make us do all the work," Alanna said.

"If you were asked to organize an election, would you?" Jerry asked.

"Not while I'm also about to start planning Gregory and Eddie's wedding, not to mention someone's got to keep you in line," Alanna replied. "Why?"

"Dunno, I think it would be kind of fun. Putting everything in order, setting up voting districts, polling places, all that," Jerry said. "Lots of moving parts, though."

Alanna ruffled his hair. "I'm sure you could do it, but you should probably be grateful nobody's ever going to ask. Seems stressful."

"Story of my life," he told her with a sunny grin. "Failing to live up to potential is a career, not a hobby."

There was definitely something unusual going on at dinner, Gregory decided, but he was having trouble determining what it was.

Milo seemed composed, but there was something slightly off in his manner. Bruno, the historian, was clearly there to follow the Ansevalis' lead, but seemed perplexed by something as well. The support staff, Ofelia told Gregory, preferred to dine in their rooms to allow the royal dinner to be a little more intimate; that wasn't unusual, and wasn't what was raising Gregory's red flags, but something was. Ofelia herself was difficult to read, but perhaps that was normal for her.

Eddie was his usual charming, enthusiastic self, and Jerry was matching Eddie's energy. Alanna had her Lady Daskaz face on, welcoming Milo as if she hadn't forgotten his existence and making small talk with Ofelia over dinner while Bruno peppered Eddie with questions about cooking and Gregory with questions about local politics. Nobody brought up the multiple elephants in the room: Galia's poor relationship with Askazer-Shivadlakia, the death of the duke, or the reason they were there. At least, not until coffee was served.

"I was wondering," Milo said, after the waitstaff had poured the coffee and left, "if you've considered what the death of Duke Tomas will mean politically for the country."

"I think it's safe to assume that I've been considering it all day," Gregory said. "Who's currently holding the reins?"

"The senior advisory council, on an ad-hoc basis," Ofelia said. "But the consiglieres aren't empowered to do much without the approval of the ducal office."

"Which is why we need to move swiftly," Milo added.

"I'm not going to lie," Gregory said, "I'm interested in who you mean by 'we,' and what swift movements you have in mind."

"Well — to install the new head of state," Milo said, eyebrows rising as if he was surprised by this. "That's why we're here. We've brought the formal paperwork, of course, although that can all be dealt with later – "

"You're not thinking of me on the throne of Galia, are you?" Gregory asked.

Milo and Ofelia exchanged a look.

"Ah. Were you…not aware?" Bruno asked.

"Aware of what?"

"His Grace died without issue, and has no siblings, but his cousin married into the Shivadh nobility," Bruno said. "His nearest heir is one of your people. We assumed you knew…"

"Oh, no," Alanna said, putting her cup down sharply enough that coffee splashed into the saucer.

"Alanna?" Gregory asked.

"I didn't even think of it," she said. "Oh, no, this is – they're not here for you, Greg."

Gregory stared at her. "What?"

Jerry was doing something mentally, one hand hovering in the air, moving up and down as if in an imaginary family tree.

"Father's…sister's…son," he said absently, then looked at Bruno. "Right? The duke's paternal aunt moved across the highlands and her son married into the duchy of Askaz. He'd be Alanna's dad. But he died years ago, so…"

"The Lady Daskaz is the next in line to the duchy of Galia," Ofelia said. "Technically, even now, you are the Duchess of the Horse of the House of Galia, whether you knew it or not," she said to Alanna.

Gregory could see Jerry and Eddie's eyes lock; he knew they were both thinking it. *Duchess of the House Horse*, he thought, panickedly trying not to laugh as all three of them struggled, for Alanna's sake, not to say it out loud.

"We had come prepared to discuss what needed to be done to invest Her Grace on the throne of Galia, but I can see we miscalculated," Ofelia said. Alanna still hadn't spoken.

"This must be a shock," Milo added gently.

"Alanna, you're going to be a queen," Eddie stage-whispered to her. "Are we freaking out good or freaking out bad?"

"Uh…" Alanna looked from Gregory to Milo to Jerry, which seemed to galvanize him.

"I think you're right," Jerry said, standing up. "This is a little shocking. To Gregory, too. I think he was expecting to have to graciously decline," he said, and Gregory saw his look – *sorry to humiliate you, please play along.*

"I have to admit that was part of it," he said. "And the political ramifications of having a meeting with Galia after such a long estrangement were also top of mind, rather than the genealogy of it."

"Obviously Alanna's going to have to confirm this with her people, and speak to our legal team," Jerry continued. Gregory resolved to forgive Jerry all past and future transgressions if he got Alanna out of this somehow. "I think we had probably better stop there until we're on more even footing."

"Agreed," Ofelia said, smiling at Jerry. "And we wouldn't mind an early evening-in after traveling, would we, Milo? Bruno?"

Both men took their cue, rising when Ofelia did; Gregory saw them to the door, where staff would escort them back to their rooms.

Once they were gone he turned around to find Alanna standing up as well, leaning into a bewildered-looking Eddie for a hug. He was hugging back, but clearly didn't know why. It was true that in any given group of people, Eddie was probably the best person to get a hug from.

"Are they gone?" Alanna asked.

"At least for tonight," Gregory said.

"Shit, shit, shit," she said, leaning away from Eddie and dropping back into her chair.

"She seems less than thrilled," Eddie said to Gregory.

"I'd definitely be in shock," Jerry said.

"Both of you, please be quiet for a minute," Gregory told them, before crouching in front of Alanna, taking her hands in his. "Hey, Al. This is going to be really complicated and weird, but I promise I am not going to throw you to the wolves. There is nothing this fixes that can't be left broken. You understand?"

She gave him a weak smile.

"What does this fix, exactly? Why is her becoming queen attached to you betraying her?" Eddie asked. "Gregory, please, I'm a clueless American."

"There is nothing that would be better for Askazer-Shivadlakia, in terms of our relationship with Galia, than a Shivadh noble on their throne," Gregory said. "A Shivadh noble who isn't the king but has a strong relationship with him, training for governance, and no spouse. It's basically bloodless conquest. I secure familial ties to the Duchess of the Horse – "

"The House Horse," Jerry blurted, clearly unable to keep it in any longer.

Alanna's face crumpled for a half second and then she burst out laughing, which was such a relief that Gregory started to laugh too.

"I saw you think it," she said, her voice high and thin. "When Ofelia said 'duchess of the horse' I saw you BOTH think it and then I saw *Gregory* see you think it."

"House Horse," Gregory repeated helplessly, still crouching, leaning his forehead on Alanna's knee.

"Okay, I'm sorry," Jerry said, still laughing. "Gregory, please, Eddie is a clueless American."

"If Alanna takes the throne, her children would still be considered Shivadh by our standards, but if she marries a Galian, then the child is acceptable to Galia as future heir. Even without kids, we become favored trading partners and close family combined, very suddenly. If she has a child, we have *influence*," Gregory finished. "That's what Alanna could achieve for us. However," he added, giving Alanna a stern look, "it also means Alanna has to quit her job, accept the throne, move to Galia, marry whatever Galian noble is least offensive, and have a baby. I'm not going to make her do any of that when Galia hasn't really got anything we want and she doesn't even want to be Duchess Askaz here in her home country."

"So there are all these shiny, great things that could happen, but only if the rest of Alanna's life sucks," Eddie said.

"Yes and no," Gregory said. "Yes, in theory, but no, because I'm not going to let that happen. All three of us are going to back whatever Alanna decides, unconditionally, regardless of the politics of it. And nothing needs to get decided tonight. Jerry?" he asked.

"I stand and wait," Jerry said, squaring his shoulders.

"Whatever else happens between now and tomorrow morning, I want you in the dining room at eight to meet with the Ansevalis. Your job is to make sure they're kept entertained."

"This is why he made me Grand Vizier," Jerry said to Eddie, taking his phone out. "Setting my alarm. I'll put some contingencies in place. Al, you want me to take you home?"

"No, I uh…I'll stay at the palace tonight," she said. Gregory stood up, offering her a hand to help her out of the chair.

"Okay, then I'm heading out." Jerry kissed her cheek. "Call if you need anything. I mean it."

"Thanks," she said. "Greg, can you walk me to my room?"

Gregory gave Eddie an apologetic look, but Eddie waved it off. He probably knew Alanna needed a moment to decompress.

"I'll see you upstairs," Eddie said. "Al – "

"If I need anything, I know," she said with a small smile. Eddie gave her finger-guns as he left.

"It's a little like having three big brothers with you guys sometimes," she said.

"We all mean well. Come on," Gregory replied, leading her out into the hallway, heading for the old nursery, which had been turned into a room for Alanna to sleep over in as a child. The bed was narrow and the bedroom itself still had a decidedly "little girl's princess room" cast to it, but Alanna had never seemed to want to change it.

"Someone's going to have to tell Nonna and Grandfather," Alanna said. "And Michaelis should probably know."

"Only if you want to. Our grandparents have no stake in it, and if Galia was going to be public about asking you to take the throne they would already have made a press release. If you really want to tell the grandparents now, I can do it."

"No…they'll be asleep, and you're right, it's not their problem, at least not yet," she said.

"It's not anyone's problem until we decide it is. You don't even have to tell Dad – he's retired and he knows it. He'll be annoyed, but he'll live if he isn't told for a few days."

He stopped in the doorway as she walked into the room; it had been made clear to him at a young age that this was Alanna's room, and he needed permission to go in. He hadn't really had to ask in years, but the habit still held strong.

"We'll get this figured out," he said.

"It's just really…I didn't even think of it," she answered.

"Nobody did. And I think…" Gregory wondered if he should even bring it up. Alanna waited. "Clearly someone in Galia did. They knew who the heir was and they got people here fast."

"What does that gain anyone?"

"I'm going to think about that. Above and beyond the fact that this is awful for you, Alanna, this is also political. It's not necessarily strange to know who the heir is, but not to tell them they are? Who gains from that? You should have been made aware, by Galia, long before now. Something to consider," he said thoughtfully.

Alanna nodded. "If I think of anything – "

"Put it in a note in your phone and try to sleep," he suggested. "We both need to be rested for tomorrow."

"Gotcha. Thanks for backing Jerry when he was kicking the Galians out, by the way."

"He made a good call. Can't say his career as a vizier hasn't been a useful one so far," Gregory said. "Goodnight, Alanna."

"Night, Gregory," she said, and he closed the door, heading upstairs, where Eddie was waiting to pounce with a hundred questions.

Alanna tried not to stay over at the palace too often, just to keep some kind of work-life balance, but she always kept some clothes in her old room. Pajamas, for sure, and a couple of comfortable outfits in case of emergency, which this clearly was. She struggled out of her formal clothes, sighing with relief, then pulled on some spare jeans and a shirt she suspected she'd stolen from Gregory at some point.

Are you awake? she texted Michaelis.

For another hour or two. How's it going? Are they still mad at me? he replied.

Mind if I come down to the lodge? Easier to talk in person, she said, hoping she didn't sound weird or desperate.

I'll be here, he answered, imperturbable as usual. She found a pair of sandals in the closet, pulled them on, and slipped out of the palace, heading for the lake.

The lakeside trail from the palace to the fishing lodge wasn't lit, but she knew it by heart, and there was enough moonlight to follow it easily. Michaelis was on the front porch when she arrived, leaning on the railing, clearly waiting for her. Retirement agreed with him, she thought; here at his home he was comfortable, barefoot, in a pair of loose trousers and a worn rugby shirt. The hard set of his shoulders that he'd had in the last few years of his reign had eased. He looked like a man on vacation, not a king.

"It's either gone excessively well or excessively poorly if Gregory's sending you here to break the news," he said, when he saw her coming.

She nodded, climbing the stairs to join him on the porch. "Kind of both, but he didn't send me."

"Did they offer Gregory the throne?"

"Not exactly." She tried to figure out what she wanted to say – had been trying the whole walk over – and she could see Michaelis waiting patiently. "Did you like being king?" she asked at last.

"I wouldn't have done it for forty years if I didn't," he said.

"But you also knew you were the best person for the job, right?"

"Well, I was unusually arrogant at twenty," he said with a smile.

"What I mean is…if you knew you were the best person for the job but really didn't want to do it, would you have done it?"

Michaelis considered her. Finally, he said, "This feels like a trick question, Alanna."

"My father was the duke's cousin," she said. "I'm the Duchess of the Horse of the House of Galia."

Michaelis nodded slowly. "There's wine inside. And harder stuff, if you want."

"Wine, please," she said. He held the door for her, following her in.

"When you texted, Jes suggested we might want some privacy. We won't be interrupted," he said, taking down wine glasses and pouring for them both, filling hers generously. She sat at the little breakfast table, trying not to gulp her wine, while he leaned on the counter and regarded her.

"I'm so sorry, Alanna," he said at last. "I didn't even think of it. I knew your father's mother had immigrated from Galia, but that was before he or I were born, and I didn't know her well. I just always thought of Mark and his mother both as Shivadh."

"Nobody else thought of it either. Gregory's suspicious that I wasn't told earlier," she said.

"He's right to be, but that's neither here nor there." Michaelis sipped his wine thoughtfully. "To answer your earlier question, no. If I hadn't wanted the job, even if I knew I was the best person for it, I would not have taken it. It's not that I lack patriotism, but there's simply no way to do the job well if you hate it. For evidence, I present to you the entire British royal family, many of the Tsars, and at least a few American presidents."

"Gregory said he'd back me if I refused the throne."

"Good. I can think of problems your being ruler of Galia solves, but – "

" – none of them actually need solving?" she asked. He nodded. "That's what Gregory said."

"He is my son. You're likely to get much the same answers from me as from him." He tilted his head. "Not that I'm not always pleased to see you, but it is a little strange you're coming to me, instead of going to him."

She nodded. "It just got a little…Eddie and Jerry were hovering, and Greg was really worried that I'd think he wanted me to take the duchy. It was all a lot. I love the boys, but you're, um." She took a second to phrase it correctly. "You've been good about letting us be adults. Gregory's always going to treat me like a sister. It's not bad, it's just not helpful right now. You know how to be more impartial."

"Yes, I suppose I see that."

"And I know if I asked Gregory this question, he'd say it was my choice and he couldn't tell me what to do, but you might actually give me an answer," she continued. Michaelis smiled. "If you were me, what would you do?"

He gave it all due consideration, puzzling out the angles thoughtfully. Finally he said, "Hm. It's nonsense, isn't it?"

"What is?" she asked.

"You can't possibly be the only heir. You might be the first in line, but if they're going up two generations of the family tree and coming back down in Askazer-Shivadlakia, they ought to be willing to go one branch further out to find a native Galian, or at least a Shivadh who wants the job," Michaelis said. "They have to make you an offer, but you can decline. And you should even be able to do it pretty diplomatically if you can offer them someone else instead."

She could feel herself slump with relief. Of course; that was an easy solution, and any of them should have seen it. Trust Michaelis, who never saw a problem he didn't want to immediately solve, to be the one to spot it.

"The real issue isn't whether to take the job, it's how to find someone else to take it," he continued. "Difficult to do that if the only information you have is coming from Galians in Askazer-Shivadlakia who clearly want you to be the one. You need more data."

His face took on a sudden, distant expression that she'd seen before – it meant he had an idea, didn't like the idea, and didn't want her to know he'd had it. She considered what Michaelis's mind might have suggested that would be so distasteful.

"But I could go to Galia," she said, sitting up straight again. "And then I'd be in Galia, and I could get the information for myself. And, being duchess, any other information we might want."

"I didn't say that."

"You didn't have to," she replied.

"I am not saying accept the duchy. But it would be possible for you to consider accepting the duchy, inspect it thoroughly in person, investigate the royal genealogy, and then renounce in favor of whoever you find," he admitted. "After that, you can come back here to tell your dear cousin the king all about your visit. I know, Alanna, that you like to be useful. That would be useful."

"Gregory would be so mad to hear you say that," she said.

"Wouldn't be the first time he's been irritated by my good advice," Michaelis said with a smile. "I also know you well enough to know that Gregory is being redundant when he reminds you that you don't have to bow to royal pressure. You'll do as you please, you always have. Very like your father that way, actually. While it's been frustrating, on occasion, you've rarely been wrong. This is up to you, Gregory is correct about that, and it's his job to tell you so. I don't have that same responsibility, not anymore. Frankly, I think two weeks in Galia, poking your nose in where it doesn't belong, would be a lovely holiday for you and very helpful to him. I'd go with you myself if that wouldn't cause an incident."

"Not very kind to the Galians, deceiving them like that," Alanna said, studying the last of her wine.

"In many ways it's kinder than the alternative – either flatly denying them and leaving them to flail, or taking up the throne and bending it to Shivadh interests," Michaelis pointed out. "Though I will say, having read the lives of your ancestors, the truly noble Askazer thing to do would be to accept the throne of Galia, raise an army and invade Askazer-Shivadlakia, take the throne from Gregory by force, and then rule both countries through benevolent yet ruthless absolute fiat. Now that is an epic in the making," he finished with relish.

"You seem very into invasion," Alanna said.

"I never got to do any invading myself. One likes to see one's protégés achieve more," he said, affecting a false modest tone.

"I'd probably have to have you beheaded," Alanna pointed out.

"Oh, I'd flee to Paris and live in genteel poverty," he said. "Gregory's the sort to fall in battle so I shouldn't worry about him either." He studied her. "Are you going to tell your grandparents?"

"I thought about it. I suppose I'll have to tell them something," she said. "It's just such a mess. They're not very happy with me anyway. They still think I should quit the job and go find a husband, start producing heirs."

"I can't throw stones there. I made that mistake myself with Gregory, trying to push him into marriage. But I thought you were getting on all right with them at Gregory's engagement ball."

"That's just how the old guard is," she said, and saw his mouth curve with amusement at not being considered part of the old guard. "You know what I mean! They were there for Gregory and so was I. We weren't going to make things awkward for him. But they're not big on family for family's sake. Family for the sake of the duchy only."

"Yes, I do know. Your grandmother was thrilled her daughter was marrying the crown prince, and simultaneously did not care much for me as a person," Michaelis said. "I think Miranda was happy to get away from her, to be honest. I'm sure your mother Ruth was, too. It's why we always insisted you spend so much time at the palace after the accident. We wanted to make sure you had someone who wasn't your grandparents helping to raise you."

She didn't blame him, but Alanna did always find it darkly amusing that Michaelis never referred to her parents' deaths directly. His wife Miranda, her mother's sister, hadn't either when she'd been alive. They always called it *the accident*. As if her parents just vanished one day, swept away by fate, instead of dying in a car crash that would definitely have killed her also if she'd been with them.

"I could just tell my grandparents I'm going on vacation," she said.

"I think probably there will be Galian press releases about your visit," he pointed out. "But you don't have to have a confrontation of any kind. Leave them a note, that'd be a very royal thing to do. Dear Nonna, gone to Galia to investigate the throne. For any questions, please see my social secretary." He sipped his wine. "Send them a postcard from Galia. Your grandfather will appreciate the brevity."

"Maybe. Maybe I just won't say anything and won't answer the phone when they call."

"Also an option. In this, not to echo Gregory, but I will support your choices. I've had forty years of handling your grandparents, there's not much they can do to me."

"Thanks." She finished the last of her wine and he took the glass from her, setting it next to the sink. "I should go back. Nobody knows I came to see you."

"I won't mention it. Although if Gregory thinks you came up with this spy job all on your own, that may color his opinion of you. He already knew I was like this," Michaelis added.

She gave him a quick hug, and let him kiss her forehead. "I appreciate the counsel."

"Remember: invasion is an option," he said, walking her to the door. "And if you decide you want to throw the Galians out of the palace, I'm happy to come help."

CHAPTER TWO

GREGORY WOKE IN the morning to a text-message alert; he rolled onto his side and picked up his phone, squinting at the screen.

Gregory, message when you're up, Alanna had texted, although she'd sent it to the group chat that included Eddie and Jerry. Eddie had stolen Gregory's phone at some point and named the group The Royal Pal-us.

I'm awake, he sent. *What is it?*

Almost before he sent it, the next text appeared. *I have an idea to present for your almost certain disapproval.*

He rubbed his face. *If you're pitching bad ideas you have to be the one to put real clothes on and come up here. I'm not wandering the palace in my pajamas.*

If I have to wear clothes, so does Eddie, Alanna said.

"I don't know where she gets these ideas about me," Eddie said from behind him, apparently following the chat on his own phone. He sat up and threw the blankets off, photographing his own lower half, clad in pajamas printed all over with flamingos. A few seconds later it showed up in the group chat.

On my way, Alanna said.

By the time she arrived, knocking as she entered to announce her presence, Eddie was brewing coffee and Gregory had pulled on a robe over his pajamas, settling into the sofa. He waved her into the nearby chair.

"You look like you actually got some sleep," Gregory said. "I'm a little impressed."

"I got the idea last night," she said. "I put it in my phone, per your command," she waved her phone, "and when I woke up it still seemed like a good idea that you will absolutely hate."

"You know," Eddie said, bringing her a cup of coffee and handing Gregory one before sitting down next to him, "it might be a terrible plan, but you may as well pitch it. The last time you screwed up,

Gregory got a husband out of it."

Alanna choked on her coffee and glared at Gregory. "You *told* him I hired him accidentally?"

"I wasn't going to build an entire marriage on a lie, even one of omission," Gregory said. "He thought it was funny."

"I did," Eddie chimed in loyally. "If I could return the favor I would. I don't know what your type is."

"Patient, handsome, and emotionally self-sufficient," Alanna replied.

"Good, cheap, and fast – you can only have two," Eddie replied.

"Good and fast," Gregory said, and then laughed when Alanna said the same thing at the same time. "We both have expensive tastes."

"I'll have you know I'm extremely cheap," Eddie said.

"It's charming you think that," Gregory told him, then turned back to Alanna. "Come on, Al, tell me what it is."

"Well, there has to be some other heir, right? There have to be alternatives. Besides, you want to know why they're so hot to get me onboard," Alanna said. "So I was thinking, I could pretend I was considering accepting the throne, demand to inspect Galia in person, dig around in the archives, maybe do a little light desk-rummaging… then renounce in favor of another heir and report back to you."

Gregory narrowed his eyes. "I'm going to strangle my father."

"How do you do that?" she demanded. "How did you know he came up with it?"

"Because any other rational human being would tell you that it's your choice while gently nudging you towards the safe and sane option, which is to say no and then stop answering their calls," Gregory said. "We had no relationship with Galia before yesterday. It's not like we could make the situation worse. Except by sending you to a *whole entire other country* to spy on them!"

"What are they going to do, arrest me?" Alanna asked.

"Yes, actually! If you're brought before The Hague for international espionage there's not a lot I can do for you."

"I can do plenty," Eddie volunteered. "Fuck the cops, I'll break you loose."

Gregory knew what Eddie was doing, and normally loved him for it – Eddie, perhaps because he was the oldest of five siblings, knew exactly when to insert himself into a conversation to relieve tension, to stop fights. It was already invaluable at parties. But it was also highly annoying when he did it to Gregory.

"I'm not saying this is a cold war on a level with, you know, the Cold War," Gregory said. "But it isn't a game, Alanna. If you are caught accessing or removing state secrets you can be prosecuted and imprisoned. Being the cousin of the king and heir to two duchies isn't going to change that."

"Okay, fine, but I can still go and look," Alanna pointed out. "I can see a lot, legitimately, as the heir to the throne, and I can get into the genealogy books to find a suitable replacement."

"And there's also a question of whether, once you say no, they'll let you come back," Gregory said darkly.

"This isn't the 17th century," Alanna said. "They won't lock me in a tower. They don't have a tower to lock me in. Send some security with me if you're worried."

He was opening his mouth to reply, because he understood he'd been suckered into turning this from a request for permission into a negotiation for support, when there was a rap at the door.

"It's Jerry," Jerry called.

"Come in," Gregory called back. Jerry put his head in.

"Thought I saw you were here, in the texts," Jerry said.

"You're up early," Eddie told him.

"Wanted to make sure I was on time for my breakfast with the Ansevalis. And I'm bored, so I'm glad you're all awake and apparently up to something," Jerry replied.

"We're discussing our options. Come sit, Jerry, you can give your opinion," Alanna said.

"Actually, I have an option I thought of to present to you," Jerry said, sidling through the door and letting it close behind him. "Okay, think on this," he said, pacing and gesturing as he spoke. "We support Alanna, of course, but we obviously don't want her to accept the duchy because we know it'll make her unhappy. I was thinking about that on the drive home last night. We'd be mad if she said yes, right? Supportive, but mad! And what would be the advantage if she said yes? Why would she do that? And then I thought, what does she get if she says yes...but then doesn't follow through?"

Gregory looked at Alanna, who was watching with an almost anthropological fascination.

"She gets an invitation to visit Galia, and she gets to go anywhere she wants in Galia," Jerry said, spreading his hands to demonstrate how exciting this would be. "Not only can she do a little light spying, she can figure out why Milo is – he's acting weird, right, Gregory? I didn't make that up in my head?"

"He is acting a little weird," Gregory agreed. "I can't figure out how."

"Me either. Pin in that. Anyway, if Alanna goes to Galia under the pretense of maybe accepting the throne, she can also find someone else to shove in front of them when she says no, so they won't even *suspect* she was lying," Jerry finished. "Now, before you tell me this is a terrible idea, I know. It's extremely unsafe. I agree. So I think she'll need an escort. I mean, definitely at least one lawyer, and if she's taking one she might as well say she's taking two and bring security along. I recommend Georgie. But also, here's the brilliance of my plan: me."

"You…are the brilliance of your plan," Alanna said.

"I come with you. I am known universally as a politically unimpressive gadfly, but I am the Duke of Shivadlakia and I have land on the border. Even if they wanted to fuck with the Lady Alanna Daskaz, they are not going to fuck with *two* royally connected Shivadh, one of whom is the grandson of a king. Also, I can accomplish quite a lot while looking extremely harmless. So what do you think?"

"Did he just…" Eddie said quietly, pointing back and forth between Alanna and Jerry.

"Yes," Gregory sighed.

"Did I just what?" Jerry asked.

"I think it's a fine plan, Jerry," Alanna said, and Jerry beamed at her. "The kind of thing Michaelis would come up with. Great strategy. I especially like the part where you come with me to keep me safe. And Gregory," she added pointedly, "did promise that all three of you would support whatever decision I made. Even if you're mad about it."

Gregory could tell he was about to lose this strategy session very badly. He had dealt with professionally trained political operatives who were easier to debate than his own family. He rubbed his forehead with his fingertips.

"All right," he said. "But let's be smart about this, because neither Milo nor Ofelia are oblivious and you're going to need to be on the historian's good side."

"Good morning," Alanna said later that morning, as she swept into the dining room. Pretty much everyone was already assembled; Milo and Bruno were standing at the sideboard with coffees, conversing with Eddie, while Gregory sat nearby with Ofelia.

"Good morning – should I call you Your Grace?" Milo asked.

"I'd rather you didn't – Alanna's just fine," she replied, taking a pastry from the tray and pouring herself a coffee. "Listen, I need to apologize for last night. It just caught me so off-guard. None of us here had thought about – oh, obviously we thought about the succession, but not in terms of our own family trees. We thought Jerry might actually be distantly related."

"Well, you are cousins, aren't you?" Milo said.

"Not by blood, surprisingly," Alanna said. "His uncle married my aunt. The real problem is we forgot my father was Galian – he was born here, and he married into a prominent Shivadh noble house."

"I know how strong the national identity is," Milo said with an easy smile. "I'm sure any Galian immigrants are thought of as Shivadh very quickly."

"Exactly. Actually, that's what's been on my mind since," she said, leading Milo and Bruno to the table. "I was thinking about – this sounds terrible, but I was thinking about the Empress Alexandra."

"The wife of Tsar Nicholas?" Bruno asked, picking at his pastry. "Brutally murdered in a revolution?"

"That went straight for the most unforgiving path," Ofelia said, amused.

"I was thinking of her because I remember in school, learning about how she became empress – she had to marry Nicholas very suddenly. She wasn't trained for it yet and she barely even spoke the language. She was never happy at court. I find myself feeling sympathetic. Galia's not Russia, obviously, but we haven't had good diplomatic relations in my lifetime. I have no idea how to behave in a

Galian court, I don't know any of the law. I speak Italian, but that's roughly what I have going for me. You have to admit, it's not ideal."

"Well, no. But we can provide training. And you'll have no lack of advisors," Ofelia said.

"I'm sure, but…I don't know either way, do I? My first reaction was reluctance, but that's not fair to me or to Galia. I'm trying to be sensible about it, but to do that I think I need data," Alanna said, making the opening with care.

Because really, as Gregory had pointed out, they wanted her in Galia. Away from the Shivadh palace, somewhere they could convince her to take the throne. Even if they had the best of intentions, Alanna going to Galia was good for them.

"I'd like to do a sort of inspection tour," she said, and Bruno was already nodding. Milo looked pleased. "I can't accept – or decide any other way – until I've had some time to learn about the country. A few weeks in Galia would help me out, and I'm sure it would…"

"Calm concerns from the populace," Ofelia said. She glanced at Gregory, who had a cautious expression on his face, equal parts hopeful and apprehensive. It was a hell of an acting job. All she had to do was convince the Galians that Gregory had persuaded her, and she just needed a little extra nudge…

"I believe this is a good solution," Ofelia continued. "It provides you with information to make your decision, and provides Galia with time to recover."

"To mourn," Milo said, his voice so dry that Alanna fought a smile. "And to make plans."

"I'm going to need an entourage," Alanna said. "Not large, I don't want to inconvenience you. I'll be bringing a Shivadh lawyer, possibly two, just to ensure any legal dealings can be handled smoothly."

"And I'd like to come as chaperone," Jerry said. Milo glanced at him, then back at Alanna. "She should have some kind of escort from the royal family. Gregory can't go, and I think we can all agree the King Emeritus probably shouldn't."

"I asked Jerry if he'd attend and provide advice," Gregory said. "He is my vizier, after all."

It looked – at least, Alanna hoped it looked – like two big ruling-class boys were strong-arming the Lady Alanna into the modern-day equivalent of a political marriage.

"We can make appropriate preparations for anyone you'd care to bring," Milo said. "Were you thinking of returning with us, or…?"

"I need to put a few things in order here," Alanna said. "If we leave tomorrow afternoon – "

"You'd arrive late, but not so late as to be uncomfortable," Ofelia said. Bruno, the historian, was watching everything curiously.

"Let's plan on that, in that case. Which happily means there's not much paperwork for any of us to review today," Alanna said. "I can attend to my work, and you and your staff can have the day off."

"Jerry's volunteered to show you around Fons-Askaz if you want, or you're welcome to make use of the palace and the grounds," Gregory said. "I won't be available for lunch, and I suspect Alanna's going to be packing, but I thought I might arrange a small going-away party – a cruise on the harbor this evening."

The Galians exchanged looks, but they seemed pleased with the outcome. Ofelia spoke first, turning to Jerry.

"I'd love to see Fons-Askaz," she said. "I'm afraid Milo probably has work – his job is not limited to office hours – but I'd be glad of an excursion. Bruno?"

"I'd actually like a few hours in your library, if it's accessible," Bruno said. "I've had questions for years about some finer points of international relations that I think documents in the library could answer."

"I could call the royal librarian – he knew he might be needed," Alanna said to Gregory. "Excuse me, I'll just let him know."

She stepped outside and sent a quick text to the royal librarian – *Confirmed request for access, please come asap* and got an almost immediate response in the form of a book emoji. She flipped over to the phone app and dialed.

"Good morning! How is your planning coming?" Michaelis answered. It sounded like he was outside.

"Gregory absolutely knew it was your suggestion, so you're in trouble," she said.

"I can take him," Michaelis said easily. A seagull screamed in the background.

"I'd pay to see that fight," Alanna replied. "Where are you?"

"Down at the beach. Jes took us out for breakfast."

"Nice work if you can get it."

"Fortunately, I can. I suppose I owe Gregory some form of apology, or at least I owe him ten minutes of berating me for it. What did he think?"

"It took some persuading, but he bought it, and we've just sold it to Galia. I leave for Galia tomorrow. Jerry's coming too."

"You're taking Gerald?" he said, sounding surprised.

"He actually had some really good points about why he should come along. Tell you later."

"It's true he's good in a pinch. Not the most reliable soul, but he never got you into any trouble he didn't also get you out of. And he's very sociable, good at making himself agreeable."

"I think one of the Galians thinks he's cute."

"All the better," Michaelis said, which irritated her for reasons she couldn't define.

"I should go, they think I'm calling the librarian."

"This cloak and dagger business is fun, isn't it?" he asked. "Be safe. Text me."

"Of course. Bye," she said, and hung up just as Milo emerged from the dining room. "Librarian's on his way for Bruno. Do you need a workspace? We have empty offices."

"No need, you provided me with a very nice suite. We don't get sea views in Galia," he said with a smile. "I'm on my way back to the suite now. I'm so glad you chose to consider the throne. You'd be a breath of fresh air."

"From what you've said so far, I think you think anyone would be," she said.

"We should speak more on that later," he said. "But yes. I think you will find at least some of Galia extremely welcoming to any fresh blood after the old duke."

"Alanna," Jerry called, and they both looked back into the dining room. "Do you know where Uncle Mike keeps the Jag?"

"Yes, at the fishing lodge, because he's using it," she replied. "If you want to drive into town, take one of the government cars."

"I'll find something better than that," she heard Jerry say to Ofelia.

"I'd say we'll try to restrain Jerry but we've been trying for years with limited success," she told Milo.

"Ofelia can handle him. She likes a challenge," Milo said. "Until this evening, I think, Alanna."

"Looking forward to it," she replied.

Alanna went to her office first, because her mind was already filling with lists of things she needed to see to, particularly things she needed to tell her assistant, Darien, who would have to step up to help Gregory while she was gone. She had to bow out of meetings for the next few weeks, set an out-of-office, and send a memo to the team outlining how to handle the media. She'd need to talk to someone – probably Milo, maybe Ofelia – about how Galia would handle her visit.

She spent an hour trying to work out what to tell her grandparents, and in the end took Michaelis at his word about handling them.

I've been offered the Duchy of the Horse of the House of Galia, including the throne of Galia. I'm considering my options and will be in Galia for a few weeks to gather more information. Michaelis can explain it better than I can, and you can ask him if you have questions. I'll write from Galia when I'm able. Call anytime.

Her grandmother, who hated text messages and emails, would appreciate the physical note. Her grandfather, who didn't like long conversations, would enjoy how short and informative it was. It also neatly cut off any suggestion that her grandparents should offer her any advice. She did love them and knew they loved her, but their advice was usually terrible, because it was always about putting the estate first. Or at least, some idealized version of the estate that existed only in their minds.

"The thing I hate when it comes to media about the nobility," she'd said to Gregory and Jerry once, incensed by the very idea of enjoying *Downton Abbey*, "isn't that they get things wrong, or that they romanticize the nobility. It's that every plot, eventually, comes down to the same thing."

"Noble marriage?" Jerry had asked.

"No. Every plot eventually involves sacrificing personal

happiness and freedom in the name of the title. The title, the estate, the continuity. If someone who is rich and powerful has to do something unpleasant, the writers have to find a reason for it, which is difficult when you're so insanely privileged. The reason they always give for the nobility having to do something they don't want to do is that they're doing it for the sake of their children, their legacy."

"Well, stability is important," Jerry had said. "It's why even when we elect a king it's a life term, eh? You can't do anything to make life better without a solid foundation."

"Sure, but when does the make-life-better part come into these stories? Everyone's always giving something up to nobly support the nobility for no good reason. It's why I hate the stupid ending of stupid *Roman Holiday*. If every generation is miserable for the sake of the next, what's the point of any of it? Why be unhappy just to pass on something to your children that will make them unhappy, too?"

Gregory had considered it, dark eyes thoughtful. "Put like that, it does sound pretty awful. Makes me glad I had to be elected."

"Wish I had to be elected, I'd refuse to run," Alanna had said. "Good riddance to the whole legacy. I'd have taken Gregory Peck over a kingdom any day."

"Who among us wouldn't be tempted?" Gregory had asked.

"Lord, imagine if I'd had to be elected," Jerry had said, and they'd laughed. "Mind you, I do love a show. I could have put on a hell of a campaign tour."

Now, trying to tie up loose ends before a weeks-long tour of a foreign country she was nominally already the head of, the irony of the situation hit home. She gave herself five minutes to feel upset without trying to rationalize it, then set the letter aside to be couriered over after she departed the following day. She locked her laptop and her desk, checked to make sure she wasn't missing anything vital, and went home to figure out what to pack for a royal inspection tour.

Jewel-toned sheath dress number eighty-one, she supposed. Pearls, heels, carefully expensive brand-neutral casual wear, tasteful athleisure. All of it on the blander end of her wardrobe, some of it downright uncomfortable.

What are you packing? she texted Jerry, procrastinating.

Loaded question, he texted back, and she smiled.

Seriously, though, I'm going very Young Conservative, do you think I should bring anything flashier? she asked.

I'll bring some suits and a tuxedo, casualwear. Wear what you want, I say. If Eddie could land Gregory wearing cargo shorts, you can snag at least an earl with capris and ballet flats, Jerry pointed out.

Very Mary Tyler Moore, good call, she said.

Instead of replying, he called; she put it on speakerphone as she looked through her closet.

"Words of wisdom in person, or just not willing to commit to writing it down?" she asked. He laughed down the line.

"Easier to talk this way," he said. "I'm still squiring the diplomat around Fons-Askaz. She's handbag shopping at the moment, which I'm enjoying pretending is a spy ruse of some kind. On that note, why pack a single high heel unless you want to?"

"I have to dress appropriately. You know how this game is played, Jerry, even if neither of us love playing it."

"Sure, but this isn't their game, is it?"

"How do you mean?" she asked.

"They know you're Shivadh. We've got a gay king and a notoriously relaxed attitude. You're also coming from a place of power – you don't have to impress them. If they want you to take the duchy, they have to impress you," he said.

"It's a real asshole stance to take," she said.

"Sometimes life forces us into the position of being assholes," he replied. "Furthermore, you know you're not taking the duchy so you don't even have to worry about first impressions. If they don't like you, so what? Oh, she didn't wear heels, pooh pooh," he groaned theatrically. "The fashion bloggers don't like what you wore to visit a country you don't want to rule and will probably never go back to? Big deal."

She considered the pile of dresses on her bed. "I can't go to Galia in Chuck Taylors and cargo shorts."

"Not with that attitude," he said. "But you're also not backpacking across the continent. You can bring two suitcases. I'll have at least two."

"One for suits, one for…?"

"Sex toys."

"Jerry!"

"Fine," he groaned. "It's for shoes. And also to bring back souvenirs. Hang on, looks like Ofelia's done. See you tonight. Oh, wear something in a cool tone – blue or purple."

She was about to ask why, but he hung up before she could.

It was early enough in the season that they hadn't had too much trouble getting hold of a boat for the dinner cruise, although Gregory generally didn't have trouble in any case. It was a trim, elegant little yacht that Simon had taken possession of earlier in the day, loading it up with fresh food from the markets in Fons-Askaz. From the look of it, Eddie hadn't been far behind Simon in boarding. As she came onboard, he was just emerging from a changing cubby at the back, adjusting his formalwear for the evening.

Gregory had once told Alanna that Eddie reminded him simultaneously of a Viking and a tree, and she had to admit seeing him in a suit was always a little startling. Sometimes it was because he looked oddly out of place in them. Sometimes it was the suit itself.

"I see that eyeball, Madam Alanna," Eddie told her, as he adjusted the cuffs of the cream linen suit, heavily embroidered in blue with vivid flowers and songbirds.

"You look like an entire museum textiles gallery," she said. "I'm not complaining, just momentarily overwhelmed."

"Well, it was this or the chef's whites I've been sweating in all afternoon. Simon punished me for making him come in today by making me do all the hard prep. You look very nice, though," he said, gesturing at her deep blue dress.

"Jerry told me to wear cool colors, I'm not sure why," she said.

"Ah! I know. Stay there," he told her, and ducked into the kitchen. He emerged again with a little paper carton with a posy in it – a bundle of small, tasteful blossoms arranged in a blue-and-gold starburst. "Florist dropped it off earlier, Jerry set it up."

"Nothing for you?" she asked. He beamed, bringing his other hand out from behind his back. It held a trio of blue orchids, arranged as an overly large boutonniere.

"Go big or go home," he said.

"Oh, Eddie," she said, laughing, and kissed his cheek. "You are the best queen Askazer-Shivadlakia has ever had."

"I'm certainly trying for it," he agreed. "Would you – "

"Ah, yes," she agreed, undoing the little pin fixed to the orchids and passing it through his buttonhole, securing the bundle in place. She opened the carton with the posy and let him pin it to her dress at the hip, Askazer-style.

"Al, if you steal him, I will have you executed," Gregory said, joining them in the corridor. "And then I'll have to find a new boyfriend *and* someone to run my life."

"Alanna wouldn't have me," Eddie said, kissing him in greeting. "Though bagging a king and a duchess in the space of a year would definitely look great in my Wikipedia entry."

"Hm." Gregory adjusted the cuffs of his uniform, the sober black touched with gold that he always wore for formal occasions. "I can't approve of you being so interesting."

"Come on, squire me through," Alanna said, taking Gregory's arm and heading down the hallway, past the kitchen and into the opulent main cabin. There was a dining table at one end and a cluster of comfortable-looking benches and chairs at the other, all facing the wide glass wall that looked out on the bow of the ship. Beyond the glass, the harbor of Fons-Askaz was serene in the early sunset. They could hear Eddie call a greeting to Jerry and Ofelia from the hall.

Gregory went to the glass wall and began opening the panels, letting the warm salt air in. He leaned against one of the posts and admired the view, hands in his pockets.

"Something something the wine-dark sea?" Alanna suggested as she joined him.

"It really is beautiful," he answered. "I spend so much time looking at – the math, I suppose? All the ways we quantify the country. Spreadsheets of dairy production and olive yields and tourist spending, train timetables and bills passing through parliament. Even when I look out the window I'm usually looking at Fons-Askaz. I can see why Dad always made so much time for the outdoors when he was king."

"You're in a very philosophical mood tonight," she said.

"Trying not to think about you and Jerry leaving tomorrow."

"We'll be fine."

"Well, I am worried about that," Gregory admitted. "But I'm also feeling sorry for myself a little. I'm going to miss you. I need my advisor and my vizier."

She patted his arm. "We're only going over the highlands. Back before you know it. And Jerry's surgically attached to his phone. If you can't get him by text, just post up a message on Photogram ordering him to call you."

"Who's calling me?" Jerry asked, strolling into the room, Ofelia following behind him. He'd changed into a fashionably nautical suit – navy blue with dark trousers, which looked a little silly but she couldn't deny was on brand. "Ah, you got the flowers," he said, gesturing at Alanna's waist.

"Yes, they're beautiful, thank you," she replied. Jerry went to Gregory, fixing an orange-petaled boutonniere, much subtler than Eddie's, on his uniform jacket. His own was already jauntily installed in his lapel, a small spray of blue-on-blue.

"And for the lovely Ofelia," he added, producing a different posy, this one of delicate purple flowers, the Galian national color. "May I?" he asked, gesturing between her dress and Alanna's. She nodded and held still while he pinned it in place.

"Bruno and Milo will be along shortly," she said, admiring the flowers. "I must say, Shivadh hospitality leaves nothing to be desired."

"I think we'd all like to mend fences," Gregory said. "Planting flowers isn't a bad way to start."

"True. Perhaps you and Bruno should speak about that," she said. "As a historian, he's aware of the fraught nature of the past few decades. He has some suggestions for reconciliation. Of course, if the duchy is to Alanna's liking…" She smiled at Alanna, warm and friendly enough that Alanna felt bad all over again. Ofelia seemed nice, and probably didn't deserve their duplicity. On the other hand, Michaelis was right – better to find someone who could serve Galia properly.

"I don't think it needs to be passed through back channels that we'd like a better relationship with Galia," Gregory said. "To that end – aperitif before dinner?"

Milo and Bruno arrived as drinks were being poured, boutonnieres already in place, apparently handed to them by Simon as they passed through. Eddie mixed himself an Old Fashioned and then one for Alanna at her request, light on the bourbon; Jerry just dropped the ship's steward at the bar a wink and got something he'd apparently requested beforehand, gold and full of fruit.

"This is a new recipe," Gregory said, offering Ofelia a tumbler of light ruby liquid, small bubbles clinging to the inside of the glass. He had another one for himself. "After Davzda had its moment in the sun last year, Eddie did a survey of Davzda cocktails."

"Mostly just dressed-up margaritas," Eddie grumbled. "Nobody has any imagination when it comes to salt in mixed drinks."

"Where was I?" Jerry asked. "You didn't invite me to your tastings?"

"It wasn't an *event*," Eddie said. "Besides, most of them were terrible. I didn't actually taste that many. You can smell the bad cocktail coming off the page on 'em."

"Pomegranate?" Ofelia asked, studying it.

"Pomegranate, soda water, Davzda," Eddie said. "I call it the Royal D."

"It's certainly fragrant," she said, sipping the drink.

"I should warn you, he doesn't care about politeness," Gregory said, as she swallowed thoughtfully. "If it's awful, he'd rather know."

"A good quality in a royal spouse, I expect," she said. "It's actually quite good, thank you. Oh," she added, as the mushroom after-flavor hit the back of her throat. "And…layered."

Eddie grinned. "I won't be hurt if you want something a little more mainstream."

"I'll suffer through," she said, patting his arm. "Milo, Bruno, what will you have?"

"I'd better not," Bruno said. "I get motion sickness. Boat should be fine – boat and alcohol maybe not."

"I'll try one of these," Milo said, and coughed a little as he took his first sip of spiked pomegranate. "Well. That's adventurous."

"Ah, and it looks like the meal is nearly ready," Gregory said, as a waiter brought out a tray of nibbles – Simon's usual well-crafted food, but nothing Alanna hadn't had at dozens of parties before. "Please. Enjoy. How did you like Fons-Askaz?" he added to Ofelia, as Bruno pulled out her chair for her. Jerry jockeyed with Milo for a second, then let the Galian pull out Alanna's chair while he sat next to her, Milo on her other side. Eddie watched the little dance, amused, and then pulled Gregory's out for him, a gallantry he normally didn't bother with. Gregory gave him a look.

"It's delightful. So quaint, just like in all the Photograms," Ofelia said.

"Oh hey, what's your handle?" Eddie asked. "Did you post at all?"

"Yes, some very pretty vistas, here…" Ofelia held out her phone for Eddie to examine.

"That reminds me," Jerry said, leaning over to speak quietly to Alanna. "Brought you something."

"You already got all the flowers," she said.

"Those are palace business. Actually, that may have been me getting carried away, but the palace is paying, regardless. Anyway, I didn't buy this," he added, handing her a small velvet envelope, a little worn-looking. "Stole it from Mom. She doesn't really wear it much but she thinks it's lucky, and stolen things are double-lucky."

"Not sure that's how it works," she said, shaking the contents out into her hand. "Oh, wow."

In her palm lay a City of Gold, a ring cut in the shape of a city skyline. Usually they showed Jerusalem – she had a Jerusalem City of Gold tiara from her bat mitzvah – but this one was clearly Fons-Askaz. The Grand Synagogue was visible on one side, the palace on the other. The line of buildings along the harbor ran from the synagogue to the palace, and from the palace back to the synagogue were rolling hills broken by a small, distant, but unmistakable outline of Jerry's ancestral home, the seat of the Dukes of Shivadlakia.

"You don't have to wear it or anything, just thought it might be a nice lucky charm," he said as she examined it. It was loose on her fingers when she tried it, but fit snugly over her thumb. "Hey, that looks good. Very post-fashion."

"Sarah won't miss it?"

"If she does, she'll know who took it," he said, grinning. "She's got rings for years, she'll be fine without it. It's not an antique or anything, I think Dad had it made for her as a birthday present one year. We have to take a little Shivadh with us, right?"

"I'm glad you're coming with me," she said, making sure she was still speaking too quietly for the Galians to hear.

"Me too. It'll be fun. And if you decide you want the throne after all, you've got me to help you pick out an appropriate husband."

"Can you imagine," she laughed.

"Imagine what?" Gregory asked, glancing over at them.

"Jerry says, if I decide to stay in Galia he'll help me find a good Galian husband," Alanna said.

"You know, I distinctly remember your horrified reaction when I asked you to find me one," Gregory said. "What was it you said? I couldn't meetings-minutes myself a partner?"

"Very traditional royal thing to do," Bruno said. "Arranged marriage for the king. You'd hardly be the first."

"That's what I told her! But I can't imagine I'd have managed to go through with it. That was a stressful time for everyone," Gregory said, and Eddie reached over to run his fingers through the hair at the base of his neck, a quick affectionate touch.

Every so often – not frequently, but once in a while – she would see Eddie do something like that, or Gregory reach for Eddie, in a way that made her heart hurt a little. Gregory was a brother, Eddie a good friend, and she was happy they'd found each other, but it made her envious. She had her hands full with life, her own and Gregory's, and what romance came her way was fine, but the Shivadh kings seemed... especially fortunate, these days, when it came to love.

She twirled the City of Gold on her finger and listened to Eddie tell the story of their first meeting, when Gregory had been so unbelievably awkward that Alanna had to high-five Eddie as his stand-in.

"I think it's quite fortunate, you falling next in line for the throne," Milo said, as Bruno and Ofelia engaged with the king about some point of obscure historical protocol and how it might apply to the high-five. "I know it's perhaps not the most politic thing to say, especially when you still don't seem thrilled by the idea."

"It's just a lot at once," she said.

"But you are extremely well-trained for this, pragmatic, with useful skills," he said.

"Duke Tomas must have at least had some kind of handle on things, to keep power as long as he did," she said.

"He wasn't elected. Who was going to remove him? And under what process? Short of mass revolt, anyway."

"And there's no parliament. Just him and his advisory council," Alanna said, considering this.

"Well…now you and your advisory council," Milo pointed out.

"Maybe," she said, not enjoying the lie at all. "But you worked for him, and Milo…I know we didn't know each other that well at school, but you don't seem like someone who bows to power for power's sake."

"It's a strange compliment, but I will take it," he said. "Galians aren't like Shivadh, you know – we don't like excitement and pageantry. We're stoics. But more to the point, Ofelia and I both watched Duke Tomas rule, practically since birth. We saw the only way to change things was from the inside. So, that's where we went."

"A conspiracy of two, eh? And you managed to get sent to fetch me?" she asked, thinking of Michaelis and his remarks about cloak-and-dagger.

"We do what's best for Galia. I hope that's not at the expense of Askazer-Shivadlakia, but if it is, it is," he said. "Your king would probably agree," he added, raising his voice a little to get Gregory's attention. "Political expediency occasionally demands sacrifice for the sake of the state, especially from those who are in a position to see it clearly."

"Alanna doesn't necessarily agree with you there," Gregory said. "And we try to keep it to a minimum. The state is made up of people, after all. Harming the people can't be good for the country."

"Milo and I argue about that sometimes too," Ofelia said. "Your father has a saying I like," she added, and Alanna felt the tension in the room jump up a notch. "A king isn't a person, he's a king – but only during working hours."

"More or less," Gregory replied, tilting his head. "Where did you hear him say that?"

"I listen to his podcast," she replied. "He has many useful things to say about governance."

"I think we were all given to understand he's *persona non grata* in Galia," Eddie said slowly.

"In some circles," she replied. "But radio doesn't stop at the border, fortunately for us. Regardless, I assume you aren't in working hours now. Or are we considered a late evening for you?"

Gregory smiled, but Alanna could see the politician in it. "This is a farewell party for two much-loved cousins. Couldn't be more off the clock if I tried."

Eddie changed the subject with his usual skill, leaning forward to observe that a chef was rarely off the clock, and he was interested in any Galian variations on Shivadh dishes. Alanna ate lightly from the courses that were served and mostly listened. She saw Simon hovering in the doorway at one point, clearly checking to see if the food was approved-of, and gave him a smile. He'd done a lot of her and Jerry's favorite dishes.

She knew she'd picked up enough politics in the palace as a child, and was generally adept enough at them, to play Gregory's sort of political games if she wanted. But that was why she worked for Gregory rather than serving as an MP, or anything more overtly political: she didn't care to. She didn't find politics interesting in the way Gregory did, or entertaining in the way Eddie had come to. Ofelia, on the other hand, seemed to be from Gregory's school of thought, appreciating the intricate challenge of it, so it was more fun for Alanna to watch her and Gregory play the game than to participate. She was still trying to make up her mind about Milo's attitude towards such things when they brought in the sorbet for dessert.

After dinner, most of the party drifted outside onto the deck. This far out on the water, the air could be chilly but the stars were bright and stunning. Alanna leaned on the railing and listened to Eddie and Jerry, who were competing to see who could make the most puns about boats.

"I keep trying to think of a way to strike up a conversation that doesn't make it sound like I'm flattering you," Ofelia said, joining her at the railing. "Unfortunately, I was trained to open diplomatic talks with a compliment. And those two are very distracting when I want to strategize."

She nodded at Eddie and Jerry, and Alanna grinned.

"You learn to listen around it, after a while," she said. "But I'm open to being complimented. Sounds like it's a royal privilege at the duke's court."

"You certainly won't lack for it once you arrive," Ofelia said. "Everyone's going to want to curry favor. Stay on staff, on the council."

"Including you and Milo. He's already made a sidelong pitch for being my trusted advisor."

"Pushy as usual," Ofelia said, sighing. "You'll need to see for yourself, I think. But when you do, I imagine your choice of who to trust will be correct. In the meantime, a little advice?"

Alanna gestured for her to continue.

"When you get to Galia, let them – let us – call you Your Grace. At the moment it is your title, and it will get you the respect you're going to need."

"Spoken as a Galian?"

Ofelia tilted her head. "Spoken as someone who knows what it's like to be the only woman in a room very full of men."

Alanna glanced past Jerry and Eddie to where Gregory was talking with Bruno and Milo.

"I take your point," she said.

"In any case, I understand you'll need tomorrow morning to tie up loose ends, but it would be better for Milo and myself to return sooner, and there's no requirement to travel together. We may leave tomorrow morning, if you don't have any objection."

"No, none here."

"Then we'll leave a driver with you, to ensure a safe arrival," Ofelia said. "I think we're looking forward to seeing how you fare in Galia."

"Me too," Alanna said thoughtfully.

CHAPTER THREE

JERRY AND EDDIE didn't often text each other anymore. It was rare that they wanted to share something with each other that they didn't also want to inflict on Gregory and Alanna, because both of them were big talkers who liked attention. Even so, Jerry knew that Eddie would be the most amused by what he'd found, so when a friend sent him a link to a Photogram post that morning, he passed it on to Eddie privately.

Someone, probably a late-shift worker at the harbor, had seen the farewell party disembarking from the yacht the previous night. Most of them were in dark clothes, but Eddie's embroidered cream suit stood out like a beacon. Eddie had his arm around Gregory's shoulders, saying something into his ear, and Gregory was turned into him, laughing, clearly enjoying himself. In the background, Alanna had Jerry's elbow, although they weren't very visible except for the little gold sprig of flowers at her waist.

Whoever took the photo clearly agreed that they looked nice; they'd captioned it "The hottest royals in the hemisphere."

I will never be over my dorky cousin's social media glow up, Jerry texted, still lying warm and comfortable in bed.

Honestly, me neither, Eddie replied, and Jerry laughed. Another message came through. *Hey, travel safe today. Can't be there to wave you off but I packed you guys some food.*

Not one for big goodbyes anyway, but thanks, I love snacks, Jerry replied, and sent a couple of food emojis for the hell of it.

He rolled onto his back, letting his phone tip gently out of his hand so that it came to rest on his forehead, closing his eyes for a last few minutes of peace. He didn't really want to think, yet, about the trip to Galia and all that entailed. He was going willingly – more than – but that was for Alanna's sake, not because he had any special desire to see

Galia. Someday he was going to have to shake off his bad habit of following where she led, but it wasn't going to be today.

His "you do actually have to get out of bed now" alarm went off while his phone was still sitting on his head, vibrating his teeth together. He silenced it and struggled his way upright, then reached back into the blankets for the phone.

His luggage had been packed and was waiting by the front door for one of the family servants to load into the car; all he really had to do was bathe, dress, and ride down to the palace in time for their noon departure. These days it made him a little itchy, waking up early and then having nothing to do, but a regular sleep schedule was more and more appealing, past thirty.

He set some music to play on his phone, bumped the audio up, and took it into the bathroom with him while he washed and shaved. That done, he dressed in a suit laid out by his valet, decent for traveling as a visiting dignitary to Galia, and set out to acquire breakfast.

His mother and the dogs had already eaten and she was no doubt in her office, seeing to her correspondence (voluminous, never quite organized, and all done in longhand). Her days rarely varied and, while he knew she was always pleased to see him, it didn't often feel as if they even lived in the same country anymore, let alone the same house.

The dogs, meanwhile, were out being exercised, yelping joyfully in one of the gardens. He wasn't quite sure why they still bothered keeping dogs after his dad, the real dog lover of the family, had passed. Still, a dozen Shivadh Hunthunds – big, noisy, curly-coated retriever types with uncanny intelligence and no fear in their hearts – did at least fill a lot of empty space in the vast old ducal seat. The long gallery from his bedroom to the reception room, full of portraits of past dukes and duchesses, echoed with his footsteps.

The reception room itself held his favorite portrait – it showed a garden party, in the style of Matisse, featuring the last few generations of Shivadh nobility. In it, his grandfather Jason sat centrally, resplendent in an old-fashioned suit of deep blue and a spectacular, neatly-kept grey beard. His sons were seated on either side of him, Jerry's father Eitan on the right, Michaelis on the left. Eitan, already middle-aged, had his arm around Jerry's mother Sarah, significantly younger than he was; both were in Shivadh blue as well. Jerry was a kid, crouched nearby to poke at something in the grass with a stick, wearing a little navy suit but with bare feet.

Michaelis, on the other side, was only a little older in the painting than Gregory was now, but he'd already been king for several years. He was in the royal uniform of black and gold, seated, holding hands with his wife Miranda, in the vivid orange of the house of Askaz. Her sister Ruth was next to her in an almost identical outfit, holding Alanna, a cherub in a fluffy pastel ruffled dress, in her lap. Ruth's husband Mark, the cousin of the infamous Duke Tomas, was sitting in the grass at Ruth's feet, in a nondescript brown suit. He was bent over a book, studying it with Gregory, a grave-faced little boy in the royal black. He'd never actually worn the black uniform as a child, but the symbolism was meaningful; everyone was already well aware by then that serious, bookish little Gregory was the heir apparent to the throne. Michaelis had protested for years that Gregory should choose his own destiny, but Gregory's mind had been made up by the age of five.

Jerry wasn't sure why the painting was in the home of the Duke of Shivadlakia, rather than in the palace. Art did tend to get shuffled from place to place, but he suspected the royal family might have found it difficult to look at, after Alanna's parents had died. Michaelis might have palmed it off on Jerry's mother. Lord knew there were enough portraits of various dead royals in the palace as it was.

In any case, Jerry had always liked it, especially seeing himself off in the corner making mischief. As they'd all begun to grow up, he'd found it entertaining to remember Michaelis and Miranda so young, to see the hints of the adults Alanna and Gregory (and himself) would become in the children in the portrait. He liked to see his own brow and nose in the severe features of King Jason, who he barely remembered.

He passed the painting by and turned down another hall to the kitchen. Their kitchen staff weren't nearly as friendly or as entertaining as Simon or Eddie, but if Jerry wasn't at breakfast they knew to leave out something he could take on his way through. This morning there was a whole carton of food – granola bars, dried figs, little sweet oranges, and a tea-towel full of pastries. Travel treats. He took the hint, tucked the box under one arm, and went back out to the reception room. He set the box on the suitcases, looked at his luggage, looked at his watch, and said "Well, hell with it."

Ten minutes later, car loaded with his bags, music blaring through the speakers, and an onion knish between his teeth, he was driving down the winding road through the western edge of the family seat, heading for the palace. He'd be early, but it wasn't like that was going to be *bad* for his reputation, and he could get underfoot and entertain himself in the palace as easily as anywhere else.

When Darien finally tapped Alanna on the wrist in the middle of their handoff meeting and said, "I can take it from here. You need to go, the car's waiting," she felt a little twist of internal anxiety.

"Jerry's probably running late," she said, but she began shutting things down and packing up her purse and laptop case.

"Jerry's been here since breakfast," Darien said with a smile. "It's fine, Alanna. I'll handle the king in your absence, and I promise not to be so competent he replaces you. Go, enjoy your visit."

She might have stalled a little longer, but at that point most of her entourage arrived. Will, one of the palace legal team and chosen to go along because he was fluent in Italian legalese, was a small tidy man with sharp, intelligent eyes, as attached to his tablet as Alanna often was to hers. With him was Georgiana, taller than him and somewhat severe, with short ruffled hair and in a suit cut a little loose. She too had a law degree, but she was also a highly-trained bodyguard, one of the very few the Shivadh royalty bothered to employ.

"Ready to enter the lion's den?" Alanna asked them, as she left the office and they turned to follow her to the car.

"It's just Galia," Will said with a sniff. "It's not like we're going behind some iron curtain. My dad goes there every year for vacation."

"What is there to do on vacation in Galia?" Alanna asked.

"Gamble, mostly," Will replied. "He likes the horses, but the casino's pretty fun too."

"Fortunately, this time we'll be in the royal quarters, not the local casino," Alanna replied. "You've both had briefings?"

Georgie gave her a curt nod as they stepped out into the afternoon sunshine. Jerry, leaning on one of the palace cars they'd requested, looked up from his phone and waved. He looked like a model in a photoshoot, lounging in a casually rumpled but clearly expensive suit, the sun picking out gold highlights in his auburn hair. Alanna was secretly glad it was Jerry going with her. Gregory and Michaelis were both astute men, but they were also very serious sometimes, and Jerry could at least take her out of herself once in a while. She twiddled the City of Gold on her thumb idly.

"Adventure awaits, Your Grace," Jerry said, pulling open the door. "Georgie, are you riding with us?"

"In front," Georgie said, then lowered her voice. "Keeping an eye on the Galian driver. Not sure I trust him with one of our cars."

"Perhaps not, but I trust you with my life," Jerry told her earnestly, as Alanna got into the car. He closed the door after her and circled to clamber into the other side, while Georgie and Will loaded their luggage into the second car, which would follow them with Will driving. Inside, the barrier between passenger seats and driver was already raised, giving them some privacy.

"Away we go," Alanna said, as the cars pulled out of the drive, heading east towards the highlands and the passage through to Galia.

Jerry was on his phone almost immediately, scrolling through social media or perhaps reading the fashion blogs; he had little patience for long car trips. Alanna watched the scenery roll past for a while, enjoying the grassy fields and groves of fig and olive trees until they began the climb into the highlands. Most of the land around them either belonged to Jerry's family or had at one time, and it was pretty country.

She turned away from the window after a while, realizing her phone hadn't had any text or email notifications in ages, panicking briefly before remembering everything was being rerouted to Darien. Jerry, who had put his own phone away, cocked an eyebrow at her questioningly but let it go when she didn't offer an explanation for her sudden rushed consultation of her screen. He returned to the laptop he'd taken out – it was a newer model that could be folded to use as an extra-large tablet, and he was working over it with a stylus, moving abstract shapes on an irregular grid.

"What are you up to?" she asked, leaning on his shoulder to watch the shapes flick around the screen.

"Just a new puzzle," he said, giving her a quick smile. "Got tired of Sudoku."

"What's the goal?"

"Still working that out, actually," Jerry said. "It's one of those games where you're not sure what you want to achieve for a while."

She nodded and looked back down at her phone, scrolling through various apps, still leaning on his shoulder. After a minute, he shifted his arm back and around her, pulling her in more comfortably against his right side, still working away with his left hand.

"What do you want to do when we get to Galia?" he asked, eyes on his screen. "I assume there'll be some sort of formal welcome, but outside of all the usual stuff."

"I thought tomorrow I'd introduce myself to the royal genealogist, so I can start looking for a replacement," Alanna said. "Then I should talk with Milo about operations. I need to know who actually cuts checks and issues permits, that kind of thing, because I need access to the paperwork, the…bureaucracy. Although that's actually lower priority. In theory the national budget is public but it's actually very difficult to access, so I'm going to work on getting that, that'll be the most helpful. I'm going to need to speak to some of the advisors too – "

"Lord, I regret asking," Jerry murmured, amused. "All in the same day, Al?"

"It's not much more than about an hour's work in terms of networking – it's just asking other people for things with delays in-between," Alanna said. "Why, what's your plan?"

"Well, since we're there for two weeks, I thought I'd play it cool and not tip our hand wholesale," he said with a grin.

"I like to get things done," she replied, mock-prim.

"I know, which makes you amazing, because there's nothing I hate more than getting things done," Jerry replied, then shook his head. "I mean, I like getting them done, but the work to get there is irksome."

"You think it's a little much to try for all at once?" she asked.

"They know you need information, but they think you're trying to make up your mind. They don't know you already have and you're just looking for proof," Jerry said. "Let stuff flow. Get lost in the offices after seeing the genealogy records and ask who you should go to for palace operations. Find out from them where the budget data lives. Or send me, your faithful hound, to charm a clerk in the house of budgets."

"Seems like a lot of work," she said.

"The cost of sneaking around," he replied. "Or the joy, depending."

"On what?"

"On whether you're me, a man who makes trouble for the sake of it," he said, jostling her affectionately.

"You don't, really, though. You get into a lot of it, but you don't make it for no reason."

"Only with the best of intentions, you think?" he asked.

"Well, you are the vizier. You wouldn't be you without a little hint of mischief," she said.

"Spice of life," he replied. He did something to his game and it lit up with various colored patterns; perhaps it was one of those coloring-book apps. "We're about to lose signal until we're down from the highlands."

"Good to know," she said, texting the group chat. *Going silent in the last internet-free place on Earth. See you in a few.*

She had books on her phone she could read, or some podcasts downloaded – there was Michaelis and Jes's latest, about Shivadh-Spanish cooking, and a few of Noah's new one with his classmates, all about boats. Boats were not, Alanna felt, inherently fascinating; she didn't share Michaelis and Gregory's love of the outdoors. But the kids were funny, and some of the history was interesting.

"Why do you suppose it is that Askazer-Shivadlakia has olives and Galia doesn't?" Jerry asked, as she tried to decide what to listen to.

"Wrong side of the mountain, maybe," Alanna said. "Gregory might know. Or someone in the agricultural cabinet, *great for growing tomatoes*," she said, as Jerry chimed in on the joke Eddie wouldn't stop making. *The agricultural cabinet? Oh yeah, had one of those for my tomatoes.*

"I'll have to ask when we get there. Good excuse to get out and have a look around, maybe," Jerry said. "Oh, perhaps the terroir for growing them is wrong."

"What do you know about terroir?" she asked, curiously.

"This and that," he replied. "Are you listening to music?"

"Just deciding what I want to listen to," she said.

"Gimme an earbud, you can DJ for me," he said.

"Gross, I'm not giving you an earbud. I can just put the phone on speaker," she replied.

"Is sharing headphones gross?" he asked. "A philosophical debate."

"Do you want the podcast I was going to listen to or do you want to be my own personal podcast?" she asked.

"You know me, I can improvise an hour's worth of content, but I prefer to save myself for a more appreciative audience," he said. "As the lady prefers."

She consulted her podcast player again and then decided on music; something with a nice thump of bass and generic lyrics she wouldn't have to pay too much attention to. Jerry hummed idly along with the music, and she scrolled through one of the books on her phone until they were back in cell range and notifications began to pop up from the Ansevalis.

"Ofelia says Galia knows we're coming," she told Jerry. He reached over to tap her music silent.

"Ofelia says Galia, like the whole country?" he asked.

"I assume so. She says to look out for crowds, but we probably shouldn't stop. Not a security thing, we've just got somewhere to be."

"They aren't playing around, are they?" he asked. "I've got snacks if we don't want to stop for dinner." He kicked his heel against something under his seat. "The estate chefs and Eddie both packed us stuff. Pretty sure Eddie made fried chicken, because he loves us."

"Maybe in a bit," she said. "Formal evening reception, 8pm, Milo will brief us when we get there. Milo says he's sorry it's unavoidable."

"It's not like we're not used to unavoidable social obligations," he said. "The lot of a Shivadh noble is a hard one."

"Yes, very difficult," she replied, gesturing around them at the car, the driver, the bodyguard in the front passenger seat. "Especially for you. You blow off social obligations whenever you like."

"You made the genuine error of allowing people to know you're reliable," Jerry said. "Now they're trying to give you a country to run. The only reward for hard work is more work."

Eventually the road down out of the mountains widened, and the occasional building started appearing again. It was only a few isolated farm houses at first, but then residential neighborhoods began scrolling past and, off to one side for a while, a golf course. The signs, when visible, were in Italian.

They passed through one small Galian town, sleepy and quiet, and then another larger one; this one had the purple of the Galian flag strung up as bunting, and a hastily hand-painted sign in the small plaza of a city center, facing the road, reading *Welcome Duchess of the Horse* in Italian.

Duchessa del Cavallo. Alanna didn't care for it. It sounded… uncomfortably operatic.

The capital city of Levaldi lay on a river that passed around it from northeast to southwest; at the bridge in the southwestern corner, a crowd had gathered. The cars were technically unmarked, without even the royal seals on the doors that some of the Shivadh palace cars had, but they did have Shivadh parking stickers on the corners of the windshields. And, well, they were big flashy cars that looked very royal.

"Time to smile and wave," Jerry said, lowering his window and putting an arm out to wave as they passed by. Alanna did the same on the other side, smile fixed on her face. People shouted in Italian, mostly friendly, and one ambitious young Galian man threw a bouquet with astonishing accuracy, right into the window. When she picked it up, the ribbon holding it together had a phone number written on it.

"Marriages are built on worse," Jerry told her, laughing.

There weren't any more huge crowds, but there were certainly people lining the streets to watch them pass; Levaldi, like Fons-Askaz, was a labyrinth of small streets cut through with big thoroughfares, full of open-air cafes and wide pavements where people congregated. There were small river-fed canals that cut through the city like efficient blades, paying no heed to what streets they interrupted, making for dozens of decorative little bridges. And everything seemed to radiate outwards from the Palazzo Cavallo, the center of the duke's power, a large domed building in the center of the city, set slightly higher than most of the buildings surrounding it. The vista was spoiled only by the giant, ugly modern casino situated directly next to it.

They took a service road up to the back of the Palazzo, pulling into a little turnaround clearly meant for deliveries to the kitchen. Milo, notified by the security gate that they were near, was waiting for them with several men and women in Palazzo livery.

52

"Your Graces, welcome to Galia," Milo said, offering his hand to help her out of the car.

"Glad to be here," Jerry said, stretching his legs and rotating his shoulders as a valet opened his door for him. "And we beat the deadline."

"Barely. Hello again, Milo," Alanna said, accepting polite cheek-kisses. "Thank you for coming to meet us."

"Yes, Ofelia tells me you got her message about the reception. I'm so sorry, the council strong-armed us into it. They clearly want you tired and off-balance for your first meeting."

"What's the advantage there?" Alanna asked, and then realized she was already treating him like one of Gregory's aides or her own researchers, there to answer questions and gather intel for her. She reminded herself that Milo was not necessarily a reliable source – and he had his own job to do in any case.

"Establishing power early, I suppose," Milo said, seeming pleased by her question. "Or one of them wants to convince you to accept the duchy and thinks he can do it tonight while your guard's down. This way," he added, leading them up a handful of steps and into a back hallway. "There's a changing room we've set aside for you – your bags will be taken to your actual rooms – "

"No – let me take that one," Alanna said, pointing at one of them. "I need a dress from it."

The man handling the bag looked perplexedly at Milo. Alanna remembered herself, repeating the request in Italian. His face broke into a grin.

"Yes, of course, Your Grace," he replied in Italian, apparently delighted she spoke the language.

"This one for me," Jerry said in less perfect Italian, pulling one of his bags after him, pre-empting a liveried attendant. "It's fine, I can do it," he told the man. Then, after a second of consideration, he reached into his pocket and found a crisp Galian cash bill. Alanna heard him murmur, "If our bags reach our rooms without being searched, there's another for you."

"Half will need to go to the officer," the man said. Jerry sighed and gave him another bill. "You're a generous man, Your Grace."

"Why not let them search the bags if they want? Nothing

incriminating in them," Alanna said in an undertone, following Milo inside.

"Speak for yourself, I might have controlled substances in mine," Jerry told her with a grin. She swatted his arm. "Why should they get to search us? They've got no business poking through our stuff."

"How did you even know they would?"

"I didn't, but I don't like it when my luggage is out of my sight, and now I've confirmed someone was going to," he replied with a shrug.

"You know, sometimes I think you have a lot more of your grandfather Jason in you than you let on," she said.

"I've just spent years stealing Uncle Mike's trashy spy thriller novels," Jerry replied.

"In here," Milo said, holding a door for them. Inside was a small office with a sitting area, a bathroom off to one side. "You can change, wash – have you eaten?"

"We had food on the trip," Jerry said, looking around him. "I assume there'll be nibbles at the reception, too. Can't drink on empty stomachs."

"It would certainly be an interesting first impression if you did," Milo said. "Anything you require that we can provide within the next ten minutes or so?"

"We'll be fine," Alanna reassured him. "Just let us get changed and maybe…if there's anyone who can stay close to us at the reception, someone to offer context…"

"I unfortunately can't escort you, but Ofelia will be escorting His Grace if you've no objections. As duchess, you're expected to attend unescorted if you're not married."

"Well, that's helpful," Alanna sighed. "Can Jerry and Ofelia stay close, at least?"

"I recommend it," Milo agreed. "I'll let her know."

He gave a little bow and left, and Alanna went to her bag, opening it and shedding her traveling clothes while Jerry changed into something less rumpled, backs to each other out of politeness.

"Thank goodness it's not black tie," he said, coming over to zip up the back of her cocktail dress. "My tuxedo is a wreck."

"We can unpack tomorrow morning and get things laid out," she said. Jerry wrapped his arms around her shoulders, hugging her from behind, and she leaned into the comfort of it for a moment. He smelled better than anyone had a right to, having spent that much time in a car. Probably something his valet did to his clothes before packing them.

"Let's go dazzle 'em," he said, and let her go, heading for the door.

When Jerry walked into the reception that evening, it was like every party his father had ever thrown, without the benefit of Shivadh liberality.

It was almost entirely men; Alanna and Ofelia were two of about a dozen women, not counting the servers. There were perhaps three times that many men, and most of them looked to be over fifty.

"It's the duke's advisory council," Ofelia said, her arm in Jerry's but her head inclined a little towards Alanna, on her other side. "Plus wives, and well-connected political hopefuls."

"Yikes," Alanna said.

"Tits and teeth," Jerry replied.

"Charming," Ofelia told him.

"Wasn't my idea," Jerry shot back, and just then there was the thump of a staff on the ground.

"His Grace, Gerald, Duke of Shivadlakia, and Ms. Ofelia Ansevali," a pair of voices announced, first in Italian and then in English, and Jerry left Alanna behind for a heart-dropping moment as they entered the room properly. All heads lifted, all eyes fixing on them. Jerry tried to radiate authority and nobility, but he suspected they'd figure out his real deal soon enough.

"Her Grace and Majesty, Duchess of the Horse of the House of Galia, the Lady Alanna Daskaz," came the same dual-language voices.

"We can drop the English if you want, by the way," Jerry said to Ofelia. "We both speak Italian. Or anyway, I get by. Alanna's fluent."

"Very helpful, and considerate. But you, perhaps, don't let on yet," she replied. "Always an advantage when they think you don't understand what they're saying."

"I like you more all the time," he said. She showed her teeth gently.

The reception wasn't all that different from various events he'd had to attend as Gregory's cousin – an introduction line, the presentation of dignitaries' wives, extremely brief small talk until everyone had at least had a chance to shake hands. Then a subtle jockeying to see who would get the ear of the duchess first. The Shivadh kings preferred dancing before conversation, but Jerry estimated roughly half of the men in the room might collapse if they tried anything more vigorous than a slow waltz. He snagged a handful of snacks that were being passed around, then lifted a glass of champagne for Ofelia from another tray, passed it to her, and looked around for the bar.

Once he'd found it, he said "Stick with Alanna," in Ofelia's ear and abandoned her. He headed for the corner, where a handful of men, on the younger end of the fifty-to-five-hundred range, were gathered around two harried looking bartenders.

"Ah, do you know how to make a Gunner?" he asked the nearest one in a low voice. She gave him an uncomprehending look, then held up a finger and tugged on the sleeve of the man working next to her.

"Repeat, please?" he said. "My English is better."

"Oh, thanks, sorry," Jerry replied. "A Gunner? Type of drink?"

"That is…ah, yes," the man agreed, cutting himself off with a nod. "I believe I know."

Jerry leaned back on the bar, snacking on the appetizers while the bartender measured and mixed, and it took about three seconds for one of the other men at the bar to approach. No-fail. Jerry grinned.

"Your Grace," the man said. "Not a champagne drinker?"

"Not allowed anymore, I'm afraid, after an incident with a fountain," Jerry replied. "It's Consigliere Riva, isn't it?"

"A good memory, given how many names you've just heard," Riva said with a sharp smile. "How are you enjoying Galia?"

"Haven't seen much of it yet," Jerry replied, accepting his drink from the bartender and dropping a tip in the glass behind the bar. "These nibbles are very good though."

"We were pleased to be able to promptly offer such hospitality. Obviously very important to make the duchess feel welcomed," Riva said. "She'll have a long night ahead of her, I expect," he added, watching Alanna and Ofelia speak with one of his colleagues.

"Ah, fortunately Alanna's used to it."

"And she speaks Italian! An added benefit, although you'll find most of us on the council know enough English," Riva continued. "Anyone who says they don't is pulling your leg."

"I'll bear that in mind," Jerry said soberly. "You aren't going to go circle with the others?" he added, watching the subtle way people tried to find strong positions from which to approach Alanna.

"No. I have no pressing concerns, and there will be time enough in council meetings to become better acquainted."

Jerry knew this score. Some of the men wanted direct access, but Riva was smarter than that. He wanted a connection, like the one he could get through the duchess's chaperone. Well, there was nothing inherently wrong with that, Jerry supposed.

He made small-talk on autopilot, and suspected Riva was doing the same, both of them with half their mind elsewhere. Jerry had his eye on Milo, who was helping to manage the crowd, moving between knots of people, shaking hands here and there. It was beginning to be much clearer to Jerry why Milo kept pinging him as off, somehow.

Milo, he decided, wasn't concealing anything specifically from the Shivadh nobility. He was concealing something from everyone, and they only noticed because they'd known him at school. Jerry even thought he could put a finger on what, generally, was wrong: Milo Ansevali was furious about something, the kind of low-banked, long-burn anger that was constant and therefore hard to see. He could only see it now because this was clearly touching on whatever enraged him. Jerry watched one of Milo's hands flex open, curve back into a fist, and then force open again as he spoke, smiling, with one of the older men casually waiting his turn to speak with Alanna.

Jerry supposed he had plenty to be angry about. He clearly hadn't liked Duke Tomas, and having brought the new duchess here, he now couldn't do much to defend her. Milo couldn't know how little Alanna needed defending, and might even be annoyed with Jerry as well for abandoning her. Certainly Milo was keeping an eye on both of them, glancing over every so often between being obviously condescended to by members of the council.

Why take the job if he hated it so much? Or at least if he hated the people surrounding him. Something to investigate while they were here, perhaps.

He turned his full attention back to the small-talk with Riva, mainly because someone new had entered the conversation – Bruno, of all people, the quiet nerd who got motion sickness.

"So good to see you again, Your Grace," Bruno was saying.

"Pleasure's mine," he replied. "I never got to ask how your research in the Shivadh archives turned out."

"Very well indeed," Bruno replied. "Consigliere Riva, did you know His Grace here is actually, hereditarily, a prince?"

"Only by certain rules," Jerry cautioned. "You'd need to be very careful making that claim in Askazer-Shivadlakia."

"You're only a prince in some places?" Riva asked, eyebrows rising.

"Well, we're democratic, as you know," Jerry said, and Riva nodded. Jerry checked on Alanna, estimating he had about five minutes before he should go back to Ofelia. "The king is declared by vote only. Can't be a king without a popular vote. But the king's children should always be referred to as royalty. It reminds people of what they had to put up with, more or less, as children of the ruler."

"But your father was a prince, properly titled, son of the king directly," Bruno said.

"Mm, yes," Jerry sipped his drink. "But that was honorary. It wouldn't pass down to me unless he became king. My uncle was king before he retired," he said to Riva, just to see what kind of reaction that got. Mostly a poker face, which was interesting. "So my cousin Gregory was prince, and then elected king. His children will be princes and princesses, or princeps, I suppose – that's the suggestion we've had for the gender-neutral, you know, going forward."

"How…progressive," Riva observed, lip wrinkling a little.

"Must move with the times. In any case, it was less confusing to refer to my father as a duke than a prince, since he was never going to run for the kingship even if my uncle left office. No interest in that kind of bureaucracy. Can't blame him."

"And now you are the Duke of Shivadlakia," Riva said carefully. "With land bordering on Galia, in the highlands."

Jerry bit down on the urge to make the old joke, *Just the one highland, really*. Instead, he smiled. "Yes! It's one reason I was so pleased to accompany Alanna. Great to see more of the place. That reminds me,

Bruno, I'd love to know if you could show me where the original ducal holdings might have ended. I believe Shivadlakia sold a lot of land to Galia and I'd be interested in seeing the areas that might have been kept by my ancestors."

"Of course," Bruno said, but he looked confused by the request. It was mostly nonsense, but it was a good reason to tromp around the country a bit, while Alanna had to put up with all of these…delightful consiglieres. "I'll see about locating some maps for you."

"Great. Consigliere Riva, it's been splendid, but I'm neglecting my date. If you'll excuse me," he said, and headed back towards Ofelia. She gracefully made space between herself and Alanna.

"Just how awful is it?" he asked.

"Not any worse than what I've seen Gregory put up with," Alanna replied. "You can have about a minute and a half before someone is going to get impatient."

"Nothing to report here that can't wait. I – " he stopped, because someone had just entered the room, a late arrival who looked like he still felt he was too early. He wore a suit that was both expensive and several years out of style, though it looked new, and the light caught the shine off his mostly-bald head, where he didn't have any short, bristling white hair. He looked faintly like an overdressed turtle.

"Is that Brasolin?" Jerry asked, indicating the old man with a slight jerk of the head. "Holy shit, what an old bat."

Alanna followed his gaze. "It must be him. I wish we'd had time to get some kind of brief on the council."

"That's Consigliere Brasolin," Ofelia confirmed, following their gaze. "Alanna, this may not be pleasant, but…"

"No, I agree," Alanna said, and Ofelia patted Jerry on the shoulder and left, crossing the floor to where Brasolin seemed to be imperiously waiting for her.

"He can't be very fond of you," Jerry said. "Or me, for that matter. If I'd thought about it I'd have brought a pie."

That got a sharp noise out of Alanna, who bit her lip briefly. "Don't make me laugh, he's about to come talk to us," she said.

"I'm going to find the video," Jerry said, reaching for his phone.

"No! Jerry, don't you dare," Alanna told him. "Seriously. You know how important he is in Galia."

"I know how funny it is watching him get hit in the face with a pie," Jerry said.

"Not right now. Behave yourself."

"Yes ma'am," Jerry replied, as Brasolin reached them.

Alanna offered her hands. "Consigliere Brasolin, how nice to meet you," she said in Italian.

Alexandros Brasolin, the overdressed turtle, took her hands and bowed over them, but when he straightened, his eyes were narrowed. Forty years earlier, Brasolin had been one of the candidates running against Michaelis for the kingship of Askazer-Shivadlakia, claiming citizenship through a Shivadh grandmother and blatantly, at least to the history books, looking for power. He'd never had a strong chance of winning against the charismatic younger son of the sitting king, but it was the pie that had sealed the deal.

Jerry wondered if Brasolin could see on their faces that all they could think of was the film footage, shown in Shivadh history classes, of a political activist who favored Michaelis, hitting Brasolin in the face with a pie during a campaign debate. One of Michaelis's first acts as king had been to quietly pardon the man who'd done it.

"A pleasure to meet you, Your Grace," Brasolin said to Alanna, also in Italian. Jerry had to give him this, he seemed sincere. "Kind of you to arrive with such speed."

"It seemed like it needed immediate attention," Alanna replied. "His Grace was young to have passed so suddenly."

"Indeed. Quite the loss. Still, there seem to be some benefits," he said. "Your presence. Perhaps a reconciliation between nations."

"Perhaps so. I'd be interested to hear your thoughts on it," Alanna said, which was something she absolutely had learned from Eddie, Jerry thought. It was a key phrase of his for when he wanted someone to feel like he was listening despite having already made a decision about what to do. "I believe Milo is setting my agenda — I'll make sure to find some time on it to speak with you further."

He gave her a nod, seemingly satisfied with this for the night, and retreated strategically.

"I'm texting Michaelis," Jerry said.

"If you really have to. Tell him from me that Brasolin has not aged gracefully."

"He has a face meant for pies," Jerry said, taking his phone out again. He shot a quick message to Michaelis, then managed to find a set of animated images of Brasolin getting the pie in the face, and sent those sequentially to the group chat. Alanna's expression didn't change as her notifications began beeping while she was being buttonholed about urgent paperwork by one of the other consiglieres.

Gregory, uncharacteristically, sent a string of laughter – *ahhahahahahah hahahaha* – and then a second message, *Sorry this is Eddie, Greg just explained it, I was holding the wrong phone.*

"Jerry, would you send a message," Alanna said, handing him her unlocked phone. "Tell them that the Duchess of the Horse simply cannot surround herself with a trio of buffoons any longer, and I have fired all three of you."

Ofelia looked amused. "Chaperone and social secretary?" she asked Jerry.

"Not as of ten seconds ago, I've been fired," Jerry said, hitting send and handing Alanna back her phone. "It's something Gregory does sometimes," he told Ofelia, more seriously. "He can't really be seen to be on his phone at official functions, so he asks one of us to send a message if he needs to. Used to be Alanna or me, now it's usually Eddie. Everyone expects Eddie to be on his phone."

"A strategy I hadn't considered," Ofelia said thoughtfully. "Duke Tomas didn't use his phone for communication."

"What did he use it for?" Alanna asked.

"Videos, mostly," Ofelia said, with a vagueness that told Jerry very little but apparently spoke volumes to Alanna, who wrinkled her nose.

"Brasolin's very powerful here, though – you aren't wrong," Jerry said, considering the room, the way people were moving and the change in dynamic since he'd arrived.

"Something we would all do well to remember," Ofelia agreed.

"Ofelia, if I want to circulate more, do you need to come with me?" Jerry asked. "I don't want to be seen to abandon my date."

"It's all right, I can handle things at this point, most of the introductions have been made," Alanna said. "Go entertain yourself, Jerry. Ofelia, do what you need to."

Ofelia looked like she was pleased, in a way, that Alanna was giving the orders. Jerry offered her his elbow.

"I think you should know," he said, as they left Alanna to some new would-be advisor, "one of my favorite things to do is meddle. It's mostly for my own amusement, but if it can serve the crown I always like it that much more. I feel there is fertile soil for that here, with you."

"What kind of meddling did you have in mind?" Ofelia asked, sounding more than mildly interested.

"I'm not picky," he said, but he narrowed his eyes, sweeping them around the room. "Wouldn't mind thinning the herd a little. Some of these fellows are just annoying Alanna, and I can't allow that."

"You'd like a target?" she asked.

"I'd like to know who the bad eggs on the council are. Not the competent ones who are just unpleasant. I want the boat anchors," Jerry said, making a little slashing motion with his free hand. "Cut 'em loose."

"I can offer intelligence, if nothing else," she said. "Introduce you to a couple of the heaviest of boat anchors."

Jerry beamed at her. "Let's have some fun, then."

It really was an endurance race, these formal occasions; Alanna knew they wore Gregory out, much as he enjoyed them. Now, after a long car ride and an evening full of introductions, re-introductions and discussions, it was starting to take its toll. But then, that was what Milo had meant – they wanted her off-balance. At least some of the council members had left early, and the longer conversations were easier, with less shifting between people and remembering who was who.

Then there was a break, someone leaving before someone else arrived, and Milo and Jerry both stepped in at the same time to block out anyone else.

"Just the man I wanted to see," Jerry said, and Milo pivoted, clearly a little startled. "I suspect you know how to get the bartenders to issue last call. Al's fading and I'm bored."

"I was about to ask," Milo said. "Technically, you can leave at any time, of course, but now would be good timing. Ofelia and I can circulate, help the exodus along."

Alanna nodded gratefully.

"If you leave through there, someone will take you up to your suites," Ofelia added, indicating the door they'd entered through at the start of the night. "You should leave first," she added to Alanna. "His Grace can go once you have."

"I'll be three minutes behind you," Jerry promised Alanna, giving her a formal Shivadh bow and a grin. Alanna, gratefully, retreated back through the door, watching as Ofelia deftly blocked someone who clearly still wanted another word with her. In the corridor behind the door, she leaned on a handy table and took her shoes off, groaning. A man in the ducal livery jumped up from a chair.

"Your Grace," he said. "Would you care to retire? I can show you to your suite."

"Please," she said. "And please say it's not far."

"Not at all, just up these stairs."

"Lord, stairs," she mumbled to herself, but he heard her; a smile flitted across his face.

"His Grace never allowed guests to stay on the ground floor," he said. "He believed the rooms were not sufficiently secure or private," he continued, as they slowly climbed the stairs.

"So what does he…did he do with the ground floor?" she asked.

"Storage. Offices. Some of it was converted for a menagerie, and the animals' kitchen and veterinary office take up a good deal of space," the man said. They reached the top of the stairs, thankfully, and he crossed the hallway to indicate a door. "Here you are."

"Thank you. Oh – my guest, Gerald, Duke of Shivadlakia – "

"Next to you on the left. Your entourage is across the hall. If you require anything, there's a buzzer on the bedside table."

Inside, there was a little sitting room with a very nice view of some manicured, parklike grounds, including what looked like a decorative iron gazebo. There was a long, wide arch leading into the bedroom – not much privacy, with no door on it – and beyond that she could see a bathroom. Across from the bedroom was a small alcove with a very basic little kitchen arrangement. She flopped on the sofa in the sitting area, wondering if she had the energy to write up notes from the night – something Gregory usually did, dictating them into his phone and putting his thoughts in order later with her.

She could probably talk them out like Gregory did, at least. She was just getting her phone recorder app open when she heard clattering from the other side of the wall, then a knock on her door. "Al, it's Jerry."

"Come in," she called. He walked in, and she smiled at the sight – shoes off, tie and jacket already gone, probably dumped somewhere on the floor in his suite. He'd popped his cufflinks, so his sleeves swung a little loose, and he had something in one hand, like a bocce ball.

"Is that a pomegranate?" she asked, blinking at it.

"It is, in fact, a mysterious pomegranate," he replied, holding it up for her to examine. "I found it sitting on my luggage in my bedroom. I don't imagine you arranged for cryptic fruit to be provided."

"No, but I love pomegranates. Very cultural, too," she said, as he put it into her palm and wandered away, exploring. "National Shivadh fruit. Someone was being thoughtful."

"You've got one too," he called from the arched doorway into her bedroom.

"Do you suppose they'd try to poison us?" she asked, laughing as he came back to the sofa with a second pomegranate. He sat down on the ottoman across from her and took his own back, considering both together.

"Well, I've been back and forth to the bar all night and you've had snacks and champagne, it seems fruitless to try and kill us with something as difficult as a pom," he said, and then laughed. "Fruitless!"

She recognized the loopiness of exhaustion in his voice. "You should get some sleep."

"So should we both."

"Agreed, but I still have to dictate my notes," she said, holding up her phone. "And I've had just enough champagne that I should have some water, too."

"Fair enough. You dutiful types," he said, putting one pomegranate aside and taking a little folding knife out of his pocket. "Couldn't be me. Anyway, go on. Your bags are in the bedroom. Talk your notes out while you're getting your pajamas on. I'll fix us a snack."

"Don't hurt yourself," she said, as he started to work the knife into the top of the pomegranate, carefully pivoting the blade around his thumb to slice the rind open.

"Not to fret, done this a million times," he replied. "Go. Sooner you get your notes in, sooner you can sleep. Ofelia said we had nothing tomorrow until ten," he added, rising and going to the little kitchen as she headed for the bedroom.

He worked quietly while she talked to her phone, her voice low enough that he probably couldn't hear more than the rise and fall of her tone. She tried to get down as much as she could from memory as she changed into a pair of sleep pants and a t-shirt, taking the phone with her into the bathroom, washing her makeup off and running a wet comb through her hair. By the time that was finished, she'd covered as much as she could think of. If it was possible to be *more* tired than she had been, she was.

Jerry brought over a plate full of pomegranate sections from the kitchen as she came back into the room; he'd rolled up his sleeves to the elbows and sectioned the fruit so neatly that there was hardly a seed out of place.

She felt a warm swell of affection for him that she didn't often allow herself. Jerry was a good friend, and she'd known as a teenager that she could have all the crush on him she wanted as long as she never did anything about it. Alanna knew how to spot a heartbreak in the making and avoid it. Still, it was nice sometimes to let herself enjoy looking. The affection was banked down low enough it wouldn't harm anyone, including her.

Jerry, oblivious to her private thoughts, set the plate down and went back to the kitchen, returning with a tray that had a carafe of water, two glasses, and a clean but crumpled handkerchief containing some slightly-dented appetizers from the reception, clearly stolen off a tray and stuffed into his pocket. He gave her a cocky grin.

"Take half an hour, come down from all the excitement a little," he said, offering her a section of pomegranate. "Want to hear all the cool stuff I learned from Ofelia?"

She did, but she also knew this was an excuse to let her be silent; Jerry could fill a room with noise for hours, effortlessly, and mean nothing by any of it. He wouldn't expect her to retain any of it, either, well aware it was nonsense. So she sat on the sofa, sipping water, eating pomegranate seeds and weird little finger sandwiches while he laid out his own evening, which sounded like a lot more fun than hers had been.

"Anyway, my Italian was never great but it is very rusty now, so just as well I pretended I haven't got any," he said, as her eyelids began to seriously droop. "I think I get the gist of most of what's being said, but I couldn't hold an intelligent conversation in Italian. Barely manage that in English," he added.

"Ah, don't say that," she said, and he cocked his head at her.

"Yeah, you're right. I usually keep up with you and Gregory, anyway, so I must do okay," he said, as if he'd genuinely considered it and revised his opinion. "And you look bushed. Go to bed."

"You too? No more mischief?" she asked, standing and accepting a hug and a cheek-kiss.

"Not tonight. I'll be up a little while yet, might unpack. Want me anywhere specific tomorrow?" he asked, gathering the remains of their late-night snack back onto the tray and carrying it to the kitchen.

"No. Well, breakfast. What time is it now?"

"Nearly one," he said, and then, clearly seeing her struggle tiredly with the math, he said, "I can set an alarm for nine."

"Not early enough."

"I won't go earlier than six."

"That's…" she frowned.

"Five hours," he said gently. "How about I come get you at seven-thirty if you aren't up. I can't imagine breakfast will be ready before then anyway."

She nodded, heading for the bedroom. "Night, Jerry."

"Night, Duchessa," he said, and laughed when she threw an obscene gesture over her shoulder at him. She could hear her suite door open and close, and then his own; she thought possibly he slammed it for her benefit, to let her know he was in for the night.

CHAPTER FOUR

ALANNA DID SLEEP that night, if not particularly well. Her bed was softer than she was used to, and the room was so quiet. Her snug little apartment in Fons-Askaz was close enough to the harbor that she was used to coastal noises in the night – waves and the odd creak of boats, the cries of seagulls.

She figured that there was probably somewhere they were meant to go to get breakfast, or that it could be brought to her room, but instead she was up early enough, and Jerry was prompt enough, that they went in search of it. It caused a flurry of excitement in the kitchen when they arrived, but Jerry charmed the head chef with broken Italian and Alanna found herself sitting at a little table at the back of the kitchen, eating brioche and drinking extremely good coffee with Jerry, a companionable little meal for two.

"It's all about twenty degrees off normal, isn't it?" he asked, watching the kitchen staff work as he ruminated. "It's like home but not quite home. Brioche instead of scones, jam from the wrong side of the mountain…" He tapped the side of the little pot of jam with the handle of his knife, where it bore the ducal Galian seal instead of the Shivadh royal arms. "Coffee's all right, though."

"It's just more Italian. The English never made it over the highlands after they took Askazer-Shivadlakia," Alanna said, opening her phone to check her Photogram feed. The palace didn't seem to have burned down without them. Eddie had posted a few more photos from the farewell cruise, including a very sweet selfie he'd taken with her, captioned "Already missing #ladydaskaz," which had lots of well-wishes for her visit to Galia. She suspected either Eddie or the staff had gone through and excised a bunch of negative comments about Galia, its relationship to Askazer-Shivadlakia, and whether or not it was stealing *their* duchess out of spite.

"Do you suppose they could make a brioche scone?" Jerry asked, as she continued to scroll. "Like a cronut, only unbearably European. A scioche. Brione?"

"Isn't that just a currant bun?" she asked absently, trying to get past all the recommended-for-you posts – then stopping and scrolling back up as something caught her eye.

"I suppose it would be. Wouldn't mind that, either. I'll make some requests, I think. I like a good pastry, but I'd like an egg even better. Anything you'd like requested for breakfast tomorrow?" he asked, but Alanna barely heard him. "Al?" he prompted.

"Sorry, I'm – have you looked at Photogram this morning?" she asked.

"Only to post, I had extremely photogenic bedhead. I try not to read my feed before nine anymore. Too much input too early in the morning," he said.

"Very mature of you."

"One does one's best. Why? Gregory post something inflammatory?"

"No, it's the algorithm," she replied. "Now that we're in Galia it's throwing recommendations for Galian Photograms into my feed and they're…strange."

"How so?"

"Well, they reference us, sometimes. More, obviously, right now, but if you scroll back…" she flipped through the accounts, curious. "There's an expression they use. *How Shivadh.*"

"Really," Jerry said, leaning over interestedly to inspect her phone, then getting up and moving his chair around to sit next to her. "How are they using it?"

"Seems to be…I'm not sure, actually. This is like when Gregory was trying to figure out what 'yeet' meant because he thought it was a dance move," Alanna said. Jerry chuckled. "It's not a hashtag, more like a saying that's just been imported to social media. Seems like it's a response to…it's like a specific kind of aesthetic, maybe?"

"Good or bad?" Jerry asked. "Are we the Beautiful People or are we the embarrassing next-door neighbors?"

"Could be value-neutral, or contextual. It seems like it refers to modern things. Maybe like avant-garde," she said. "Like they're saying, if something is progressive, or even just new and shiny, it's Shivadh, but that isn't always a good thing. I've never seen it before. Comms should have briefed me on it if they're aware of it."

"Maybe because we ignore Galia as a rule?" Jerry said, leaning his head on her shoulder, still watching her scroll through Galian Photograms. "What I want to know is how Eddie doesn't know about it."

"Almost all Galian Photograms are in Italian, and he doesn't speak Italian."

"Ah yes. I believe the excuse he gave was *California Public Schools*," Jerry said, amused.

"He's monitoring half the social media in Askazer-Shivadlakia anyway, unfair to make him do Galia as well. Definitely unfair to make him learn Italian when he's already learning Hebrew."

"Is he?" Jerry asked. "He hasn't mentioned that."

"Gregory said he didn't have to convert, but I think he's secretly very pleased he's trying to."

"Those two are going to raise some real weird kids," Jerry said.

"Strange to think about, isn't it?" Alanna asked.

"I suppose. Wonder if the ducal line will end with me like it did for old Tomas," Jerry said.

"Why? You're not a particularly objectionable man like he was, and Shivadh men often have children late in life, especially in the nobility. You're only thirty."

"Yeah, Dad was over fifty when I was born. Still, not being particularly objectionable and actually being marriage material are very different," Jerry said. "I could get married tomorrow if I wanted, but whoever it would be, she'd only want me for my title. Hard to find someone who'd take me on non-titled terms. Anyway, I have hang-ups."

Alanna leaned back and looked at him. "Like weird kinks or something?"

"No – oh, maybe. I don't know what lies in my subconscious, and I refuse to excavate. No, I get hung up on people, and usually for really terrible reasons."

"Huh. How Shivadh," Alanna said to him, and Jerry grinned. "Anyway, this whole Photogram thing is exactly the kind of information we thought we could find and make use of. I'll send a brief to comms and ask them to take a look."

"Ah, and I suspect the Ansevalis are looking for us," Jerry said, leaning back and lifting an arm. Alanna followed his gaze and saw Bruno Sheff in the kitchen doorway, clearly looking for something, probably them. "Bruno! Sheff! Over here!"

"There you are," Bruno said, dodging deftly past hurrying staff members to reach them. "Milo just went to fetch you both for breakfast and found you missing. I said I'd help the search. But I see you shifted for yourselves," he added in amusement, taking in the remains of breakfast strewn across the table.

"The Shivadh palace keeps an informal house," Alanna told him. "But if there's somewhere we ought to be…"

"Well, not ought, exactly, but Milo would like to brief you on the day's agenda, that kind of thing," Bruno said. "Come with me?"

"Do you usually breakfast in the Palazzo Cavallo?" Alanna asked, as he led them out of the kitchen and down a hallway.

"I live here," Bruno said. "Perk of the job – the Palazzo has housing for about half the staff who work in it. There's a dining room we eat in, that's where I'm taking you now – although in future we can have meals brought to your room if you prefer. Duke Tomas ate in his rooms, or in the menagerie patio."

"Someone mentioned that last night – he kept a little zoo?" Alanna said.

"Yes – we put you in a suite that looks out on it. It's very pretty, if…" Bruno considered how to word it. "Old-fashioned," he decided.

"I don't mind eating with the staff," Jerry said. "Seems more useful."

"It would be seen as very democratic of you," Bruno told Alanna. "Whether that's the impression you'd like to give is up to you."

"Seen by whom?" Alanna asked, and Bruno gave her a surprised look.

"Shrewd question. Depends on who you'd like to see you there. If you were to, say, post an image of yourself with the staff to Photogram, the people of Galia would no doubt appreciate your, ah, common touch? In a good way. The consiglieres might feel markedly different – like you weren't respecting the office. That said, very few of them have that sort of nuanced understanding of the younger generation. Or know what Photogram is."

"We'll eat with staff until further notice, but I'd appreciate no Photograms for now," Alanna said.

"I'll make sure it's understood. Most wouldn't anyway; the Palazzo has some stringent rules about photography on-grounds."

"Lord, have I already broken a rule?" Jerry asked.

Bruno's mouth quirked. "I think bedhead selfies are exempt," he said. It occurred to Alanna that it was a little strange an archivist should be aware of what Jerry had posted that morning, but she set that aside for now. Milo had said Bruno was a fan of Eddie's; perhaps that extended to Jerry as well.

The staff dining room wasn't at all the institutional canteen she expected; it was an airy, high-ceilinged affair with tall windows, fitted with decorative grilles on the outside. Inside were a series of round wooden tables and comfortable-looking brocade chairs.

"Ah, you found them," Milo said, rising from his seat. "Thank you, Bruno. Would you let Ofelia know?"

"Already done," Bruno said, waggling his phone. "I'm afraid I can't stay, but it was good to see you again, Duchess Alanna. Duke Gerald, I'm working on those maps," he said to Jerry, and withdrew.

Milo led them to one of the round tables, past a few other staff members who gave them covert curious looks. Alanna noticed Will and Georgie dining at a table near the window and gave them a wave.

"Sorry we slipped our harness," Jerry said, settling in, lightly making their excuses. "We weren't sure where to go. Bruno told us we can eat breakfast here most mornings?"

"Yes, by and large – you can almost always get a meal here, any time of day. There may be one or two breakfasts that local concerns would like you to attend, but we can go over all that," Milo said, turning to Alanna. "Have you eaten? I can wait to review your schedule for the day."

"We ate in the kitchen. By the way," she added, "someone left pomegranates in our rooms last night, do you know anything about that?"

"Oh! Yes, sorry, I arranged that. Didn't remember to tell you."

"As gifts go, a little cryptic," Alanna said, but she gave him a reassuring smile.

"Was it? I know they're a particular Shivadh symbol. I thought it would be a nice touch of home, and maybe a decent snack after the reception."

"He's got us there," Jerry said to Alanna.

"We did appreciate them," she agreed. Milo looked pleased as he opened his folio case and handed them each a printed schedule.

"Ordinarily the council meets from ten to one every day," he said. "Luncheon, then individual meetings and paperwork and such in the afternoon."

"Three more hours with the council this morning sounds excruciating after last night," Alanna said, consulting the agenda. "But it does say here that I'm due for only half an hour today."

"Yes – I agreed with your assessment," Milo said. "The council can carry on without ducal approval for a few weeks, at least, before things start to catch on fire, so you won't be obliged to attend every meeting for the full time. The duke rarely did, after all. This morning is just to familiarize you with the proceedings. We've scheduled a tour of the Palazzo for the morning, and then a driving tour of Levaldi in the afternoon. Some of the younger nobles have asked you to dinner tonight, which should be a lot lower-impact than last night's reception, but you can decline and rebook if you think it's a bit much."

"No, the dinner sounds fine," Alanna said, "but I'm not sure I want two tours today – and I actually…" she took out her phone, consulting it. "I have a list of things I'd like to do and see as well, beginning…"

She trailed off, because Milo had laughed –quietly, clearly trying not to, but all the same. When she glanced at him, he shook his head.

"Apologies, it's only – I think your job for His Majesty in the palace was very similar to my job for His Grace here in the Palazzo," he said. "It's just pleasant and a little funny to find you appreciate the, ah, operations of it all."

She smiled back, pleased he'd recognized that she might be a duchess by birth but was an administrator by trade.

"Now, what's on the agenda you made?" Milo continued.

"Introductions at ten to the council is fine," she said, looking through her notes. "I'd like to meet with the royal genealogist after, if I can – I'll bring Jerry for that, and maybe get some printouts for our legal team, just to confirm that everything's in order."

"Certainly. Bruno can help, he shares an office in the archives."

"And I think we talked about a review of the national budget?"

"That's a little sticky, but I'm working on it," Milo said. "Won't have it ready for you today. The lower you go in a bureaucracy, the tighter people tend to hold on to their paperwork."

"Then let's push the tour of the Palazzo to this afternoon, after lunch. Where is this dinner – here?"

"No, they've booked one of the nicer restaurants in town."

"Oh, perfect, then I can see at least a little bit of Levaldi, and I'll do the official tour some other day."

"Certainly. Anything else?"

"Those were the big priorities. I'd love to see some kind of information on the major industries in Galia, there's not much available online," she said. "Maybe tour some factories or farms or similar."

Milo considered this. "Off the top of my head, it's almost entirely hospitality. Casino, restaurants, hotels, golf courses. We're heavily – perhaps overly, but that's just my opinion – invested in tourism. There's some agriculture, but it's on the outskirts. Not much manufacturing, but I can arrange for you to see what there is."

"What do you think we should be invested in?" Alanna asked. She saw Jerry mouth 'we' to himself as he fiddled with his phone.

"I'd like to see something along the lines of the Shivadh model. More food production in-country for the country, more luxury exports. We couldn't work quite the same way, but there are steps we could take to be less wholly dependent on gambling for our major revenue stream. The money coming into Galia is mainly from casino tourism, and most of it goes right back out again because we have to buy food and goods from outside our borders."

"You've put some thought into this," Alanna said.

"Couldn't avoid it, in my job. And Duke Tomas didn't want to hear it, so I've had a lot of time to refine the pitch," Milo replied.

"There goes that bid for trusted advisor again," she told him, and he shrugged, guilty as charged.

"I'll arrange your new schedule for today and begin setting up a few future meetings based on what you've said," he told her. "Jerry – " He caught himself, shook his head, and smiled. "I mean, Your Grace."

"Ah, Milo," Jerry waved it off. "Unless Brasolin or that other guy – "

"Riva," Milo said knowingly.

"That's the one. Unless they're in the room, Jerry's fine. You've seen me in my underwear at school, I think we can stick with first names."

"Regardless, would you like to be duplicated on Her Grace's schedule, or have one of your own?" Milo asked.

"If you can give me her schedule, a driver who speaks English, and a key to the front door, I'll entertain myself most days," Jerry said. "Although – is there anywhere off-limits around here? I'm a notorious wanderer and I get lost easily."

"Most of the council have offices on the fourth floor," Milo said in measured tones. "They tend to be a little touchy about their privacy, and legally of course could have you arrested for being in an office uninvited – that's a matter of national security."

"Good to know," Jerry said thoughtfully.

"The casino also has very strict security, but they make a point of having friendly staff, and I'm sure I could arrange a backstage tour, if you'd like one. But if you really want to stay out of trouble I'd simply stay out of the way of the consiglieres. Power in Galia is compressed down into the hands of a very few, but that makes the balance very precarious."

"Ah, yes. Ofelia and I had some discussions about that last night. I appreciate the warning," Jerry said.

"And – importantly, this is for both of you – if you encounter a locked exterior door?" Milo pointed at a door, or what had once been a door, leading out into the courtyard. It had been sealed off with a couple of decorative horizontal bars across it. "Don't try to open it or get around it. If they're locked, they open into the menagerie."

"Well, I think I can handle a few birds, or some roe deer or whatever you keep around here," Jerry said.

Milo studied them both. "Perhaps you should come with me."

He stood, gathering up his paperwork, and led them towards the far end of the dining room.

In one corner, facing outward, was a door that wasn't locked or barred; Milo pushed it open easily, then swung another, slightly heavier door open in the little foyer on the other side. It led into a peculiar sort of outdoor corridor – a long walkway through the grass of the courtyard, hemmed in by thick wrought iron bars that arched over top of them, forming a tunnel. A few birds were perching on the bars, chattering to each other. Most of them took off in flight when Milo passed nearby, or fluttered over to an ornamental birdbath nearby.

"Oh, this is the gazebo you can see from my windows," Alanna said, following him. "I didn't realize there was a walkway to it. It's beautiful ironwork – is it historic?"

"Relatively new, but done in a period style," Milo replied, sounding a little grim. "The menagerie was put in when the duke came to power. He's been augmenting it over the years. There are some roe deer, actually, in the northeastern enclosure," he added to Jerry. "The birds come and go, but there's food and clean water, so they mostly stay. There was a capuchin monkey but he, ah, passed a while ago. Some wild rabbits got in, bred ferociously, and never left, but they're not an enormous concern."

"Why all the bars, then?" Jerry asked, as they reached the gazebo. Milo opened his mouth to reply, but Alanna's soft, sharp intake of breath interrupted them.

Because she had seen the obvious, evident reason for the bars, both on the windows of the ground floor and surrounding them now. A pair of amber eyes gleamed at her from a thatch of tall, waving grass that blocked some of the nearby windows from view.

"Ah. Yes. That would be why," Milo said, following her gaze.

"That's a tiger," Alanna said, hating how high and tense her voice sounded. Jerry tucked the knuckles of his left hand under his nose, cradling his elbow with his right, clearly a stress reaction. "That's a tiger on, like. On a lawn."

"That's Athena," Milo said. "She's very mellow most of the time, and she doesn't like to attack the bars. You're in no danger, as long as you're in here."

"She's massive," Jerry said. "Is it just that we're closer than we'd be in a zoo, or is she unusually enormous?"

"She's Siberian – they're a big breed. Duke Tomas acquired her about fifteen years ago as a cub. Hand-raised her, until he got bored of doing it and hired someone else to. He was very fond of her, though,"

Milo said. There was something hard and unpleasant in his voice.

"How big is her enclosure?" Jerry asked, processing this with a lot more speed than Alanna. She was still caught in that amber stare. She could see for herself how harmless the tiger was currently – lying on her belly, paws tucked in front of her like a housecat, simply watching them from the shade of the grass. But she could also see those paws were about twice the size of her hands, tipped with wicked claws.

"Not nearly big enough," Milo replied. "But she is the reason you should not go through any locked doors into the courtyard. It's her territory. Here, or on the private patio, she can come to you and that's fine, I suppose, if you want to get up close. Anywhere else in the courtyard, she'd possibly consider you prey. She got over the fence into the roe deer enclosure a few years ago and went straight for the humans feeding them, not the deer. Close call."

"This can't be good for her," Alanna managed.

"It's not great for us, either, I feel," Jerry said.

"No. But the duke was fond of her, or claimed to be, and it's shockingly difficult to rehome a tiger raised by humans," Milo said. They both looked at him. "I wanted to propose sending her to a preserve or at least a better zoo. He wasn't going to listen unless I had a solid plan, and I couldn't ever get that far along. The only people willing to take her were private wildlife parks that weren't any better, and now even a lot of those are closed."

"Poor trapped thing," Alanna murmured.

"She'll try and eat you if you annoy her, so keep your sympathy measured," Milo said. "But yes. It's not ideal."

Athena chose that moment to chuff loudly, a noise between a growl and an indignant huff. Her eyes closed in a long slow blink as she rolled over onto her side, claws raking the air.

"Duke Tomas must have been an extremely unlikable man," Alanna said. She looked at Milo. "He's eternally on my shit list at this point, so don't mince words if you don't want to. I certainly won't be, at least with you and Ofelia."

"I think he was morally bankrupt, not very bright, corrupted by power, and driven by his hungers," Milo said. "I was close enough to his inner circle to have heard the story about the last Shivadh state visit – do you know what happened?"

Alanna nodded.

"The thought of anyone punching the duke in the face is the kind of thing that keeps you warm at night," Milo said. "You'll find I'm not alone in wanting to shake your uncle's hand. I disliked working for His Grace intensely. But he was never going to leave power, and someone had to be his brakes."

"And that was you?" Jerry asked.

"Me, Ofelia, a few others. Believe it or not, he could have been worse, these last few years. Still no idea why he hired us, given he had to have seen we were working in our best interests, not his, but for whatever reason..." Milo gestured haplessly.

"What about his council?"

"Mostly men like him, if not quite on his level when it comes to being an appalling person. They do not want you here for your liberality of spirit or your progressive ideals," Milo told her.

"Yeah, that's been made clear," she replied.

"And they have a level of power that means you can't just wholesale clear them out and bring new people in. But there are more...aggressive things that could be done, with a strong hand on the wheel. Which is why Galia needs you. Your Grace," he added, as if he'd overstepped his bounds.

Alanna felt a little thrill of sensation run through her – not excitement or pleasure, but not precisely fear. Her objection to being the Duchess of Askaz had always been that it was so pointless – her grandparents paid someone to manage the land, and otherwise did very little for either good or ill. Being the Duchess of the Horse...she didn't care for power, but she did care about fixing things, and there were things here to fix.

"Well," she said briskly, turning away from the tiger and beginning to walk back towards the dining room. "As long as I'm here, I should make a start, whether or not I mean to continue. I'll look into getting her removed from here myself."

"Very good, Your Grace," Milo said. "I'll send you my notes, so you won't duplicate my work."

Jerry's phone beeped, and when he consulted it he frowned.

"Ah, left something in my room," he said. "Listen, I'm going to run up and get that and handle a few things – meet you for the big genealogical summit? Milo, where should I go?"

"I'll send someone for you," Milo said, making a note. "Just be in your suite around ten thirty. About the rest of the menagerie…"

"The water and food for the birds can stay," Alanna said. "I'm fond of birds. We'll deal with the rest of the animals once Athena's been handled."

She wondered, as Jerry ran off and Milo took notes, if this was what Gregory felt like most of the time. There was a certain charm to it.

It would be especially funny, she thought distantly, if she came all this way, only pretending she was considering the throne, and then took it after all.

Bruno was in the office of the royal archives when they arrived; to Jerry's delight, he was leaning back in an office chair, twirling slowly, firing rubber bands at a hook mounted in the ceiling which already held several. When Milo cleared his throat from the doorway, Bruno nearly fell out of the chair.

"Ah!" he managed, righting himself. "Good morning, Your Graces! Happy to see you again so soon."

"Keeping busy, I see," Milo said.

"Composing my mind. A very important part of the research process," Bruno replied.

"Be kind, Milo, the poor man's stuck in here all day," Jerry said, peering around. Unlike the bright, comfortable royal library of Askazer-Shivadlakia, the archives of the Palazzo were in a squat, long, narrow room that buzzed faintly with fluorescent lights. Smelled nice, though, like archives often did, all dust and, what was the stuff? Lignin, the stuff in paper that made old books smell the way they did. A cluster of desks near the entrance spoke to a communal workspace, though Bruno was the only one there. The stacks behind the desks vanished into darkness, but they looked clean and well-organized at least.

"It's hardly a chore," Bruno said with a smile. "Although a brisk walk in the sunshine is occasionally recommended. Milo said you'd like to look over the genealogy," he added to Alanna.

"Just to make sure everything's in order. And I don't know much about my father's people – the duke's people, I suppose – so I wouldn't mind a little tour of his side of the family," she replied.

"Of course. Well, you have a couple of options," Bruno said, "starting with the fact that the royal genealogist is a volunteer position and he decided not to come in today."

Milo rubbed his face. Jerry grinned sidelong at him.

"That said, as long as you don't actually need any specialized research done immediately, I can get you access to the files," Bruno continued. "There are several ornate family trees on paper, there's a book, or we've been working on digitizing the complete tree. We're waiting to connect with a couple of other countries to link our people to theirs, but that shouldn't be a concern for you. I assume if you need to go into your family tree on the Askaz side, you know who to call."

"More or less," Alanna agreed. "If you could give me access to the digital version, I should be fine."

"Let me show you how it works," Bruno said, guiding her to a chair at one of the other desks and pulling his over. "Your Grace, can I help you first, before Her Grace and I dive in?"

"Ah, I'll just wander, if that's okay," Jerry said, gesturing at the stacks. "I mean, not if you think I'll break or nick something, but I promise to keep my hands in my pockets."

Bruno matched his gesture with a smile. "The fragile stuff has been archived; you can't do much damage unless you steal something. If you can find something left worth stealing, you deserve to get away with it."

"Very permissive. Love that in a librarian," Jerry said, and wandered off into the stacks, listening with one ear while Bruno showed Alanna how to move around the digital family tree.

"Do you suppose I've got any hidden cousins or aunts or things?" she asked, and he heard Bruno laugh.

"It's possible, but if so they're not on the tree. Further out than first-cousin? Probably, and those we could find."

"Like who? How would I find that?" she asked.

"There's a macro, actually. The program itself will go up the tree and come back down with your closest relatives, then those further out, and further out."

"Is that how you found me?"

"I didn't find you," Bruno said, still sounding amused. "But you weren't hard to locate – not like we needed the macro. Especially since I've been staring at this thing for months, inputting new names."

"Why new names?"

"Filling in blanks. We're always finding new information. That's why this is here," Bruno said, and Jerry leaned around a shelf, trying to see what he was pointing at. He couldn't see much, and Milo seemed to be watching him, so he ducked back into the shadows.

"See, if you click on Duke Tomas, you get this ghost that shows up," Bruno said. "Well, we call them ghosts. It's a hidden family member you don't see unless you click."

"But that's a child," Alanna said. "I thought the duke didn't have any children."

"He doesn't, that we know of. But the Guard of the Horse was in his office after he died, and they found a letter that mentioned an heir. No name, no gender, no mention of who the heir's mother was. For all we know it was some kind of code or joke, but it hardly matters. We put in a space for an heir, should one pop up, and that lets us put this in…" he clicked something, "which is a list of known female associates of the duke who might have had a child with him."

"He…certainly got around," Alanna said in a measured voice. "My goodness, there's a second page."

"There's a fifth page," Bruno sighed.

"Huh. And nobody's found any other mentions?"

"Not so far, but the duke's got about fifty years of paperwork to go through," Milo said.

"Surely this interferes with my succession, though," Alanna added. There was a silence long enough that Jerry looked out again. Alanna was looking back and forth from Milo to Bruno.

"Even if there is a child, it's out of wedlock, so their claim would compete with yours but not preempt it," Milo said at last. "And we can't delay on the off-chance we come across them someday. You're still the legitimate heir. And you've got the support of the council."

Jerry held his tongue, but only just; it was such a good opening, but Alanna had to be the one to say it –

"Be that as it may, I don't like this," she said. "I don't like even the whisper of an idea that there might be competing heirs. Can something be done about finding them, or disproving their existence?"

Jerry punched the air, just a little, making sure he couldn't be seen doing it. Of course she'd said the right thing; Alanna never failed.

"As of right now, you are the duchess, and your request is reasonable," Bruno said. "If you'd like to make this a priority, we certainly can. As long as I have permission to say it's ducal business."

"Of course. Use what resources you need. In any case, it does seem like everyone's very excited for the idea of me taking over," Alanna said, quieter now.

"And why not?" Jerry asked, emerging again from the shelves. "They saw you ruling Gregory with an iron fist and thought, *we'll have a bit of that.*"

"Jerry, don't make it sound dirty," Alanna said.

"Can't help it; I was born for innuendo. Speaking of, Milo, you really shouldn't have to babysit us. Bruno can keep us entertained. Or I can entertain Bruno," Jerry added. "Al, you're good, aren't you?"

"I'd just like an hour with the genealogy," she said. "Then I'd love to see some of the archives, if you're willing to show me around."

"I'm at your service, Your Graces," Bruno said, nodding at Milo.

"I'll come retrieve you for lunch – if you need me, you know how to reach me," Milo said. Jerry sat in the chair at the desk opposite Bruno's and stretched, preparing to do what he did best: talk absolute nonsense in the most distracting way possible and for extended periods of time, while elsewhere other people got up to the important business.

They didn't really get the chance to confer in private that afternoon; lunch, it turned out, involved Alanna hosting a gathering of the consiglieres' wives, including looking at a suspiciously large number of photos of unmarried sons (and one daughter, which she thought was rather brave of the mother). Jerry cooed over grandchildren, looked at a few unmarried daughters himself, and distracted people whenever she gave him a particularly desperate look.

The tour of the Palazzo Cavallo – complete with a much closer look at the menagerie grounds, which didn't improve with exposure –

took up most of the afternoon. They only had about an hour to get ready for the dinner, most of which Alanna spent trying to wash off the crazy of the day. There'd be time for her to discuss the paperwork with Jerry later; she'd already photographed printouts of the family tree and sent them to the group chat, copying Will, the palace lawyer. She emerged from the shower to find Eddie and Gregory had filled her text notifications, texting each other while sitting in the same room. At least it was about the problem at hand, but still.

She hadn't mentioned the mysterious possible child, wanting to see if Bruno would find more about them first.

There were a few likely candidates to take Alanna's place, at least, but they were all Shivadh – when the nobility of Galia had a fall from grace or lost all their money, they tended to jaunt over the highlands, settle in Askazer-Shivadlakia, and become normal, everyday people in the way a noble just couldn't do in Galia. Her father's mother had done exactly that. So had a lot of other Galians loosely related to her father. Those names were fine, possibly useful, and Will was vetting them to make sure none of them were obvious criminals. But none were the bullseye she was hoping to offer.

Then Gregory looped Michaelis into the group text, and the genetic nerdery of the royal family took over. Michaelis was sure he could find someone on the Galian side if he could talk to a genealogist of his acquaintance in Milan.

How do you know a genealogist in Milan? Jerry asked, which must mean he was nearly ready to go.

Mind your business, Michaelis replied. *Shouldn't you be escorting Alanna somewhere?*

She grinned and typed, *He should indeed. I'm ready to go when you are, Jerry.* She turned off her notifications and was on her way to the door when Jerry knocked. "Come in!"

Jerry put his head in. "Ready to be dazzled?"

"Am I ever," she sighed.

He stepped into the room, spreading his arms grandly. He was wearing a deep purple crushed-velvet dinner jacket, over a purple shirt and patterned purple tie. The trousers, at least, were black.

"I call it my 'When in Rome malicious compliance' suit," Jerry said. "I'm leaning so hard into Galia that I lean right back out again."

"That's a heavy philosophical statement to put on a crushed velvet dinner jacket," she said, but she took his arm and collected up her purse. Out of habit, she opened it and let him drop his phone in. Half a dozen lost phones in the last decade meant if he was going out with her, his phone went in her purse. He'd tried carrying his own bag for it, but when he did that he just lost the bag as well.

There was a car waiting, with a Galian driver at the wheel. Georgie was leaning against the car, talking to the driver.

"Good evening, Georgiana mine," Jerry called, beaming at her. She smiled back. "Are you coming along?"

"Only if you like," Georgie said. "I cleared the attendees, and the restaurant's fine," she added in an undertone to Alanna.

"I'm sure it's safe," Alanna said. "Take the night."

"Phone's on, though. If you need me, call."

"We'll be home by midnight, Mom," Jerry told her.

"Grounded if you aren't," Georgie replied, and waved them off.

It wasn't a long drive, though the route to the restaurant did take them past the casino. Jerry tilted and twisted his head, trying to take it in as much as possible, while Alanna watched the other side of the street, where a busy public park was full of people out for an evening stroll.

She knew exactly one person in the room when they walked in – Carlo, the son of a count on the council, who'd been at the reception the night before with his father. At least it was a very small crowd, only about eight people, and Carlo introduced them around as they seated themselves at the long, dimly lit dinner table.

At that point it got…slightly surreal. Very surreal, later, but when she considered it, she felt that was probably when it started.

She knew, of course, that Eddie's Davzda cocktail recipes had been put on Photogram, and she knew that he was famous; she'd been a fan before she'd hired him for Gregory's coronation. But long exposure had converted him from "famous person Eddie Rambler making cocktails for Photogram" to "my best friend's weird boyfriend who occasionally makes terrible drinks." When the servers brought an entire round of Davzda cocktails, clearly based on one of Eddie's early experiments, she shot a confused look at Jerry on her left. He was busy trying not to bump elbows with the woman sitting next to him, who looked like she honestly wouldn't mind bumping more than that.

"Shivadh fashions are en vogue right now," Carlo said, seeing her expression. "Did you not know?"

"We all want to drink what they drink, wear what they wear," one of his friends said, and it was true that she was in the latest style Alanna had seen in all the stores in Fons-Askaz. "Nobody wants to be a stodgy Galian stoic anymore."

"I can't say I've seen much of Galia that I didn't see from a car window, but you have a beautiful city," Alanna replied. "Surely Galia has a lot to offer."

"Maybe," a man who looked like he was probably a less interesting version of Jerry said. "Maybe more, if you become duchess."

"Aren't you going to?" someone asked, and Alanna wasn't sure how to respond to that. She was saved by Jerry, who leaned in and shook his finger at them.

"No peer pressure, friends," he said. "Al's just here to make sure she's the woman for the job. Now, if you really want to know what's fashionable in Askazer-Shivadlakia, I can show you a new drink that's making the rounds, a pomegranate soda…"

"He's very protective of you," Carlo said to her, while Jerry talked at the rest of the table. He'd spent most of the day talking; Alanna hoped he was hydrating.

"Jerry just can't stand not being the center of attention," she told him with a grin. "Very trying, me being up for the duchy."

"He holds court well enough," Carlo said, as food began to emerge from the kitchen. "All right, everyone," he added to the table at large, "Time to show Her Grace a good meal and then a good time. Dozhine," he said, lifting his glass, and they all toasted and drank.

"This is what they mean when they say *How Shivadh*, I think," Jerry said, leaning in. "I think we are the cool kids, Al."

"Well, what do I do with that information?" Alanna asked.

"Milk it for all it's worth. I plan to," Jerry said, and turned away again to ask his seatmate something.

It was, actually, a nice dinner. Alanna didn't get out to many meals with people her own age that she didn't actively work with. She had friends in Fons-Askaz, but – like her – most of them had pretty intense jobs, and it was rare they could all get together at once. The Galians were a little eager to please but they were also lively people who had a lot of opinions and suggestions, and they seemed to like both her and Jerry not just for what they were but who they were, at least by the time the meal was winding down.

Several of them had taken their drinks out onto the restaurant's terrace after the meal, and a handful were at the bar, which at that point left just her, Jerry, and Carlo, their nominal host and emcee. Jerry announced he was going for a drink, but Carlo said, "I wonder if you'd stay, just a moment."

"Ah, sure," Jerry said, settling back down.

"As much talk as there has been tonight of Shivadh culture, I have to admit, I'm a Galian through and through," Carlo said. "I don't like to waste time and I haven't much sentiment in me, when all's said and done."

"You're a rare bird in the nobility, then," Alanna said with a smile.

"Perhaps. The point is, many people in Galia do want you to take the duchy, and if you did, you'd need connections – a guide, someone who can arrange nights like this," Carlo said. "To make sure you meet the people you ought, and that you're in good company."

"I appreciate that, but Milo – "

"Is a good man to have at your side in a finance meeting or a treaty negotiation," Carlo said. "I'm talking about something deeper."

Alanna steepled her fingers, because she could not believe that she knew what was coming, and also could not believe it was coming. "You'd better be a plain Galian, in that case," she said.

Carlo grinned. "I like that, a plain Galian. Very well. It may come across as hasty, even importunate, but if you do take the duchy, I'd like to be the first to make you an offer of marriage. Obviously a political contract, but I think in time I might be able to charm you sufficiently for more," he added, with the shit-eatingest grin she'd ever seen.

"Can I ask why I'm here?" Jerry said, into the silence that followed.

"I wouldn't dream of proposing a marriage like this without the presence of her chaperone," Carlo said. "You represent all of Askazer-Shivadlakia standing behind her. If you disapproved, the thing would be a non-starter. I know that."

"Ah," Jerry said. "Al, do you have some input on this?"

Alanna tried to decide if she was offended, and came to the conclusion that she wasn't – this big dumb son of a count didn't mean any harm, he just had a practical view of the world and thought she might, as well.

"Carlo, this is honestly one of the nicer things anyone in Galia has done for me since I got here," she said, and Carlo looked pleased. "You put together this whole little soiree just to welcome me and pitch yourself as the guy who can help me out. I appreciate that. But I'm afraid I can't even promise you I'm going to accept the duchy, and if I do, I have to give everyone a fair chance."

Jerry's face, trying to suppress laughter behind solemnity, was priceless.

"Of course I'll keep you in mind. You're a very strong contender. But this will be a long audition process, you know," she continued.

"Very wise of you," Carlo agreed. "You understand my expediency, however."

"Completely. Does you credit. And dinner has been lovely. But as I'm sure you can understand, today's been long and I'd like to consider things a little more. Would it be absolutely a mood killer if we went home?"

"Of course not." He took one of her hands and kissed it. "Especially if it helps keep me in your thoughts. And if you have any desire for another dinner, or a tour of the finest nightlife…"

"You'll be the first person I call," she promised. "Jerry?"

"Yeah, I'll get the car," he said, voice suspiciously strained. "Back in a flash."

He was uncharacteristically silent until the pair of them were in the car, doors closed, on the way back to the Palazzo Cavallo, and then he turned to her and cracked up laughing.

"That was," he said, "the best proposal I've ever been a part of. That was *mental*. Positively medieval in the strictest sense, proposing a business marriage in front of your chaperone. I wanted to ask him for his prospectus. I bet he has one. I bet it's a headshot on the cover and a bunch of impressive financial statements inside."

"Hey Alanna, how did your first day in Galia go?" Alanna asked, in a passable imitation of Greg, which set Jerry howling. "Oh, not bad. We met a tiger. Count Carlo proposed to me."

"Oh, no, when his dad kicks it he'll be Count Carlo." Jerry gasped with laughter. "Make way for Alanna, Duchess of the House Horse, and her consort, Count Carlo. It's a cartoon."

"You should have tried to accept," she said.

"What, accept him on your behalf?"

"No, you should have – "

"Pretended he was proposing to me!" Jerry clutched his chest. "I can't believe I didn't think of that! Next time. Bound to be a next time. I'll start a pool."

"What if Carlo's the one, though?" Alanna asked. "What if he's my soulmate?"

"Stop, I can't breathe," Jerry wheezed. He thumped his chest and then shook himself to calm down. "Hoo, wow. I hope every night in Galia is this fun."

"I don't think I could take this much fun on a regular basis," Alanna replied, and Jerry regarded her from where he had propped himself up in the corner of the seat. "But I do have a job for you as vizier. From now on – I'm serious, no joke – your job is to run off anyone you see trying to propose to me."

"Nothing easier," he said, folding his hands over his chest and relaxing. "Unless you give me some kind of secret signal. If you tug on your earlobe it means *I like the look of this one, let me take him for a spin first.*"

"Yeah, that's fair," she agreed. "Just in case."

"Not to be an elitist monster, but also your grandmother would have kittens if you married a mere count."

"Someday I'm probably going to marry a commoner. I can only hope that doesn't kill her," Alanna said.

"Very respectable in Askazer-Shivadlakia, the nobility marrying commoners," Jerry said. "She'd probably be fine with you marrying a fishmonger or a schoolteacher or something. But it's got to be one or the other. High rank – higher than a count, anyway – or no rank at all."

"Lord, is that what you're getting from your mother?"

"It's what I hear her saying. Not to me directly. I don't think she often considers my love life, which is probably for the best."

"Well, you're a boy. Different standards."

"Yeah, that blows for you, for sure," he said. "But you always say you haven't got time for a husband anyway, so I suppose the poor tailor you could have married will have to marry the baker instead. Would you consider a noble, or is that an automatic disqualifier?"

"I don't automatically disqualify anyone, until they give me reason," she said. "But – you know how it is. We're different."

"Are we?"

"You and me. I work for a living, I'm not part of the party set."

"I am," he said, puzzled.

"Maybe you're in it, but you're not part of it, not the way Count Carlo is. You're the vizier to the king," she said. "I know we all say it's a joke, but Gregory really does value your advice and your presence. There are other peers in Askazer-Shivadlakia, some very highly trained, and he doesn't make any of them come to the official royal events."

"That's just because Eddie likes me."

"Eddie does like you, but Gregory needs you. And me," she said, a little satisfied. Nice to be needed, after all. "So we're special. Well, maybe not special – maybe different. I couldn't marry most of the Shivadh nobility. I'm related to half of them and three-quarters of them are boring. I mean, have *you* ever had a steady girlfriend? One you'd consider settling down with?"

"Haven't been looking for one," he replied. "But I see your point. Do you think," he began, and then pressed his thumb to his lips, as if preventing himself from saying something. "Ah. Do you think Eddie's got a sister who'd have me?"

She laughed. "I do wonder. He has several siblings, one's bound to work for one of us."

"I look forward to meeting them someday. A whole family of Eddie Ramblers would be very entertaining," Jerry said. "Hey, can I get my phone back? I need to send a few texts."

She passed it over and unlocked her own while he tapped away. The group chat about the family tree had been lively while they'd been at dinner. It looked like Jes and the royal librarian had become involved. And, she noted, Michaelis's phone was still autocorrecting "Theophile" – Eddie's real first name, which Michaelis insisted on using – to "trophies". She was pretty sure Eddie had somehow done that to his phone on purpose as a prank.

"Are you texting the chat?" she asked. Jerry had been texting for a while.

"Ah, no, just a pal of mine," he said, looking up briefly. He tipped his head back, arching a little to crack his spine. "Going to sleep well tonight, at least, I hope. Milo send you tomorrow's schedule?"

"Yes, but it starts at ten a.m. again, so I'm not looking at it until breakfast," she said resolutely.

"I do like Galian hours," Jerry yawned. "Nothing nicer than beginning the day halfway through the morning."

It wasn't even that late, but Jerry was definitely crashing by the time they got to their suites; he mumbled a sleepy goodnight at the door and disappeared into his rooms. She sat up for a little while, texting with the group, but the chat status window said he'd turned off notifications.

Jer's in bed early, Eddie said. *For him, at least.*

Tell you about it next time I call. He had a long day of playing decoy for me followed by the best laugh we've had in a while, Alanna replied.

Miss you both, love you both, Gregory sent.

Go to bed, children, Michaelis added, so Alanna did.

CHAPTER FIVE

THE NEXT FEW days did become a little less crowded, or perhaps she became more accustomed to what was expected of her. Milo was still trying to wrestle a budget out of the finance office, and Bruno reported that his people were researching, and sometimes speaking to, the duke's old *amores*, but no children had turned up so far.

Otherwise, Alanna felt that things were going as well as she could expect. In the mornings, she attended the council meetings, though she was asked to leave the room when they were discussing sensitive matters she wouldn't have access to unless she actually took the throne. In the afternoons, she went into town, shopping and exploring, or touring factories and offices. She did get the backstage tour of the casino, where Jerry almost got arrested five separate times for going places he shouldn't and generally enjoyed himself hugely.

And it was pleasant to be out in Galia, because the people *loved* her. Jerry, too. They were starved for a royal they could feel happy about, and the Galian passion for Shivadh culture wasn't confined to Galia's upper classes. Shivadh fashion, Shivadh food – no wonder Galia bought so much of their seafood, with trendy little Shivadh seafood joints on every block. You could go into a gift boutique in Galia and buy posters of Gregory, most of them slightly pixelated prints bootlegged from high-resolution photographs, or vintage posters of Michaelis from the early days of his rule. She couldn't imagine what Duke Tomas must have thought of that, if he knew about it. She knew what Michaelis thought of it, because Jerry wouldn't stop texting him photographs of the old posters and getting endless grumbling in reply.

There were no other dinner offers from eager suitors, but she did meet a lot of the unmarried sons of the council. Ofelia suggested, as a joke, that she should keep a shortlist of contenders. Milo, the kind of brother who leaned into his sibling's madness, started one. As promised,

Count Carlo held top position.

On Thursday, with an afternoon that was mercifully empty, she curled up on the sofa of her suite with her laptop and tried to make progress on Project: Rehome Athena.

Milo hadn't been kidding. Alanna had Will working on the legal paperwork they'd need to ship Athena anywhere in the world, but there weren't a lot of places she could go. According to her patchy records, she was not only captive-bred but inbred, as many captive tigers were. They were kept as exotic pets with enough frequency that zoos didn't need to look very far to get one, and didn't want Athena anyway.

It felt weirdly personal. She could see the metaphor, that she and the tiger were both snared by this stupid situation, that Galia and even the Duchy of Askaz were enclosures too small for her, that she wanted meaning they couldn't provide. Well, she couldn't know if Athena craved a deeper, personal satisfaction she couldn't get from being a pet in a courtyard, but if you were going to project emotions onto a tiger, you might as well commit.

Now that she knew to listen for it, at night she sometimes heard Athena chuffing in the grass. It was oddly comforting. And it was still satisfying to work on getting her out of there, even if she wasn't making much headway. It felt like a little slice of her real job, waiting for her back in Askazer-Shivadlakia.

She was just reflecting on this and wondering if she wanted to eat something before dinner when there was a knock at the door, and Jerry's voice – "I have tea!"

"Come in," she called, and Jerry entered with a tray of food and a small teapot set on it.

"Dinner's not until nine tonight, I guess because whoever we're eating with isn't sure his balls are big enough and just had to make us wait an extra two hours for a meal," Jerry said.

"Not like Milo to allow that kind of nonsense," she said, shuffling paperwork and half the contents of her purse to one side on the coffee table.

"Ofelia's going to be there, so I suspect he's more important than first blush," Jerry said. He offered her a plate of crackers with various toppings. "You certainly do settle into a place, don't you?" he asked, sifting through the paperwork idly.

"Casting aspersions on my organizational skills?" Alanna asked.

"Not at all. Complimenting your ability to make yourself at home in strange worlds," he replied. "You've moved in. I still feel like I'm here on tolerance. Any progress from Bruno on the hunt for the missing heir?"

"He's ruled out a lot of names," she said. "He feels there must be a more efficient way to do it."

"Have we tried one of those DNA test things?" Jerry asked. "Upload spit to a database and see what it pushes out?"

"I think they're holding that as a last resort. You need a lot of DNA for it, I guess, and it's very public. Can you imagine what would happen if we uploaded his DNA and a dozen matches popped up?" she asked. "Chaos."

"Still, it'd be efficient. And extremely fun," Jerry added with a grin at her. He sat in the wing-chair at one end of the coffee table and leaned forward to pour the tea. "Anyway. Tomorrow's Friday; I was wondering if you'd given any thought to dinner, or attending shul while we're here."

"I hadn't," Alanna said regretfully. "Do you think we ought?"

"I'm of two minds. On one hand, I like a nice Shabbos dinner, and I'm sure the kitchen would do something passable, but I know your family doesn't really observe," Jerry said. "And shul could be…how to put this."

"Gregory's had to deal with some ugliness as king," Alanna said. "From outside the country, I mean."

"I suppose that's part of it, but also…it doesn't quite feel right, does it?"

"It's not our shul, and we haven't given them any warning," Alanna said. "Galia isn't Askazer-Shivadlakia, either; I'm sure we'd be welcome, but it would draw a lot of attention to the community here. Better not, this week. Maybe next. I would like a quiet dinner, though. Especially because Saturday night – "

"Ugh," Jerry groaned, leaning back, tea cradled in his lap. "That's right, the Eligible Bachelors' Ball."

Technically it was simply a formal reception to invite prominent Galians who weren't on the council; not just the nobility or the politically connected but business owners, wealthy citizens, prominent local figures. As Ofelia had put it over breakfast one morning, it was actually to introduce Alanna to every acceptable marriage prospect between the ages of twenty and fifty.

"I tried very hard to discourage the council," Ofelia had said. "But they're extremely focused on finding someone to tie you off to. Pin you down here, ensure the child's half-Galian, all of that. I imagine this has occurred to you, too."

"What would the council say if I told them I didn't want children?" Alanna had asked. "Not saying I would say that – I wouldn't mind kids, someday – but just to tweak them."

"Have you ever tried to tell a male relative you're not living to give birth?" Ofelia had asked. "Did you get the you'll-change-your-mind head pat?"

She had, from her grandfather. Ofelia had smiled at her expression and spread her hands.

"Better get a nap in on Saturday afternoon," Jerry said, bringing Alanna back to the present. "If I'm going to spend all evening shoving your would-be husbands off you."

"Well, it'll be public and pretty formal. I don't think anyone will get aggressive. Why don't you call up Carlo? I'm sure he'd help," Alanna said. Jerry laughed.

"He probably would. Actually, he'll probably be there. Ah, and Milo's just sent tomorrow's schedule," he said, consulting his phone. "Want the rundown?"

"Please."

"Bruno wants to see us at nine. Apparently he's finally got that map for me. You've got a morning jaunt to the boutique with Ofelia to do final fitting for your dress for the ball on Saturday, and then you're requested to attend the council but only from noon to one – ah, probably because you've got lunch with some of them afterwards."

"Which ones?"

Jerry made a face. "Riva and Brasolin."

"What the fuck," Alanna said, although without particular surprise. Riva was fine – stodgy, conservative, boring, but fine – and Brasolin was obnoxious but intelligent; neither of them seemed to like her much, but both of them did seem to want her on the throne. It was obvious they also didn't like each other, even though they had common interests. She thought both were angling to be her vizier, or whatever the Galian equivalent was, and wouldn't let the other see her alone.

"After lunch, you're booked in with Milo for something called Finance Review, which might be that budget you've been wanting to see," Jerry said. "Ah, and nothing planned for dinner. I think I will ask the kitchen for something a little special, if you're fine with it."

"Yes – a taste of home would be welcome, I think."

"Mm, I'll talk to the chef," Jerry said. He leaned back in the chair, studying her. "How are you holding up? Busy days for you."

She considered the question. "Well, I'm sleeping like the dead now that I've gotten accustomed to the mattress," she said at last. "They are busy days, that's true, but I like the work. I could do without the consiglieres, but if I actually took the job I could bring in fresh blood."

"I wonder. There's a power dynamic I don't think we fully understand. If you punted Brasolin to the curb, what could he do to you? What does he know, and who does he influence?"

"I haven't a clue," Alanna said.

"Me neither, but if he could ruin you it'd be good to know before baiting him. And presumably if you took the job you could find out – have someone prepare dossiers, like the palace research office."

"It does…" She thought about how to say it. "It offers a better understanding of why Gregory keeps the staff he does, I guess. I know why he has me, but I always wondered if he actually absorbed all the research and data and reports that I arrange for him to have. I think he must, though. I certainly am," she added, nodding at the paperwork.

"Better you than me. Sounds exhausting."

"I don't know," she said. "I feel like I'm good at it in the same way Gregory is. It feels satisfying, like putting a jigsaw puzzle together. Being honest, I think I'd be really good at ruling Galia," she said to him. "It'd be slow going the first few years, because the place really hasn't been well governed in ages, but I think I could create change here. And it's easier when you don't have to convince a full-on parliament, like Gregory does. If my word were law? The things I could do."

Jerry laughed. "Don't get corrupted by power."

"That's why I'd have you, to keep me humble," she said.

"Court jester! Gosh, even better than being a vizier," he said, but the amusement in his eyes dimmed.

"Don't want to be my jester?" she asked with a knowing look.

"No, that'd be fun," he said. "I'd ditch Greg for you in a heartbeat. But Galia isn't my home, is more what I was thinking. I'd need either very generous vacation or to be allowed to telecommute. That'd be funny, though. Get a tablet, put it on a little motor scooter, I'll just roll about the halls from my bed in Askazer-Shivadlakia."

"That would certainly take me out of myself," she said with a smile. "All right. It's not going to happen, anyway; we have plenty of names to suggest when I renounce. So right now, I'm going to enjoy these very nice snacks you've brought me, thank you, and keep working on finding a new home for a tiger."

"Want me to go?"

"No, finish your tea at least, and I'd rather you stay. If you haven't got anything to entertain yourself with, I can give you work."

He held up his phone. "All the world in my pocket, I'll be fine. In fact, I'm going to be Alanna to your Gregory and send some important emails," he added.

"Like what?" she asked suspiciously.

"You just do your work," he told her, nose in the air. "Your vizier has machinations to put into motion."

"Emailing the chef to request no pork ribs for Shabbos?"

"Something like that," he agreed with a grin.

Admittedly, she might have told Jerry that she was fine, and that was mostly true, but Friday did put it to something of a trial.

Alanna was accustomed to having to buy dresses for various galas, although Gregory tried to give her as many breaks from the formal events as he could. She did like wearing nice things, it was just… tiresome to always be *made* to. The dress fitting she went to with Ofelia, for her formal gown for the ball, would have been more fun if she didn't know she was going to be auditioning potential spouses all night.

"At least they're the ones in the meat case, not you," Ofelia said philosophically.

"Are you sure about that? I do feel very put on display."

"Yes, but you have the whip hand."

"Kinky," Alanna said before she thought about it, and Ofelia laughed. "Sorry, that was probably inappropriate."

"I like that you feel you can say such things. Milo might be pleased you're a strong political pick – trained, noble born, intelligent, all the rest – but I like that you're a pleasant person," Ofelia said.

"I think that's a compliment?"

"I just mean I think you and I could be friends, and we could both use one."

"Very much the truth," Alanna agreed, as the dressmaker circled around behind her. "Wish you could come to lunch with me today."

"Ah, Brasolin doesn't like me, and you'll have your hands full with Brasolin and Riva disliking each other already."

"What's his reasoning? For not liking you."

Ofelia looked away politely as the dressmaker zipped Alanna out of the dress, and she went to change out of the edifice of engineering that was the bra the dress needed.

"On one level it's as simple as being a woman in politics," Ofelia said, disdain in her voice. "He thinks it isn't their place."

"He likes me, though. As a candidate, if not personally."

"Yes, he does, thankfully," Ofelia agreed. "I think it's also that…he's not fond of me and Milo. You know they call us the Jumped-Up Ansevalis. We have ideas above our natural station."

"I thought you must have some kind of link to the upper class. Milo went to Institut Alpin. You have to be connected to get in there, let alone pay for it."

"Askazer-Shivadlakia has a scholarship program, though, yes?" Ofelia asked. "High-achieving Shivadh students can apply for the king's aid in admission? Milo got in through something similar here."

"Oh, I suppose I hadn't thought of that. I didn't know Milo was there on scholarship."

"Not through the school, no. The state paid for him to attend."

"But not for you?" Alanna asked.

"It's the girl-in-politics problem, but I'm not particularly upset about that. I never wanted to board. Didn't want to leave Galia, and our mother thought it best if I was educated here in any case. I had a scholarship to a very good school as well, just…locally."

Alanna pulled her shirt on. "All right, I'm presentable. Doesn't seem to have hurt your prospects, anyway. Whoever takes the throne, you'll be right there, won't you?"

"I hope so. Without ego, I think Galia needs people like me and Milo."

"I don't disagree," Alanna said. "And we ought to get back so I can go have my unpleasant hour with the council and then my even more unpleasant lunch."

People snapped pictures of them as they left the dressmaker's arm-in-arm; Alanna appreciated the fact that Ofelia tried to shield her, at least a little, with medium success.

"If this keeps up you'll be a fashion idol like I am," she told Ofelia. "Stick with me and you'll go places, baby."

"That's the idea. I'm only in it for the fame," Ofelia replied, amused. "Driver – back to the Palazzo Cavallo, if you would."

Alanna reflected later that Gregory – and Ofelia – would have enjoyed the lunch with Brasolin and Riva. She could see the undercurrents of the conversation, could tell when they were jabbing at each other and at her, and she could ignore the latter. But she didn't like that kind of business, all sly innuendo and nothing productive. She did her best to block it, which she could see frustrated and surprised both of them. She suspected they were as relieved as she was when Bruno came to get her for the finance review.

"A word of advice, if I may," Brasolin said, catching her elbow firmly as she bid them goodbye. Alanna looked down at her arm pointedly, flexing a muscle, and Brasolin let her go. He didn't look apologetic, let alone apologize. "You must understand whatever you see of the budget is not the full story. Galia's economy is an intricate one, and it takes time and depth of knowledge to understand how it functions. Do not be misled by simple columns of numbers."

She resisted the urge to pat his head just to piss him off. "I'll bear that in mind. Admittedly my MBA comes from a French school, not a Galian one, but I do feel Université Paris Dauphine is equally good at imparting a nuanced understanding of columns of numbers."

"Just so we understand each other," Brasolin said. Riva, who was being helped into a jacket by a valet, looked murderous that Brasolin was getting a private moment with her.

"I think we do, thank you," she said. "I really must be going, however. Do have a lovely afternoon, both of you."

Once they were outside in the hallway, on their way to the archives, Bruno shook his head.

"People who have to deal with Brasolin should be issued tasers," he told her. "If he grabs you again, I'd yell *ouch* and jerk away. Or give Duke Gerald permission to object on your behalf. He seems the type who'd challenge someone to a duel over you."

"Much as I'd love to, it's not diplomatic," she told him. "And the more he talks, even if he's giving me a creepy touch, the more I learn."

"He hasn't tried anything ugly with you, has he?"

"No – I think he's the sort to treat a person as a trophy, not as a toy. Fine distinction, but a fortunate one for me."

"Let's see if we can't show you a few interesting columns of numbers," he told her, holding open the door of the archives.

"I'm looking forward to it. You and Milo both wear many hats around here these days," she added, as Milo looked up from pushing two desks together to make a sort of improvised conference table.

"How so?" Milo asked, pulling out a chair for her.

"Well, Bruno here is a historian, seems to do most of the genealogist work, and is helping you present the national budget, such as it is," she said. "And you're social secretary, political advocate, and paperwork wrangler all in one, plus now financial advisor. I also think Ofelia's somewhat overqualified to take me to get a dress fitted, fun as it was. One might accuse you of a conspiracy," she added with a grin.

Milo looked perturbed by the idea, but he looked to Bruno and not to her; Bruno ignored the look and also the implication, which she hadn't meant seriously but which Milo seemed to take as such.

"Like Askazer-Shivadlakia, Galia is small," Bruno said. "I'm sure the Shivadh palace has people like us. Young strivers, or in my case simply people with extensive interests in very boring subjects."

"Like finance?"

"It's similar to history, in some respects. Cross-references, citations, research," Bruno replied.

"In that case, you'd better show me what you found," she said.

It didn't take long to see, first, why staff hadn't wanted to part with the data. Second, she could now see why Brasolin had warned her not to trust in it. The longer Milo and Bruno talked her through it, the worse it looked.

Galia was running at a deficit and had been for years, despite the presence of a massive casino and an uptick in tourism, which Milo thought was overflow from Askazer-Shivadlakia. There was an issue with inflation, not easily solved, and an issue with the hoarding of wealth by the upper class – the consiglieres and their families. Duke Tomas hadn't seemed to give much of a damn, but even if he'd wanted to fix things he'd have been hamstrung by the economic power of the other nobles. He would have needed a fast, large, and discreet infusion of cash to keep Galia going another two or three years without defaulting on loans or stopping payment on civil services. The data wasn't complete, but she didn't see how more information would make it less dire

"This is what nobody wanted me to see," Alanna said.

"Some of it is speculation," Milo admitted. "We don't know for sure that there isn't a secret Swiss bank account somewhere we could fund Galia on for a decade. And His Grace never seemed troubled by concerns about money."

"An indictment in itself, perhaps," she remarked.

"If you'd like my opinion as a historian," Bruno began. Alanna waved him on. "Some of the senior advisors – probably led by Brasolin – have been setting him up for years. If he hadn't died he would have had to go to the consiglieres for a very large loan. Then they'd control Galia – and the succession. They could still do the same to you. They're aware you could go to the Shivadh government for money, but only if you understand the finance side enough to know you should."

"Just how stupid do they think I am?" she asked.

"Very," Bruno said. "Unfortunately. It's no reflection on you. Most of them just assume you're an inexperienced young woman. Not to flatter you, but they're not accustomed to a noble who is also both intelligent and well-educated."

"The question is what you want to do about it," Milo said. "Seeing all this – it's bad for Galia. On the one hand I wouldn't blame you for turning around and going right back to Askazer-Shivadlakia."

"And on the other?" she asked.

"You could be the woman who saves our country," he said. "For what that's worth. You have the power to right a listing ship with about a million people on it. Not to lay a guilt trip on you."

She rested her forehead on one hand, elbow propped on the desk. "Appealing to my work ethic is a real dick move, Milo."

"Unfortunately I can't appeal to your greed or vanity, like I did with Duke Tomas," Milo said with a small smile.

"I need to think about this," she said. "Not about what it changes, although that too, but about the budget itself. Can you send me the documents, Bruno?"

"Of course. Review at your leisure, you understand the work," he said. "Now that we have certain keywords and codes from these documents, I can start ferreting out others, too, but there's no point unless it's going to be helpful. If you find something you want more information about, do let me know."

"Thank you. Thank you both for your work on this. It must be… frightening, to have uncovered it."

Milo and Bruno exchanged a look.

"It's not great," Bruno said. "But worst case…if we leaked it…"

"Please don't, not yet. Maybe we will have to but – it wouldn't help right now, and people might panic."

"Could Askazer-Shivadlakia help?" Milo asked.

"To an extent. It's a risk I'm not sure Gregory would take, to fully fund what Galia would need. But we could do some kind of structured loan for part of it, or a guarantee of purchase if Galia issued bonds," Alanna said. "Gregory knows other heads of state he could speak to about funding. Whatever happens, we can't let the country founder. I will find a solution for this. Don't let it keep you up at night."

"You should take your own advice," Milo said, rising when she did. "Can I get you anything else?"

"I think I'm just going to take a walk," she said. "Still learning the palace layout. Who knows, maybe I'll find a secret treasure room."

"If you do, call me. I'll show up with a wheelbarrow," Bruno said.

Alanna left them in the archives and took a roundabout way down to the courtyard, following a complicated route to a back set of stairs that had windows looking out on the city – it was stuffy, but the windows appeared to be rusted open, and every time she passed one of the narrow openings she got a whiff of fresh air. And the stairwell, she knew, opened into a hallway that would take her through a mostly unused wing of the building, out to the menagerie garden.

This was clearly where the duke had gone to see Athena. Her enclosure, though small, was grassy and had a pond in it; at one end was a high metal grille in the same style as the gazebo, which blocked Athena off from a patio attached to the building. There was a gate in the grille, with cavorting tigers on it, and a key in the gate; Duke Tomas used to let Athena into the patio to keep him company. Athena saw her at the gate and came over to inspect her. Alanna didn't get too close.

"Another couple of years and he'd have had to sell you off, I imagine," she told Athena, who regarded her with deep amber eyes that gave away very little. "Bet you're an expensive beast to feed. And it's awful to be owned by someone like him, isn't it? Doesn't love you. Definitely hasn't given you the home you should have."

Athena chuffed softly.

"I'm working on it. Try not to maul anyone before I can find you a nice big preserve," she said. Athena, apparently resigned to not getting to come into the patio, flopped down and rolled onto her side. Alanna tapped one of the little tigers in the gate with a hand, like she could comfort Athena through it, and went away again.

As she was heading back towards her own suite, a text message buzzed her phone – Jerry, asking if she was still stuck in finance with Milo and Bruno.

No, just got out, she said. *It's bad news.*

Care to tell me? Come to mine. Or don't, if you want to digest. Dinner in an hour, you can always tell me then.

Be there in a few, she said, and added a tiger emoji on a whim. He messaged back with a roast beef emoji, which was so tasteless that she laughed as she knocked on his door.

"Come in!" he called, though he wasn't visible as she let herself inside. "Just got out of the shower, avert your eyes."

"Were you texting me in the shower?" she asked. "How do you keep the phone dry?"

"I was bored. I do it all the time. Put it on a ledge outside the shower and voice-to-text," Jerry replied. "The places I've texted you from would curl your hair."

The suite was a mirror of hers, with the same wide, no-privacy archway between the sitting room and bedroom. She could see him moving around, towel slung on his narrow hips. She went to the little kitchen to get a drink and give him the privacy to dress.

"I think I'll go casual for dinner tonight, since it's just us. If that's all right with you," he continued.

"That's fine," she agreed, filling a glass at the tap.

"So, your peek at the budget with Milo – is it just scary, or is it Necronomicon-level bad?"

"There are some gaps, but Milo wanted me to see what there was, at least, and I'm glad he did. What I could see was food for thought. It's not good. We might have to bail them out."

"You think Gregory would go for that?"

"Depends on how. It'd be a good thing to do, but none of us are stupid, and Galia's in real trouble. Gregory won't bankrupt us to save them, and he shouldn't have to. Milo and Bruno think Duke Tomas was being set up for a bailout by the consiglieres, who could control him with large loans. Probably high-interest ones."

"What absolute dickheads. The council, I mean, Milo and Bruno are fine," Jerry replied. "How'd lunch go with the chief dickheads, by the way? I'm mostly decent, you can peek."

"It was fine, I guess. Actually sort of validating," she said, turning around to lean on the counter. "Handled myself very well against them, I thought. I don't know that they expected that."

A flash of color caught her eye as she turned; next to the sink, sitting in an empty drinking glass, was a slim cardboard carton – orange, with a white sleeve. She paused, saw him pass the bed with a shirt in his hands, and turned back to the little carton in the glass.

"Of course you did fine with them. Bet you're glad we're done with business for the day, though. I know I am. I am very tired of neckties," Jerry continued, monologuing in muffled tones as he pulled the shirt over his head. "I should have packed sweaters, nothing says casual-formal like a nice sweater, but I thought they'd be too warm…"

She listened without paying attention, reaching out for the carton. Printed in large blue letters on the sleeve were the words *Adderall* and below that, (*Amphetamine*). She opened one end, without even thinking about it. Inside was a half-empty blister pack of pills.

"…don't know if it would be considered gauche to go clothes

shopping again, because…" Jerry's voice came back into her ears, closer, as he emerged from the bedroom. He trailed off, and when she looked up from the carton, she saw him watching her.

"Ah," he said, guilt etched on his face.

"Jerry," she said, taking the blister pack out, showing him the empty pockets. He opened his mouth, but didn't speak.

"You brought this across the border?" she asked. He blinked at her. "Party drugs right now, really? Amphetamines? Thought you'd do some intense clubbing?"

"There's," he managed, almost rallying his usual light tone, "…nothing wrong with clubbing. You learn a lot rubbing elbows with the locals. And other parts."

"I know you like to have fun, but this is really dangerous stuff," she said. Her heart was in her throat – this was more than a small problem, if he had to bring this kind of thing with him. "Jerry, this is – are you drinking when you take them? Or is this what you're doing instead of drinking now? Where did you even get – "

She stopped, because she'd looked down at the carton again, and it had a label stuck on the sleeve on the other side – legal disclaimers, dosage instructions, and the name of the patient prescribed. Gerald ben Eitan Dux Shivadlakia, his legal name.

Mr. Shivadlakia, he'd said, a long time ago, joking about it. *Didn't even have to compete for the title.*

"Who prescribed this for you?" she asked, anger mounting.

Jerry closed his eyes and rubbed his forehead. Alanna waited.

"My therapist," he said.

"Like some kind of pill mill, or – "

"Alanna, my psychiatrist prescribed it," he said, voice terrifyingly loud for a second, an echo of the basso-boom she'd heard from his father Eitan when he was angry. "He prescribed it." He lowered his voice. "For my rampant, previously undiagnosed neurodivergence."

It was the way he said the word that convinced her – the way he half-laughed on *neurodivergence*, stumbling over it as if he wasn't used to saying it out loud. He probably wasn't, she realized. She stared at him, at a loss for words.

"It's not fake," he added, looking down at his hands, flexing in front of him. "And not an excuse to get drugs. Honestly, if I couldn't get illegal drugs without a doctor, what kind of life have I lived – "

"Like – it's really for…?" she managed.

"Yeah," he said, looking back up at her. "Go figure. Fucked up, right?"

"Jerry – I'm so sorry, I just – "

"You and everyone else. It's a natural assumption," he said lightly, like he was talking about the weather and not something heartless she'd just done, assuming he was high when he was *medicated*. "I mean, I'm me. Like you say, the drinking, the partying. Having fun."

"How long…?" she asked.

"Since last year. Right around Gregory's coronation."

"That recently? How? You went to one of the best schools in the world – "

"Where they are invested in assuring the parents that we're all very normal, and tolerant of misbehaving children," he said, gesturing with one hand. "I went to a school so good they didn't need to diagnose me. They just gave me average grades and graduated me. How can I possibly need medicating? I speak four languages and play polo."

He dropped into a wide wing chair, bending forward to lace his hands over the back of his neck. She came to sit on the edge of the sofa cushion, knees almost touching his.

"How'd you find out?" she asked quietly.

He laughed a little and leaned back, meeting her eye for the first time. "You're not allowed to be mad at me when I tell you. You were the one snooping in my meds."

"The box was on the kitchen counter."

"Forgot to put them away this morning. Ironic, sì?" he asked.

"Jerry."

"Fine. How I found out. I was dating a woman, nothing serious. I don't have a pill problem, Alanna, but she did, which no, I didn't know when we started seeing each other. Although it's not like that's to my credit, wouldn't be the first time I've made dumb choices when it comes to women. But I was having a shitty week and not hiding it well. She gave me a pill, said it'd take me out of my head for a little while."

The idea of Jerry having a bad week felt foreign – like he floated through life ignoring all the crap other people had to deal with. Which was probably something he'd cultivated. Alanna realized she was still holding the box, and set it down on the end table.

"It wasn't even this," he said, gesturing at it. "She had Ritalin. I thought hell, why not, maybe it'd help."

"Help with what?"

He shrugged. "Whatever it was that the drinking wasn't helping with anymore? Or the not-drinking, at that point. I'd gone dry that week because I was starting to be concerned, which is a big reason it was such a bad week. But I didn't feel high when I took the pill. I felt weirdly functional. Like I could see clearly for an hour. And I'm not stupid, I knew that was potentially a big problem – I'm given to understand that's also how *cocaine* makes you feel – and it could be dangerous."

He picked up the box and studied it, then got to his feet. "Stay there. I'm not done, I promise, but if I don't put this away while it's literally in my hands, I'm going to forget again."

She nodded, and he kept talking as he walked into the bedroom, stowing it wherever it was normally kept.

"So I did some research," he said, voice raised so she could hear him. "Turns out, the way I felt taking a party drug is the way most people just feel all the time. It's fortunate that I wasn't drinking, actually. It made it more effective, enough for me to notice. That's not how these meds work for some people. Lucky me, I guess."

He returned, dropping back into the chair, legs stretched out.

"I talked to a guy and got some tests done and it turns out that impulsive behavior, alcohol misuse, and poor academic performance are all symptoms of being a useless royal cousin *and* ADHD," he said, folding his hands over his stomach. She could see how forced his relaxed pose was, but now wasn't the time to call him on it. "My therapist says given what I've told him, my mother should get tested, but try talking to her about stuff like that."

"And you didn't tell anyone?" she asked.

"No real reason to," he said. "I'm not active in the government, so it's not impacting policy or endangering Gregory's administration. Haven't got a partner to tell, and it'd only cause problems with my mother. It doesn't affect you guys at all, except I'm more likely to be on time for things and remember birthdays now."

"So Gregory doesn't know."

"No. It felt weird to imagine, you know? Walking into a room and announcing it. And I'd rather everyone think I was unreliable and now I'm improving, than treat me like I'm sick or stupid or something. I'm used to being unreliable."

Alanna got up and went to the chair, poking him to make him scoot over. She slipped into the gap he left and put an arm over his shoulders, leaning her head against his.

"I have never once thought you were stupid," she said. "Silly, maybe, but not stupid. And I don't think you are now. I'm thrilled that you got help you needed and I'm upset you had to do it alone. And, honestly, a little angry at Institut Alpin right now. Mostly mad at myself for yelling at you. I'm sorry."

"I'd have made the same leap to conclusions you did, knowing me. And another school would just have drop-kicked me and I'd have ended up at Eton or something," he said, with a dramatic shudder. She laughed, more because she knew he wanted her to than because it was funny. He was quiet for a while, then turned into her a little, nose brushing hers. "I gotta ask, Al. Are you going to tell Gregory?"

"Of course not. Not my news to tell. But he's not just your cousin, he's your friend, and he cares about you," she said. "If you want me to tell him, so it won't be weird for you, I could. No big deal between you guys that way."

"Yeah, maybe, but that's not your job. No urgency to it, anyway. He and Michaelis both think I'm just trying to turn over a new leaf, and that's mostly the truth. I get so much *done* in a week now," he added, turning away again, body relaxing a little. "Next year the duchy's going to turn a profit on olive oil because I hyper-focused on olives this year."

"Oh, no," she said, realizing what he was saying. "Michaelis has always griped at you about doing better with the estate and staying out of trouble, that must have been – "

"Alanna," he said, gently. "Michaelis sometimes shows he cares by noticing my fuckups, yes, but it's not a big deal. Now I know there's a reason for at least some of them, life finally makes sense. He's even been kind of impressed by me, lately. Fun to take people by surprise. Anyway, I'm *less* angry and sad than I used to be, and I didn't even used to be angry or sad all that often. Please do not be angry and sad on my behalf now. Or if you are, dump it somewhere else, okay?"

She considered this, nodding. "Okay. Fair. But you can tell me when you feel that way, you know. And I'm glad about the stopping…"

"Drinking?" he asked. She nodded. "Yeah. That took a little time to sort out. Not super proud of not handling my champagne better at Gregory's engagement, but I misjudged my tolerance, that's all. Funny story to tell. Did I ever thank you for saving me from drowning?"

"You fell face up in an ornamental fountain," she said.

"Still. Thanks."

She kissed his temple. "Tell me how I can help, when you need it. Otherwise I promise not to let it be weird between us, okay?"

He leaned into her, nodding. "Solid deal. Right now, though, I'm supposed to be helping you," he added, leaning back again. "And more importantly, taking you to dinner."

She knew what it was — a change of subject meant to move them away from something delicate and painful, a sign that he'd had enough and needed to back away. She climbed out of the chair carefully.

"We could have dinner here, if you want," she said, gesturing at the table by the window where she'd eaten a few hasty meals in the past week. "Little more private than being served in the dining room."

He considered this, then shook his head. "Unless you want that, I'd rather go to the dining room."

"No, I don't mind," she said. It was understandable; sometimes you needed a reason to pull yourself together.

"You know, after the finance review I went down to see Athena this afternoon," she added, as he got his shoes on. "I told her she was a very expensive and annoying child. She didn't seem impressed."

"Poor kitty. Nobody loves a spoiled tiger," he replied. "I say we throw the gates open and let her loose. Hell with Cavallo, it's Palazzo Tigre now!"

"As amusing as it might be, it probably wouldn't be very good for Athena in the long run," she said.

"I suppose you're right. Still, it'd keep the annoying consiglieres to a minimum." He held the door for her, following her out. "Let's talk about something happier. I did get out to see the old land today. Very pretty. Galia isn't doing enough with what natural beauty it has left."

She took his elbow, which seemed to please him, and smiled and half-listened to his idle chatter until they reached the dining room.

CHAPTER SIX

ALANNA DIDN'T BACKTRACK to the topic of medication at dinner, for which Jerry was grateful; she didn't seem inclined to ask him anything more about it afterward, either, which was probably kind but possibly also because it sounded like she'd had the longest day ever *before* finding his meds. They were quieter than usual, both of them.

It had been incautious of him to leave the meds on the counter for several reasons, not least that any Galian who didn't like his presence could probably use them against him. At least it had only been Alanna who'd seen them. The way their conversation had gone didn't exactly make him want to tell anyone else, but it did feel good to have someone in his corner that the national health service wasn't paying to be there.

After dinner was over he left Alanna at her suite, probably to go over the budget numbers again. In his own suite he changed into his pajamas and settled on the bed with his phone in his hands. He had plenty of options if he wanted to reach out – he could message the group chat, call his psych, or go next door and tell Alanna he'd like to keep her company after all. She'd let him; Alanna was good like that.

Instead he opened his contacts list, tapped Eddie's name, and hit dial.

"Hey, bud," Eddie answered on the second ring. "How's foreign affairs? You're on speakerphone, by the way."

"Hi, Jerry," he heard Gregory's voice, fainter.

"Hey," he said. "Good to hear you both. Thought I might get through on your phone easier than on Greg's."

"Good call," Gregory said, closer now. "Business or pleasure?"

"Oh, the pleasure of hearing you boys' dulcet tones, mostly," Jerry said, wondering what to say now that he had them on the phone. "Al's probably going to be up half the night with some spreadsheets. I didn't want to pester her."

"You know, if we have to lose her to another job," Eddie said, "at least it takes a whole country to replace Gregory as her boss."

"It's not even a very good boss," Jerry replied.

"Ah! You don't like Galia?" Gregory asked. "I thought Alanna was enjoying it, at least in part."

"Galia's fine. Galia's government is a hot mess," Jerry said. "Might be something in the water, I feel like a mess myself."

"Oh?" Eddie asked. "Rough day?"

"Not as rough as Al's. More a rough week. I did go to boarding school for years, I know how to be away from home," Jerry said. "But a week here, all I want is to run back over the mountains."

"That sounds about right, actually," Gregory said.

"How do you mean?"

"You were always homesick that first week back at school," Gregory said. "You didn't eat, you moped around."

"Did I?" Jerry asked, trying to recall.

"Don't you remember? Pretty much every year," Gregory said.

"Maybe I didn't know I was doing it."

"Wouldn't surprise me. I used to come sit in your room and share my snack box treats with you, and you just acted like you were humoring a weird little brother."

He did remember that. "Sure. A well-loved weird little brother, but that's definitely how you came across. I thought you wanted to hang out with me because I was cool."

"I did, and you were," Gregory admitted. "But mostly it was that Al and I knew if you weren't eating my snacks you pretty much weren't eating, that first week every year. It was fine, I had fun and you always got past it eventually."

"Blasphemy," Eddie said. "Wish I'd been there. Trash Tower all day every day."

"I do love the Trash Tower," Jerry said wistfully.

"I'll stock up on chicken wings for when you get back."

"Thanks, I'll enjoy it and Al will enjoy being grossed out by it. Anyway, how's the palace? Things ticking over all right?"

"As much as they ever do," Greg agreed.

"Michaelis and Hugo are locked in mortal combat," Eddie added.

"They're having a spat over wine for the wedding," Gregory said.

"The wedding nobody is yet planning and Eddie's probably going to have to cater himself?" Jerry asked, eyebrows drawing together.

"Hugo, in his official capacity as palace sommelier, thinks we should have a Syrah for the reception," Gregory sighed.

"Hugo is out of his mind," Jerry said, beginning to enjoy himself. "Uncle Mike's never going to go for a red. He doesn't like tannins and also liquids that stain clothing. Although there is room here to pick a fight with him over why he's dictating the wine at your wedding when you are a full-on adult. He was barely an adult at his *own* wedding."

"Look, Hugo is a workaholic who only gets to shine when we're throwing big parties, and Dad's retired," Gregory said, but he did sound amused. "If it keeps them busy I'm not going to wade in."

"I am," Eddie said. "I'm a wader. Not that hot on Syrah either."

"Wish I could be there, I'd help," Jerry said.

"I'm going to try to distract them by asking Michaelis to host Greg's birthday party at the lodge this year," Eddie said. "Then they can argue about new, different inconsequential things."

"What else is life for?" Jerry asked. "Glad we'll be home soon, I miss the chaos."

"Just another week," Gregory agreed. "And you both know to call if you need anything. Personal or royal."

"Yeah, will do. I'll keep you posted. Night, boys. Don't do anything I wouldn't do."

"Too late for that," Eddie said, and Jerry laughed as he hung up.

It was a good reminder that one more week and they'd be home, and everything would go back to a new normal that he'd just been starting to enjoy in the past year. He could figure out the rest of life when he wasn't sharing a wall with a tiger and fending off petty nobility trying to weasel their way into Alanna's good graces.

The petty nobility did keep on coming, and Saturday night got a little out of hand. Not unmanageable, especially compared to most of his twenties, but definitely wilder than he'd anticipated.

He could have planned for it better if he'd thought of it ahead of time, but Jerry knew himself to be the sort of person for whom inspiration strikes at the last possible minute. In this case, it was half a dozen dances into the ball on Saturday, watching Alanna smile politely and suffer through whatever pitches the eligible bachelors were making as they waltzed with her.

It was a nice party, generally. Good food, open bar, decent music for dancing, and company that knew how to make itself pleasant. Alanna looked amazing; Ofelia had picked out a gown in purple and gold, just on the tasteful side of vivid, sleeveless to show off her shoulders and the elegant rise of her throat. The dress accentuated her figure, fitting to the curve of her hips, with the skirt of the gown flaring off to cascade to the floor. She looked, in the best possible way, like an exotic bird meant to be strutting through a jungle somewhere. Jerry was considering paying Ofelia to pick out all of Alanna's dresses from now on.

But it was also difficult, watching people he couldn't even consider competition try to make nice with Alanna. It wasn't like he'd ever been brave enough to suggest himself as an appropriate consort for the Someday Duchess of Askaz, despite her being one of the more significant hang-ups he'd had in recent years, so he was well aware he couldn't think of her as his, even though he wanted to. Watching everyone else suggest themselves as consorts for the Duchess of the Horse was somewhere between absurd and excruciating. She even seemed to enjoy dancing with a few of them.

So he was trying to focus on something else, anything else really, when he ran into Carlo while he was picking up a second mocktail from the bar, the bartender giving him a smile and a wink.

"Your Grace," Carlo said, nodding at him pleasantly. "How are you enjoying the festivities?"

Technically, of course, Carlo being only the son of a count, Jerry was still Your Grace to him; it struck him as funny that a noble elite with a good deal of money like Carlo had to call him by the same title a palace staffer would. Or even funnier – Milo sometimes slipped and called him Jerry even in front of strangers, because they'd known each other at school, but Carlo would have to be given permission for that.

Which also made him wonder if perhaps Carlo was the answer to a question they hadn't been asking.

"Oh, Jerry's fine, you know. I don't stand on ceremony," he said.

"It's really Alanna's party. I'm just window dressing in any case."

"Aren't we all? Her world, we're just dancing in it," Carlo said. "But you must at least find it amusing, all this fuss over a friend."

"Honestly, it's always been her world that I'm just dancing in," Jerry said with a grin. "And she's supposed to be flirting with all the men tonight, so I can't even chaperone her properly."

"Tedious for you," Carlo remarked, considering it.

"Yeah, but isn't it all? Much rather have a night on the town, but duty calls."

"Well," Carlo said consideringly, and Jerry glanced at him. "I'm sure in Askazer-Shivadlakia you must have the concept of an after-party."

"In Askazer-Shivadlakia, I *embody* the concept of an after-party," Jerry assured him. "Why, are you planning one?"

"There are enough of the younger set here that I could," Carlo said. "Say we leave in an hour or two, after most of us have had a chance to woo the duchess. You and I and some others could find somewhere a little louder and more interesting to be."

"In that case I'll be here at the bar, getting warmed up," Jerry said. "Come find me when it's time to go."

"I'll just have a few words with a few friends," Carlo agreed. As soon as he was gone, Jerry leaned over to the bartender.

"Whatever I order in front of anyone else, you keep giving me these," he said, pointing at the drink in his hand. "Everyone who serves me tonight gets a bonus if you manage it."

"His Grace is generous," the man observed.

"His Grace needs to leave here sober," Jerry replied.

"Be careful of that one, then," the man told him, nodding at Carlo. "Go out with him and the drinks get a heavy pour."

"I'll bear that in mind and order my own," Jerry replied.

He slipped away from the bar briefly, near the end of a song, and cut in between dances with the universal "I only need a minute" gesture at Alanna's next partner. He leaned in close and put a hand on her waist, as if paying her a compliment.

"I'm about to make trouble," he said.

"Jerry, not here – "

"No, I promise," he told her. "But I've got a line on something and I need to be a little bit visible to do it. Whatever you see here or on Photogram tonight, I promise you two things."

"Okay," she said slowly, leaning back a little to look at him.

"One, I know what I'm doing, and two, I am not drinking," he said.

"Lord," she sighed. "What are you doing?"

"Impressing Count Carlo, ironically," he told her. "That dress looks amazing, by the way. Your boobs are out of this world."

"You're an ass," she said. "But thank you, I thought they looked great."

"Dance your butt off, and don't worry about me," he told her, and then stepped back, gesturing for her next suitor to come up while he went back to monopolizing the bar.

He actually managed to leave the ball pretty quietly when the time came. He'd planned, if necessary, on picking a minor fight with someone and getting thrown out, but Carlo just said, "Hey, time to go," grabbed him, and began towing him calmly towards the door, both of them staggering a little.

"We're leaving in shifts," Carlo said, once they were in the corridor beyond the ballroom, which was significantly cooler and didn't smell like people sweating in formalwear. "We've got time for a cigarette and to have the car brought around before everyone else joins us."

"Hope you've got a ride, I'm not fit to drive," Jerry said, as they walked out onto the front steps. There were several cars, with various drivers and attendants lounging around on them – a few were playing cards on the hood of a BMW, and Jerry kind of wanted to join in, but he made himself accept a cigarette from Carlo and inhale just enough to get it lit, puffing the smoke in his mouth so he wouldn't cough.

"We're not savages," Carlo laughed. A woman in a ball gown joined them, and Jerry offered her his smoke. "Of course we have drivers."

"Should I change?" Jerry asked, indicating his tuxedo. "Should any of us?"

"No. We go out like this, people will know we were at the Palazzo. Very good tables, very strong drinks," Carlo told him.

"Can't hate that," Jerry agreed. "What's the plan?"

"Early yet," Carlo said thoughtfully. "I think karaoke, at least until midnight. Then better dancing than this," he added, nodding in the direction of the ballroom. "Not that I am not still charmed by Her Grace, and I hope my name still tops the list – "

"I've seen the list, it does," Jerry grinned.

"Splendid. But I don't think she loves this any more than we do. Ah! Would she come meet us, once her duties are discharged?"

"I doubt it – she's going to be exhausted. Maybe some other night," Jerry said.

"Perhaps we should make you Duke of the Horse instead," the woman smoking his cigarette suggested. "More stamina than Her Grace."

"I'm just less useful, so I don't spend all my energy doing the work," Jerry told her.

"Leaves plenty for us," she said with a wicked grin.

By the time a pair of limousines pulled up, Carlo had amassed a dozen people for the party, some familiar from the dinner, none without a title of some kind to their or their parents' names. Carlo packed them into the cars with the care of a DJ setting up a night's set. He knew where he was going, too, which Jerry appreciated in a party manager.

The karaoke bar they ended up in was loud, not just with music but with voices raised to be heard above it, and the English of the lyrics and the Italian of everyone else started to grate on his nerves almost immediately. He liked a nightclub; he liked the wall of sound that could shake you out of your body, get you out of your head. He used to need that a lot more than he did now, though, and even then he'd never liked karaoke. It felt too much like a form of ritual humiliation.

Still, this was where Carlo and his friends had dragged him, and they did manage to find a corner booth that was at least mostly shielded from all the…sound.

They'd also all been drinking at the ball, and more in the car, and after an hour in the karaoke bar most of them were hammered. Jerry had learned very recently how uninteresting it was to be sober in a room full of drunk people, but it was also terribly useful.

He stirred his soda water – "Davzda soda, hold the D," he'd said to the bartender, laughed at his own joke, and then tipped extra because they had to put up with him – while he waited for the right moment. Didn't take long; most of them wanted to talk about Alanna anyway. In

Italian, which made it a little difficult, but he found if they spoke Italian and he spoke English back, mostly the message got across.

"She's so glamorous," one of the women sighed. "It's internal beauty, you know. Not that she's not pretty! But she obviously doesn't care what anyone thinks of her. Such confidence."

"She's the coolest," another woman agreed. "But His Grace is cool too," she added, leaning against his arm. Her hand kneaded his thigh under the table, and he smiled down at her.

"You never know – if Al stays, I might have to stay too," he said. "At least for a little while, to make sure everything's stable. There's a lot to worry about, big job like this."

"That's the great thing, though," Carlo said. "She worked for the king! She knows what to do."

"Mostly. She can't control everything," Jerry said pensively. Carlo really never could resist rising to a lure, he decided.

"What does she need?" Carlo asked, and then turned away to hiccup discreetly. "What kind of help could be provided?"

"Oh, this and that. Milo's doing a great job – " Jerry broke off, distracted by a snort from Carlo. "What's wrong with Milo?"

"Nothing," Carlo said. "Sister's all right, too. But neither of them, you know, *are* anyone."

"Hard workers, though," Jerry said, determined not to pick a fight with Carlo over Milo and Ofelia when he had more important information to wriggle out of him. "And he's helping Alanna with the big problem."

"Dirty," one of the women put in.

Jerry faked a laugh. "Not a problem like that, and don't go spreading lies," he told her. "No, it's this issue of the duke's other heir."

"Other heir?" Carlo asked, eyebrows rising.

"Sure. Apparently there's some kind of rumor that His Grace had a kid. No evidence of it, nobody's come forward, but it makes us all nervous, you know? What if she does stay in Galia and a year from now some kid pops up? Who gets to keep the throne?"

"That old story," one of the other men waved a hand dismissively. "It's like the. The whatssnames."

Jerry waited patiently, volunteering nothing. Irritating drunk people was the most fun you could have if you weren't drinking yourself.

"The princesses," the man finally managed. "The Russian ones."

"Anastasia!" another said, snapping his fingers. "Yes, it's like that."

Someone new got up on stage to sing and the music changed beat. Jerry resisted the urge to rub his temples.

"It's a dumb old rumor," the man continued. "Just persistent, because people like the idea. Oh yes, old Duke Tomas has an heir somewhere. Very romantic. Even if he did, so what? It's not like they'd be acceptable."

"Why not?" Jerry asked.

"Have to be low born, wouldn't they?" Carlo said. "I mean, your people go in for that, all this lord-marrying-the-milkmaid and such. Can't be having it in Galia. I wouldn't care personally but the council wouldn't allow it."

"Why would they have to be low born?" Jerry asked. "Explain to a poor Shivadh, whose grandfather was an immigrant."

"Your grandfather was a king," a woman said.

"His mother was a foreigner. Greek, married a Shivadh. Anyway, we aren't talking about my parentage – my other grandfather's grandfather owned the land this bar is built on, probably. Why would a duke's by-blow have to be a commoner?"

"You don't get a noble lady pregnant, or if you do she takes care of the problem," Carlo explained. "But the old goat chased the help, and anyone else he could chase. No, if he's got a bastard out there, it's the son of a cook or a chambermaid. At best, some professional woman in Levaldi he set up with an apartment somewhere."

"He kept mistresses that way?" Jerry asked. The woman sitting next to him slid her hand up the inside of his thigh, apparently enjoying all this talk of mistresses, and he gently rested his hand on hers, shifting it to the top of his leg.

"Not many, but when he did, no expense spared, so they say," Carlo told him.

Jerry made a thoughtful noise. Most of the women on Bruno's list had been nobility. He wondered how one would even go about making a list of non-nobles. Start with the staff, he supposed.

Carlo raised a hand, signaling a server. Without even ordering, he received a tray of shots. Jerry tipped a finger over the top of his, and when everyone else leaned back to swallow theirs, he let it pour out over his finger onto the floor, then wiped his hand across his face.

"Did the old man have any particular favorites, do you suppose?" he asked, once everyone had recovered from the shot. "It's wild he managed all that while ruling the country."

"If he did, they can't have been the jealous type. He always had two or three on a string," someone remarked. "Some of the staff at Palazzo Cavallo were there for thirty, forty years, so if they minded they can't have minded too much."

Jerry had his own thoughts about that, but he set them aside and let the conversation happen around him. Nothing much else of use got said, but it did help paint a fuller picture of the duke's proclivities. By the time midnight hit, he was yearning for either a vodka neat, just to numb the senses a little, or an aspirin for the headache.

"Hey," he said, catching Carlo as they made their slow way out of the bar, heading for the first of a likely string of clubs. "I think I'm going to peel off. There's a waitress in there who doesn't know she's about to be swept off her feet by the Duke of Shivadlakia."

Carlo grinned at him. "Well, you gave us an excuse to come out tonight, I won't blame you. Got a way to get home?" he asked, which was actually very thoughtful.

"Oh sure, I'll call my driver. Give everyone my regards."

"Have fun," Carlo said, patted his cheek, and fortunately left.

Jerry about-faced and headed for the back of the bar; he pushed through and into the brightly-lit kitchen, dodged down the length of it, and emerged into the alley behind, which was quiet except for the bass thump from inside. One of the bartenders was standing in the alley, smoking and chatting with someone, and looked alarmed as Jerry leaned against the wall, taking in a few deep breaths of nice, cool fresh air.

"Are you all right, Your Grace?" he asked in English. Jerry blinked at him.

"How do you know who I am?" he asked.

The man gave him a sardonic look. "You're the cousin of the Shivadh king – the fun one. Everyone knows who you are."

"Oh. Thank you, that's very nice of you," Jerry said.

"Are you ill? You don't look well."

"Just stepping out for some air, had a little too much a little too fast," Jerry told him. He took out his phone and texted Georgie, which he probably should have done earlier. *Sorry in advance. Are you awake? I need a pickup.*

"I can bring you water, if you like," the bartender said. "Or something to eat."

"Thank you, but I'm fine," Jerry told him, smiling. Galians, he decided, were mostly decent people once you got past the weird inner layer of nobility the palace surrounded itself with.

"Would you mind a selfie?" the man asked, and Jerry laughed.

"No, of course not," he said, and the man stepped in close, holding up his phone and snapping a picture of them both that did look pretty flattering. "Uh, if you post that anywhere, please say I was the life of the party and not sadly standing in an alley waiting for my ride."

The man nodded agreeably, and Jerry's phone pinged.

Not a problem. Where are you? Bless Georgie.

He sent her a map with a pin-drop in it and went to the mouth of the alley to wait for her. Within ten minutes the car was pulling up; Georgie was at the wheel, Will in the passenger's seat.

"Georgiana, whatever we pay you, it isn't enough," he said, climbing into the back. "I'd kiss you but I absolutely reek."

"Who says I want a kiss from you?" she asked, amused. "Wouldn't say no to a raise, though."

"I'll talk to Gregory. Will, did she drag you along for a reason?"

"Off-chance you were under arrest for something," Will said, turning around to grin at him. "Besides, going in pairs is safer, in case it was a trap. Georgie has a twisty mind."

"Someday one of you is going to be kidnapped, and then you'll be glad I'm so paranoid," she said. "You royals drive me nuts. No security detail, no alarms anywhere in the palace, the King Emeritus just wanders into town whenever he pleases…"

"Not at midnight, Georgie, I'm begging you," Jerry pleaded. "I'm sorry I didn't warn you sooner I'd probably need a ride, but I didn't know and then I didn't think. Hope I didn't get you out of bed."

"No – your friend Milo saw you leaving. He let us know you might need a ride at some point, so we waited up."

"Very useful, our Ansevalis," Jerry mused. "Back to the Palazzo, if you would."

Georgie nodded and pulled into traffic; she and Will spoke quietly together and left him alone. He closed his eyes and breathed.

"I should tell you," Georgie said, as they pulled through a security gate and back up to the palace, to the kitchen entrance, "the ball's over. Staff said they saw Alanna heading for your room."

"Nasty gossip?" Jerry asked, sitting up sharp.

"Oddly enough, I don't think so. They seem to think you're the older brother," Will said.

"The third wheel," Jerry replied, rolling his eyes, and they both laughed. "Thanks, I'll make sure she sleeps in her own bed tonight."

"I think we'll all be happy to be home soon," Georgie said.

"You don't know the half of it," Jerry agreed. "You can both go to bed. And sleep in tomorrow, for sure. We will."

"Goodnight, Your Grace."

He passed through the kitchen on the way to his suite, lifting a plate of savory pastries left over from the ball and taking them along.

Alanna was asleep on his sofa when he came in. He considered her – cheek on one of the throw pillows, hair in disarray, makeup still on, his robe wrapped around her over the ball gown – and went to wash, so he wouldn't upset her with the smell of him, and also a little so he wouldn't try to hold that picture in his mind for later. She woke as he was damply pulling on some pajamas in the other room.

"Hey, I'm back," he called. "You'll get the worst kind of cramp sleeping there."

"Sorry, I thought I'd wait up for you," she yawned.

"Sorry I'm so late," he replied, settling next to her. "Do I still smell like desperation, cigarettes, and cheap booze?"

She sniffed him. "No. Why? I thought you said you weren't drinking."

"I wasn't, but I smelled like I was. I had to get Carlo and his entourage loaded. Fortunately they were already on the way, and he paid."

"What exactly were you doing?" she asked. He leaned back, spreading his arms over the back of the sofa.

"I had the idea that – much as we like Ofelia and Milo, much as they know – they work in this life, they weren't born in it," he said. "They don't run with the young nobles, the Bright Young Things.

119

Bruno neither, he's an academic."

"I think that's to their credit."

"So do I, but it means there are things they don't know. Things you or I would know, for example, that say – Jes's kid Noah wouldn't, or Eddie. Not their fault, it's just a class divide that it's hard to get over."

"Oh, fair enough."

"So I thought I'd see if Carlo knew anything about this supposed heir. Maybe there are rumors. Maybe there's someone in their set who claims to be of higher birth than their rank suggests. There's always one asshole in a group like that who tells you a secret, then tells you not to tell anyone, and everyone knows and nobody believes it," Jerry said.

"Find out anything juicy?"

"One thing," Jerry said. "Nobody knows if he has a kid or who it would be, but Carlo insists it has to be the child of someone outside the peerage. Staff in the Palazzo or someone who works in Levaldi. He'd be more cautious with someone in the nobility, and so would they. And I see what he means, as elitist as it is, but I think there's another angle Carlo isn't thinking of."

"I should hope you'd see angles he wouldn't. He didn't strike me as very bright."

"I don't know, he might have depths. I don't strike a lot of people as very bright either," Jerry pointed out. "I think what Carlo's missing is that a woman of the nobility doesn't need a royal heir to maintain her status. But if you are, say, a chambermaid, and you have the duke's child…well, he'd set you up, wouldn't he? He might send you away, but he'd make sure you didn't want to tell anyone. Especially if they were around our age – born in the era of the paternity test."

"Doesn't make our lives easier," Alanna said. "Just widens the pool."

"Yes, but there's somewhere to start. Bruno can look at payroll, see what women on staff might have had an affair with him. I can ask him, if you want," he said, taking his phone out to add it to his notes.

"Thanks," she said. "How'd it go, partying with Carlo's crowd?"

"How do you mean?" he asked.

"You sound exhausted," she said gently. "And you look sad, Jerry."

He studied her. "I am tired," he said. "It was the kind of loud I don't love. Hard to pull my usual tricks when I'm translating Italian in my head half the time." He rubbed the back of his neck. "I'm not sad. I just have a headache, and I'll be glad when we get to go home."

"If you need to go back, you know you can," she said. "I can handle Galia on my own."

"Don't you miss home?" he asked.

"Of course, but we text with Gregory and Eddie all day, and I know we'll be going home soon. And I've got you here," she said.

"And I've got you," he replied. "Anyway, I can handle it, it's only another week. I just miss the palace. I wanted brunch from Simon this morning. The food here's good but it's not his cooking. Also, Galians will put bacon in literally anything they can fit it into."

"I'm sure you'll be forgiven if you accidentally get a bite of pork," she said.

"It's not that – all right, it's that a little – but mostly it's that bacon is gross," he replied. "It tastes like being downwind of a bonfire. Mleh," he added, showing his tongue.

She laughed. "Fair enough. Anyway, you should get some sleep and I should take this makeup off. This was good work. Much more useful than me dancing with a bunch of men who are only horny for the throne I'm supposed to sit on."

"Oh, did you get to dance with that one lesbian who wants your throne?"

"I did! She's delightful, actually. No aspirations to royalty, just came to make her mother happy," Alanna said. "We're going to have drinks next week. You can come if you promise to behave. For now, go to bed."

"Yes, yes, I'm going," he sighed, pushing himself up off the sofa. "You too. Sleep in tomorrow, if you can. I'll talk to Bruno."

"Leave the poor man alone, it's the weekend," she said.

"Mysterious heirs wait for no weekend," he told her, walking her to the door. "I'm going to have awful karaoke dreams all night. Go get your beauty sleep."

She gave him a hug in the doorway and then walked back to her own suite; he managed to make it to the bed and flop down on it, face-first, but he didn't quite get a pillow under his head before he was asleep.

CHAPTER SEVEN

THE JOKE ABOUT karaoke dreams proved prescient; after the first crash, Jerry woke up around two am and from there onward didn't get a full solid hour, but also didn't feel awake enough to get up and do anything about it. He just roamed around in the bed, with various snatches of pop music stuck in his head, until he startled awake one last time around eight and gave up, fumbling for the bedside buzzer he hadn't used since they'd arrived.

"Yes, Your Grace?" came a tinny voice.

"Please save my life, bring me coffee," he mumbled.

"Of course, Your Grace," was the reply, and a few minutes later, while he was sitting up on the edge of the bed and trying to determine how well he could stand, there was a knock at the door.

"Come in," he called, and one of the staff entered with a tray – a carafe of coffee, cream and sugar, plus a plate under a domed cover.

"In bed, Your Grace, or in the sitting room?" she called.

"Ah. Sitting room," he said, staggering upright. She set the tray on the table by the window and began unloading it, pouring the coffee, adding cream and a spoonful of muscovado sugar, just how he liked it.

"You are a delight," he told her, and she smiled.

"Our pleasure, Your Grace. I took the liberty of bringing up breakfast, as well," she said, unveiling the plate. Underneath were eggs, toast, and fried potatoes, unusual for Galia; next to it, he noticed, was a little bowl of ice chips with a smaller bowl of fruit salad in it. The general Galian breakfast was pastries-and-fend-for-yourself.

"What did I do to deserve all this?" he asked, beaming at her.

"Chef likes you," she replied. "And we're all very pleased you've taken so well to Galia. We hope maybe when Her Grace is invested as duchess, you'll consider visiting often."

"And how do you know I love Galia so much?" he asked,

plucking up the fruit salad and stuffing his mouth with apples.

"You should look yourself up on Photogram this morning," she replied. "Will that be all, Your Grace?"

"Yes, thank you, and please send my thanks to the chef," he said. "I'll leave the tray outside when I'm done."

She gave him a bow and left, and Jerry pulled out his phone.

His hashtag was pretty busy even at the quietest of times; not Hollywood Celebrity busy, but he got out and about, even once he'd left off the more frequent partying, and people were always taking pictures. Eddie posted up a lot of pictures of him too, though he always checked in first. This morning, however, it was party city.

Jerry's exciting night at karaoke was laid out in all its glory from evening well into the wee hours, with exclamations of *partying like a Galian!* and plenty of admiring comments, mostly in Italian. Like once he'd gone out drinking, they could claim him. And yes, there was the photo taken in the alley with the bartender. He hoped his bartender friend got some real street cred out of that.

Someone had also snapped the moment he'd put his hand on the excitable young woman's, under the table, and moved it from crotch to leg – but they'd caught it before he'd moved it, so it did look like he was having an excessively good time at karaoke. He sent that one to the group chat with *I swear I was just removing her hand* and dug into his eggs.

I'm telling Michaelis, Eddie replied.

What are you, a cop? Jerry asked.

You all realize I'm still receiving these messages, Michaelis texted. Jerry double checked and, sure enough, he'd messaged the genealogy chat by mistake.

I would very much like to be removed but I don't know how, Michaelis continued. Jerry had a suspicion that Michaelis knew how to do a lot more on his phone than he pretended, but he'd never been able to prove it. Before he could reply, Jes chimed in.

Kind of like Jerry and the young lady's hand.

Jerry pressed the edge of the phone to his forehead and closed his eyes. It buzzed, rattling his teeth.

Be nice, he did me a favor last night, Alanna said.

He was still typing out *Thank you, at least someone vindicates me* when she texted a second time.

And I see the evening had a happy ending.

Jerry set his phone face-down on the table and ignored the cackling series of texts that followed.

Once he'd finished breakfast and was feeling fully awake, he spent the morning working his way down his to-do list. Over the past few days he'd thrown notes in there at random, which he now had to puzzle out and deal with, along with the recurring action items like answering his email. The email itself ate up a significant portion of the morning, but at least the urgent stuff got taken care of. He had a handwritten letter from his mother, too, which he replied to using some stationery he found in a search of various drawers. At least he could just put that out with the breakfast tray and a note reading *Please stamp and mail.* He wasn't sure he was up to trying to find a post office.

Alanna had lunch with Milo listed on her calendar for eleven-thirty, and he technically wasn't on the invite, but he didn't figure they'd mind if he sat in. With the five-minute warning going off on the calendar, he slipped out of his suite and knocked on Alanna's door, pushing it open when she called for him to enter.

"Oh! Hey, sorry, I was expecting Milo," she said, looking up from where she was settled in a wing chair with her computer. "How'd you sleep?"

"Poorly, but I also got roasted by everyone I know on group chat this morning, so life's going great," he said, smiling to take the sting out. "Hope at least one of us slept well."

"I've still got dents in me from that ball gown, but otherwise I'm doing all right," she said. "You know, I'm glad you didn't, but you could have gone home with that girl, if you wanted."

"I can't explain to you how much I didn't want to," he said. "Besides, going home with her would have meant two, probably three hours of going out with her, first."

"Anyway, Galia adores you, and if you want a nightcap tonight you could probably have your pick," she said. Jerry was trying to decide how best to reply to that when there was a knock on the still-open door to the suite, and Milo arrived.

Jerry had seen him, so far, only in formal clothing for state affairs or in the slightly rumpled suits of a royal functionary; he'd apparently broken out something special for lunch, charcoal dress slacks and a soft knit sweater-vest over a dress shirt, all of which made Jerry narrow his eyes. He knew that outfit. He'd worn that outfit on first dates.

"Your Graces," Milo said with a small smile, but he looked as perplexed to see Jerry as Jerry was, very suddenly, annoyed to see him. "You've had a pleasant morning, I hope. You're a big hit with the karaoke crowd," he added to Jerry. "Though nobody seems to have video of you singing."

"Couldn't find my signature song," Jerry replied.

"I'm sure if you make a request, every bar in Galia will leap to obey," Milo replied, and turned to Alanna. "Ready for lunch, or do you need a few minutes?"

"Mostly, but I suspect we're not staying in the Palazzo," she said, gesturing at his outfit. Jerry realized Alanna looked very nice too, in a simple, pretty sundress that showed off her shoulders, and began to wonder if he *actually was* the third wheel Georgie had joked about.

"I thought you might like some fresh air after last night," he told her. "There's a park that cuts through the city, the grand promenade, and a stroll around it would be nice. Very good restaurant at the northern end – authentic Galian fare, lots of fresh fruit and good bread."

"Huh," Jerry said, hearing himself and a little bit hating himself, but doing it anyway, because he saw where this was going. "Sounds delicious. When do we leave?"

Alanna and Milo were both watching Jerry with something between suspicion and annoyance.

"Ah," Milo said, glancing between them. Jerry just kept smiling. "As much as I'd love to show you both the grand promenade – this is awkward – I had intended it as a date."

Alanna's expression at Milo flat-out saying it would have been funny if Jerry wasn't standing slightly outside of his body, watching himself do something terrible.

"That is awkward," Jerry agreed. "I know that, Milo. I was trying to be subtle as well."

"About what?" Milo asked.

"Preventing it. Look, I like you, and I'm sure Alanna does too," Jerry said. "But you can't think you'd be an appropriate marriage if she does stay in Galia."

Milo seemed dumbstruck by this. Alanna, however, had rarely

been dumbstruck in her life.

"*Excuse* me?" she said.

"Well, we are being political, aren't we? And this is why you brought me, you know," Jerry said, talking faster so she'd have less space in which to interrupt. "I can't advise it, Alanna. You know they call him and Ofelia the Jumped-Up Ansevalis. It's an awful name!" he said, holding up a hand to stop Milo from talking. The funny thing was, it worked; Gregory used to joke that the Dukes of Shivadlakia bred for charisma, but there was something to the idea of eleven generations of imperious, grasping egotists producing Gerald ben Eitan, who struggled with basic math but could shut up a room simply by holding up a hand.

"It's an awful name," he repeated. "But I'm telling you this, which is nothing you didn't know, because it's a sign of what would happen. If Alanna stays here, she's got to marry someone with real status and power and Milo, that's simply not you."

"You," Alanna said, her tone icy, "are advising me on policy, Jerry, not on my love life."

"Unhappily, this is both," Jerry said, shoving his hands in his pockets. "The Duchess of the Horse cannot marry a palace administrator. Back home? Perhaps. Our king's marrying a cook."

He overplayed it there, and saw it. Alanna's whole expression changed to one of confusion.

"In any case, here, she's going to need at least a count, and hopefully someone a little brighter than Count Carlo," he finished. "She can't waste time pretending she could be with you in anything other than an adulterous situation."

Milo's mouth was open, eyes darting back and forth between them.

Alanna stood and shot Jerry a glare, going to Milo and taking his hands in hers.

"Milo, I'm sorry. Jerry is being insufferable and he does not speak for me," she said, and Jerry finally located his ability to shut the hell up. "I said yes when you asked because I'd like to go out with you. I'd love to go to the promenade. But right now it's clear that Jerry and I need to discuss some of the finer points of protocol he just violated, and that may be a long discussion. We're all tired after the ball last night, too. So I'd like you," she said, bouncing their hands together a little for emphasis, "to give me some time. We'll talk about this at breakfast tomorrow, and I'll take a promise of a future trip to the promenade this coming week, if you would do me the honor."

Milo bowed lightly over their hands. "As the duchess likes," he said, without a tremble in his voice, and Jerry had to respect him for that one, because if someone had done to him what he'd just done to Milo, he'd be *livid*. "Your Grace," he added to Jerry, and if there wasn't a tremble, there was a lot of venom.

They were silent until the door clicked shut after him, and then Alanna said, "Went too far with that crack about Eddie."

"Oh, is that where I went too far?" Jerry asked lightly, wondering if he could still get out of this.

"You towering asshole," Alanna said, so probably not.

When Jerry opened his mouth about Milo, she'd wanted to punch him. When she heard what he was saying, she'd wanted to murder him for a hot, angry second. Until he called Eddie a cook, and then she knew something else, something darker and weirder, was at play here.

Because yes, Eddie was technically a cook, but he was actually called a chef, a title he'd earned, and both of them knew it. Jerry had been in the room at least twice when Gregory had gotten mad at gossip blogs for calling Eddie a cook. Jerry knew better and respected Eddie too much to insult him so offhandedly. And Jerry, who had grown up in the nobility and gone to an elite boarding school and spent a decade with the party crowd, absolutely knew how to find the tender places and jab a blade into them.

Jerry wasn't a bully, but he knew how to act like one, and he would bully anyone threatening her – but he had zero reason to do that to Milo.

"You towering asshole," she said, turning to fully face him. He was pale, arms at his sides, not nearly as casual as he was pretending. "Why the hell did you do that? He asked me out!"

"Yeah, exactly," he replied. "You're not staying here, Alanna, and if you did you couldn't – "

"That's beside the point and you know it. So what if I'm not staying here? That doesn't mean I can't date someone from Galia!"

"You think he'd leave Galia and come running across the highlands to be with you?" Jerry asked scornfully.

"I'd like half a minute to find out. He wanted a first date, Jerry, he wasn't asking for the throne."

"Good, because he's not getting either."

"Go fuck yourself," Alanna said. "You don't decide that. Even if it's a matter of *policy*, you don't choose who I go out with, and you don't get to make assumptions about Milo's pretensions to rule."

"Oh, for the love of — I didn't run him off because I think he wants the throne, of course he doesn't want the throne, have you met him?" Jerry said. "What he wants, apparently, is you."

"Even better," she snapped. He looked like he'd been slapped. "Do you know how many people want me for me, Jerry? You're in the same messed-up boat and you know what we deal with! You've said it yourself, nobody's taking you on non-titled terms. You're being — you're being so stupid about this I feel like it has to be intentional."

"Intentional that I don't want someone else asking you out? Of course it's intentional!" he threw his arms in the air, frustrated.

She opened her mouth and then caught herself. Something about what he'd said —

"Someone else?" she asked.

"What?" Jerry yelled.

"Don't yell at me, that doesn't scare me," she retorted. He at least looked a little abashed at that. "You said, 'someone else.' You don't want *someone else* asking me out," she repeated.

"Yes?" His voice was quieter now, but he still seemed confused.

"Wait, just…" she rubbed her forehead. "If Milo isn't a fortune-hunter, if he's just a guy who likes me and wanted to take me to a nice lunch, and you couldn't let that happen…why not, Jerry?"

A muscle jumped in his jaw. Gregory did the same thing when he was preparing to lie — usually to himself. Michaelis did it too, although he had better control over it. It was a very subtle tell, one most people didn't notice. Jes did, but Alanna'd had to explain it to Eddie.

"Okay," Jerry said finally. "You know what, you're right, that was — that was shitty of me," he added, clearly working hard to get the words out. To his credit, he sounded sincere. "That was a real asshole thing I did just now. Milo didn't deserve it just because he clearly sees how great you are, and it was way over a line with you. I'm not the duke of your social life. I'm sorry."

It was a little startling, and it almost put her off the line of thought she'd been following. None of the royal family liked to admit when they were wrong, and for him to do that without trying to misdirect or put off taking blame meant something else was going on.

"But why did you do it?" she asked. "If it was such an asshole thing to do, Jerry…"

He ran a hand up into his hair, letting it rest on top of his head. He closed his eyes. "Because I didn't want him going out with you, but it's not up to me," he said. "Fuck, this isn't how I wanted to do this."

"Do what?" she asked.

"Nothing," he said, muscle jumping in his jaw again. "It's fine."

"Jerry – "

"Sorry," he repeated, lowering his hand. "I'll talk to Milo, I'll apologize and tell him I was out of line. I will fix it."

"I think what's happening right here and now is way more important to fix," she said slowly. "But I don't actually understand what's happening."

"I'm being a dickhead," he said, voice careless. "Still happens sometimes, unfortunately."

"Impulsivity problems?" she asked, trying to match his light tone.

"I'm trying to take responsibility for my actions, so yes, but also no." He gave her a tired grin. "Look, here's what's happening. I overstepped and you called me on it, which you are extremely good at doing. You were right to do it, and I'm sorry. So as long as you accept my apology, or at least let me work towards making it up to you, we're fine."

"Okay." She took a breath in, exhaled. "I do accept your apology as long as you give Milo one as well. So we can hug now, right?"

He laughed. "Is that what you want?"

"Yeah," she said, going to him, and he folded her into himself the way he always did, warm and familiar. She leaned back just a little so she could rest her forehead against his.

"Now stop lying," she said quietly. His entire body tensed.

"For fuck's sake, Al," he finally said, voice as quiet as hers. "For someone who's so relentless, you are absolutely oblivious about what you're even chasing. You're making this worse than it has to be."

"Why?"

"Because I'm in love with you," he said. It was a shock hearing him say it, even if she'd been hearing him carefully not say it for the last five minutes. "You are the person I'm hung up on. And that makes it so much worse. I don't own you, I don't have any claim on you at all, and I ran Milo off because I was jealous and worried you'd like him more than you like me. *What* an asshole."

It was difficult to catch her breath, and her throat had tightened too much to speak. He began to disengage slowly – leaned his head back, loosened his arms around her shoulders.

She swayed forward and kissed him, a little off-kilter but hard enough he jerked forward into it instead of slipping away. He caught her head in his hands and leaned in for a few intense seconds before he pushed gently, and she let him escape for the moment.

"Al," he said softly, eyes on her face, like he was looking for something specific. "Do not do this to make anyone but yourself happy. I'm dealing with this, you don't have to – you don't owe me anything."

"You know, Michaelis says," she started, and then had to swallow. "He says you and Gregory do this."

"Do what?" he asked, genuine confusion on his face.

"You treat me like I don't always do exactly as I please regardless of your opinion," she said. "Have you ever seen me kiss anyone I didn't want to kiss?"

"Well, I haven't been there for all of them," he managed. She hooked two fingers in the collar of his shirt, knuckles pressed up against his neck. She could feel his pulse thud against her skin.

"Do you think I would hurt you?" she asked. "Lie to you just to make you happy this briefly?"

"No," he admitted, and let her kiss him again. "No, I – I'm just…" He waited until she was done kissing him, "…not used to getting what I want this easily. Not when it's important like this. And especially not when I've just been a towering asshole."

"This has absolutely not been easy in any way," she told him. She kissed him again and started using her fingers at his collar to work the button free.

"Ah, I don't…" he started, and then she could almost hear it happen – somewhere in his mind, a loose gear clicked into place. His whole body relaxed against hers, one hand sliding around to cup the back of her neck, the other dropping to her waist to hold her against him. "I could be easy," he said.

"Could be cheesy," she retorted. He laughed.

"Sure, that too. Um, say the word and I can stop," he added, "but otherwise I would love to make the last ten minutes up to you and then prove a couple of points in my favor."

"Yeah, kinda counting on that," she agreed, and let him pull her slowly towards the bedroom of the suite.

It was a roar that woke her, late that afternoon. The sun was moving towards the horizon, and sometimes in the early sunset hours Athena would feel compelled to roar, for whatever reason – maybe calling out to see if she could hear another tiger, maybe at the lengthening shadows, or maybe just because she was waking up after sleeping most of the day.

Alanna stretched a little, slowly, conscious that there was another body in the bed; she didn't want to risk waking him yet. He was lying on his stomach, face mostly concealed by the pillow it was pressed into. His left arm was flung over her waist, hand curved into the blanket.

The signet ring of the duchy of Shivadlakia, the only jewelry he wore, was heavy and loose on his index finger, and had slipped around so the seal hung inward. It wasn't like the City of Gold he'd loaned her, a pretty ring with a bad fit – he'd had the ring sized to his index finger when he inherited it after his father died, and he wore it constantly enough that it should sit properly. He must have lost weight, and he didn't have a lot to spare.

She turned carefully onto her side, facing his hand and the ring. He shifted, turning as well, arm curling inward to pull her close from behind. The soft breaths behind her told her he'd done it unconsciously.

If he'd found out around the time of Gregory's coronation, then he'd been dealing with this for a year. He looked all right, even out of his clothes, not especially starved or frail. He looked great out of his clothes, actually, but she saved that for later consideration. All taken together, maybe he was healthier now. He'd stopped drinking, he said. He'd certainly started showing up to palace breakfast looking less rough, but she wasn't sure when. He'd had some drinks since, at least –

Although, honestly, it would explain the drink he'd had on the yacht at their going-away party. It had been something pre-mixed, with fruit in it – but that didn't mean there was alcohol, too. It might have been orange juice for all she knew. And at the anniversary ball, he'd had what looked like a cocktail when they were only serving wine. Until the proposal, when the champagne was poured.

Thinking on it, she could pick out a dozen times she'd seen him with a drink she had assumed was alcoholic. Always mixed drinks, never wine or beer. Even in Galia, she didn't know what was in his glasses.

She twined her fingers in his, fiddling the ring into its proper place, and lifted his hand to kiss his fingertips. This time he did wake, but with a kind of slow calm that said he knew he was somewhere safe.

"Wha'sat for?" he asked, throat raspy from sleep.

"Gold star for overachieving," she said.

"First time for everything," he mumbled into the nape of her neck. Then, a little more alertly, "Of course, never leave the lady wanting."

"That too. But I was thinking about your little game with the cocktails," she said, rolling over to face him. His eyes opened a fraction wider than they had been, curious. "You've been drinking juice for months."

"Yeah, more or less," he agreed, hand coming to rest on the nape of her neck, his arm curved around her shoulder blade. "Told you I was handling the drinking better, shouldn't be a shock."

"Bribing bartenders?"

"Tipping bartenders. They don't care what they make me. At this point, at least in the Shivadh palace, they bring me the soft stuff automatically. The bartenders here all know my drink now too, but I still get the odd glass of wine handed to me."

"What's your poison?"

"It's called a Gunner. Lemonade and ginger ale, mostly. Easier to make than a lot of cocktails, tastes fine, looks nice."

"Seems like a lot of work for you, though, always trying to get a mocktail on the sly. You could just say you're off alcohol. You know none of us would hassle you about it."

He laughed quietly. "I suppose, but that's hardly *fun*. I like pulling a fast one for the sake of it. I like cocktails, even the mock ones. The lack of alcohol doesn't impact the aesthetic. I like fruit juice, too."

"That's a point. You must be getting lots of vitamins."

"Every party's a smoothie," he agreed, yawning.

"Your ring is loose, though," she said, turning it on his finger, one way and then the other. "You're okay, right? Healthwise?"

"Yep. Fewer drunken 3am kebabs and more horrible morning runs with Greg, that's all," he said. "Nothing to worry about, promise."

"So how long has it been?" she asked.

"Since what, I started running with Greg? Feels like a damn eternity, I assure you."

"Since you got sober," she said, smiling to soften the harshness of the question.

"I'm not," he said. "I mean, not the way you're thinking. I didn't join a group or decide on abstinence or anything. I still have a drink now and again. But not very often, and not very much. When you're no longer frantically self-medicating, it gets easier. At least, for me."

"That makes sense, I suppose," she said.

"Thank you. But to answer what I think you're actually asking, I got on meds about ten months ago. That's when the self-destructing stopped. Hard month between stopping drinking so the drugs could work and getting the dosage right, but I got through it."

"And none of us noticed."

"Yeah, but that was on purpose," Jerry said. "I made myself scarce. It was right around the time Jes and Noah moved into the lodge, so Uncle Mike was…"

"Distracted," Alanna suggested.

"Yeah. You and Gregory were still figuring out how to run the palace in practice. Eddie was very new. Easy to disappear for a while, especially since we could text, so it didn't even feel like I wasn't around. Actually pretty great timing, though I say it myself."

"This will be the last time I say this, I promise," Alanna said, "but I wish you'd told me."

"I know, dear heart," Jerry said, nosing into her shoulder, kissing it before pulling back again. His voice had a certain tone to it, like the pet name was a little daring of him, like he wasn't sure even now that he was allowed. "Maybe I should have. But sometimes you gotta grow up on your own. I knew that if I came to you and asked for help, I'd get it. It wasn't about not trusting you. It was about whether or not I could stand on my own for a little while. And all of this is awesome pillow talk," he sighed.

"I like that name," she said, uncertain how to respond to the rest of it, wanting to reward him for the endearment in any case.

"What name? Dear heart?" he asked.

"Yeah."

"You would always have been dear to me. Even if we never…" He gestured between them. "Like, love has many floors to it, and I've been on this landing between the two of them, with you. But the foundation doesn't disappear just because you climb the stairs. On the other hand, if you never go upstairs, it's still there. Just…empty, for now."

"Very poetic."

"Comes naturally to Shivadh men," he said with a grin. She smiled back. "I didn't do any of this specifically for you, but the last couple of months I've felt like I could deserve you, and that's been pretty…uh, cool," he said. "For lack of a better way to put it. You were always going to be someone I loved, but you weren't always someone I would have been good for. I was at least that self-aware. I was just, you know, picking my moment."

"Took your time," she said gently.

"What's the saying? It was a calculated risk, but man am I bad at math?" he said. "There was just a lot going on, and then the damn Duke of the Horse goes and kicks it and we end up in a whole separate country where suddenly everyone sees you like I've always seen you. Or if they don't, they're still angling to get close to you. And honestly…" He tilted his head against the pillow, studying her. "I didn't know how you felt. Realistically I still don't. I hate to ask this after the fact but do you even know? How you feel about me?"

"If you think I didn't care about you and still – "

"No! It's only that I have been deliberately working to figure this out and that's not actually something a lot of people do, or need to do. So I don't know if you think this is love, or that's too fast, or this could be love but I'm coming on kind of strong, or it's definitely something really deep…I don't know. Inscrutable sphinx," he added, and kissed the palm of her hand, so he couldn't be too worried, she decided.

"I think," she said slowly, "that this was probably a very rash decision that is going to pay off big time for you."

He laughed. "It's a good place to start from."

"Also," she added, "if you asked me to marry you here and now, I would lose my shit, say it's too fast, and run away, and that'd be smart."

"Wow, Al, I'm not – "

"And then tomorrow I'd come back and say yes," she said, rubbing his cheek with her thumb. He looked stunned. "A week ago I would have said I knew you better than anyone else does, except Gregory. Now there's – a whole new part of you that you've been building with your own hands, and I'm the only one who's really seen any of it, and I'd like to see more. A year ago if you'd asked me out I'd have said yes. Would have been a mistake, but I would have done it anyway. I had a huge crush on you in school, and I got past that, but it's not like I don't know I love you. I am more than willing to spend some time figuring this out, whether that's a functional love, but – I don't think this is actually all that sudden for either of us."

"Well," he said thoughtfully, and then, "Fuck me, that's pretty great, Al. Oh, hey – hold on," he said, and rolled out of the bed. Alanna watched him hop into his underwear and pull his shirt around his shoulders, then dart towards the little vanity where she'd laid out her makeup and jewelry. He picked something up and returned, hands behind his back as he sat cross-legged on the bed next to her. He brought his hands around to show her two level fists, a traditional Shivadh marriage proposal. They'd watched Gregory pull this on Eddie, not long ago.

She looked at his eyes, not his hands, and there was humor in his face but also a weird, desperate earnestness.

"The Dukes of Shivadlakia have long engagements," he said. "We can take years, if we want. You and I don't have to ever marry. We can take our time and then decide we just want to be together, or even that we're not meant for each other and break up. But I would love to make our incredibly rash decision official. Even if it's only for us."

She sat up, kissed his cheek, and rested her fingers on his left hand. When he turned his hand over, she looked down and took the City of Gold ring out of his palm.

"First try, good job," he said.

"You're left-handed, it wasn't rocket science," she replied.

"That is the beauty of me – I will never be rocket science," he told her.

"Are you going to work on self-esteem with your therapist at any point?" she asked, sliding the ring on, and his mouth dropped open.

"Catty!" he managed. "You are cruel to your affianced! Cruel to poor Gerald! Also yes," he added. "I have been. And he's going to be super happy about this, you have no idea. I've been having a slow-motion nervous breakdown since we left Askazer-Shivadlakia and I owe him a win."

"Good," she said. "Should I – would it have been better if someone else came with me instead of you? So that you wouldn't be dealing with all this, I mean."

"No," he said firmly. "I wanted to come. I wouldn't have let you leave me behind. And look," he said, lifting her hand to kiss the ring on her thumb. "Big win."

"We're such…such nobility," she said. She'd have to talk to Jerry's mother Sarah, get the ring sized or maybe have a new one made. Eventually. No hurry. "Thirty seconds of courtship and we're engaged."

"Don't look now, but that's title number three for you. You officially have a collection," he said. "You are three whole duchesses. Galia through your father, Askaz when your grandmother dies, and Shivadlakia because you seduced that poor, witless Duke Gerald. You can't have every duchy in Europe, Al."

"I could if I wanted," she replied. She turned the ring so that the engraving of the palace was facing up, the Grand Synagogue on the other side tucked snugly against her palm.

"Yeah," he agreed, and she saw an entire future for both of them in the look he gave her. "You probably could. I'd help. Given the damn ring's not going to fit on the right finger, do you want to play it cool or tell the world?"

"We can't, not yet," she said. "Not until Galia's been dealt with."

And that was a sobering thought; she could tell he felt the same in the way his face darkened.

"We are behind enemy lines," he agreed. "Okay. Good call. I should mend fences with Milo regardless, and the sooner the better. *He's not the enemy.*"

"No. But at least now you can explain, if you want. Why you were such an asshole to him."

He let his head fall back, staring at the ceiling. "Making amends blows. But yeah, I'll go say I'm sorry."

"Shower first," she told him, and he smiled and kissed her ring one more time, then got off the bed to go wash.

When Jerry emerged from the shower, Alanna was on the phone with Gregory, hopefully not immediately telling him they were engaged, although he supposed it was a good sign for the future if she was. He held up a finger, tipped to one side, and raised his eyebrows, a question mark of sorts. She shook her head and mouthed, *paperwork.*

He dressed enough to be presentable, then found his phone in the sitting room and opened a text window to Milo.

I owe you a million apologies and probably something expensive, he wrote. *Alanna isn't making me do this, I know I was a huge asshole and you didn't deserve it. I will come to wherever you are to make good, unless you'd rather it be in public at breakfast tomorrow.*

He could see in the status bar that Milo was reading it, and then tapping a reply; when it arrived it was better than he deserved. *I'm still in the Palazzo. In the archives. Please do not bring anything expensive.*

Jerry waved for Alanna, who said, "Hang on," and held the phone away from her face. "What's up?"

"Going to see Milo. Wish me luck," he said. She gestured for him to come over to the bed, then kissed him when he got close enough.

"Be a grownup about it," she said, and he smiled and nodded and called "Hi Greg!" loud enough for him to hear, then left while Alanna was laughing with Gregory about Jerry's irreverence.

The archives were cool and mostly dark; when he arrived, Milo was sitting at Bruno's desk, feet up on the edge of it, working on a laptop propped on his thighs. He closed it and set it aside, fixing Jerry with a level look.

"First," Jerry said, "I am going to say that while I did not mean a lot of what I said, I still meant to say it, and that was really stupid and wrong. I don't think you're a jumped-up file clerk, I think you're one of the best people working in this cursed place, and I said all that because I knew it would piss you off."

"Well, you aren't wrong," Milo allowed.

"Whatever anyone says, I think you'd probably make a great Duke of the Horse, and either way it's not my job to tell Alanna who she can or should date. Having met some of her dates, you definitely are a cut above the crowd."

"Still haven't heard an *I'm sorry*," Milo pointed out.

"I am," Jerry said, coming to lean against the edge of the desk. "I'm really sorry I hurt you, Milo. I shouldn't have done that."

"Thank you. I'm glad you realized it. I assume with a hand from Alanna."

"Even as I was doing it I knew I was being an asshole, so lord knows why I kept on," Jerry said. Milo tilted his head, his glare going more studious. "I think...you understand how special she is."

"You care about her."

"Well, yes. Not sure if this is evident, and it's no excuse, but I'm in love with her," Jerry said.

"Suspected that much when you started in on me," Milo agreed. "It did not make it more pleasant, Jerry, I have to say."

"I can imagine." Jerry studied the ceiling, sighing. "But I like you, as does Alanna, and both of us need you. I did you dirty for no good reason. So I need to know how to make amends, as much as I can."

Milo made a thoughtful noise, and Jerry glanced at him. There was a lot of emotion on his face.

"I think you and I are working at cross-purposes but for the same goal," Milo said. "So perhaps it's time to put some cards on the table. I can't tell you that I was acting out of romance when I asked Alanna out. Do I want to be duke? No. Do I want some other idiot to be duke? Even less. I don't want us to have a Duke of the Horse. I want us to have a real government, with open elections. That's what Bruno was doing in your archives when we came to the palace, you know."

"What, having an election?" Jerry asked, and then snickered.

"I have known you were stuck at twelve years old since we met when you were thirteen," Milo said.

"Then you were an astute judge of character for an eleven-year-old. Everyone else expects me to be an adult, which is frankly a lot of responsibility."

"Bruno was – still is – studying Gregory II, the man who democratized a kingdom," Milo said. "He's working on a long-range plan to do the same for Galia. I know Alanna doesn't want to be here. I think she's trying to figure out a way to get out of being duchess. While I want to help her, I also think perhaps she ought to know that even if she becomes duchess, we don't intend to let her stay on the throne."

"I hope this is less beheading and more impeachment," Jerry said.

"Or they might try to elect her once we get that far, who knows? The point is, until we can put the elections in place, someone's got to take charge and if it's one of the old guard, we're just…fucked. Jerry. Really, really fucked."

"Mm. So you and Bruno – and I assume Ofelia?" he asked, and Milo nodded. "Are trying to make sure power keeps moving away from the council and towards you."

"Well, that makes us sound a little craven, but essentially. If it helps, we don't want it or intend to keep it. But if not us, then who?"

"So – when I told Alanna in the massive fight we just had that I thought you liked her for her, and didn't want the throne, I… misjudged."

"I do like Alanna greatly. I'd do a decent job as a husband," Milo said. "But I'm already seeing someone and also not attracted to her, so yeah, we were both being assholes, just in different ways."

"Now I'm intrigued," Jerry said. "Who catches the eye of the covert revolutionary Milo Ansevali?"

Milo gestured at the desk he was sitting at. Jerry blinked.

"You and Bruno?" he asked. Milo gave him a small, curt nod. "That explains a few things."

"Does it?"

"Sort of. Both of you raised some red flags for us. Nothing bad, just…unusual. Greg and I thought you were acting weird, and Alanna was kind of wondering what Bruno's deal was," Jerry said. Milo looked away, seemingly in thought. "But if you two are together and awkward about hiding it, or even just awkward about hiding all the plotting, maybe that's why. Is it okay, you outing him to me?"

"He won't mind. He's not in the closet, it'd just be…difficult for my career if I was out," Milo said. "But I don't think you're the kind to use that against us, all recent evidence to the contrary."

"No, I wouldn't do that. And I can see why you wouldn't want it gossiped about in Galia. You've already got a bunch of people taking aim at you. I thought you'd have higher sights than an archives nerd, but I have to admit Bruno's very nice. And he presumably was cool with you making a play for Alanna," Jerry added with a grin.

"I don't feel great about that, but we're working to save a country," Milo said, and then inhaled. "Uh, in *full* disclosure, he's not a historian. I mean. He is. But that's not why he's here."

Jerry leaned forward. "Then why's he here? Unless it's one of those *I could tell you, but then I'd have to kill you* deals." At Milo's expression, he sat back again. "Uh. Is it?"

"Bruno's a member of the Guard of the Horse," Milo said. "He's a spy. Sort of. No, that's not a good word…" He shook his head. "The Guard of the Horse is supposed to be the elite guard for the duke. There's a large faction that hated the duke, though, including Bruno's brother, who's pretty high up in the Guard. He brought Bruno in, undercover. The Guard's been working – with us, that's how Bruno and I even met – to make sure whoever succeeds the duke is…different. He's spent two years in the palace, trying to find ways to fix this *mess*. And then the duke dropped dead and Alanna fell into our laps. We thought if she had reason to stay, stronger than just knowing how much trouble we're in, she might accept long enough for us to organize free elections. But we could see her pulling back, so I was supposed to be an attempt at bait to keep her here."

Jerry rubbed his lips with his thumb. "Wow. Milo. That sounds stressful."

"Little bit," Milo agreed. "But desperate times."

"Alanna won't thank you for it."

"I didn't expect she would," Milo said with a sigh. "And in the cold light of you kicking my ass just now, it looks more and more like a bad, dumb, panicky idea."

"Was Bruno even trying to find a direct heir, like she asked?" Jerry said.

"He was, actually, still is – a Galian heir would solve some problems. And then Alanna could go home and report back to her king," Milo said, with a sharp grin.

He'd guessed, then, that they had ulterior motives for being here. Well, no point in obfuscating now. "Politics," Jerry said, shrugging.

"That's an excuse, but we've both had a rough weekend, so I'll give it to you," Milo said. "Besides, if I thought Gregory had ill intentions, we'd have kept Alanna out of the sensitive information."

"I'd like to see you try," Jerry said. "But no. You know Gregory. He's a diplomat, not an empire-builder. He wasn't lying when he said he'd like to have better relations with Galia."

"Good. We want that too."

"Then I also happen to have some new leads for Bruno to chase down, if you'd like to carry them along," Jerry said. "I talked to Carlo – the party count?"

"Ah, Carlo. He's dim but harmless. Useful in his way."

"Glad my assessment is confirmed. He says there are rumors the duke had a direct heir, but he doesn't think the mother was nobility. The Bright Young Things all think if he had kids it was with the help – Palazzo staff, or a professional in town. The kind of person who might use a child to maintain their position, or even just the kind of person he wouldn't be as careful with as he would someone in the peerage."

"That makes…actually a lot of sense," Milo said. "He definitely seduced the staff. Some willingly, but I'm sure there were some who just wanted to keep their jobs. What a creep he was. I almost wish he'd lived to see himself get dropped into the shit by Brasolin and his ilk."

"Anyone come to the top of your mind?"

"A few. I'll talk with Bruno and get back to you," Milo said.

"As apologies go, this was super productive," Jerry said, as Milo stood to walk him to the door.

"How's Alanna? Still furious with you? I should probably talk to her, say I'm sorry. But if she's still breathing fire, maybe it can wait."

Jerry clapped him on the shoulder. "She's quick to heal. I'll be fine, I'm going to go talk to her now. I'll clue her in on all this, if that's okay. That way when you do say sorry, at least you won't have to go through this twice."

"Yes. She should know. Thank you," Milo said.

"As you may remember from school, I have a lot of experience being dumb and panicky," Jerry told him kindly. Milo gave him a rueful grin. "You go have a nice evening with Bruno, don't work too hard, and tell him he doesn't have to worry about losing you to the duchess."

"He'll be thrilled," Milo said drily.

When he got back to the suite, Alanna was dressed again, slouched on the sofa, staring at the ceiling.

"I am exhausted," she announced. "You speak to Milo?"

"Boy did I," he replied. "Not to annoy you and then insult you but apparently his motives were not pure."

She threw an arm over her eyes. "Can anyone in Galia just say what they mean?"

"Apparently not. He's dating someone else. He was trying to lock you down so he could marry you, become duke, overthrow himself and you, and institute a democracy. It's extremely exciting and, yes, also very tiring, and explaining why he owes you an apology even bigger than the one I owed him might take a while," he agreed, sitting next to her, wrapping an arm around her shoulders and kissing her hair. Then, realizing he could, he pulled her arm down and kissed her properly.

"Just what I need, more excitement," she said. "At least now I don't have to worry about letting him down easy."

"No, indeed not," Jerry agreed.

"Gregory sends his love, by the way," she added. "He just needed to know where some files were and Darien's off because it's Sunday. Took us some time to get to them."

"He'd be lost without you. As would I."

"Nice to be needed," she said. "I didn't tell him about us."

"Seems like a face-to-face kind of conversation," he agreed. "Maybe after we've been dating for more than an hour."

"That's what I thought. So now what do we do with ourselves?"

"I sent Milo home to his *amore*. We could stay in and I will do my best to entertain you. Or we could go get dinner in the dining room, it's coming up on mealtime. I think we should go out, though. Be seen around Galia. I'll take you to a steakhouse, load you up with protein, and make you laugh," he promised. "I can tell you what Milo told me in the archives, it's a lot of good gossip. I also have extensive questions about your very offhand remark that you think I didn't notice, about having a crush on me at school."

"If I let you take me out, will you promise not to ask me about that until we're both at least fifty?" she asked.

"No, but I promise not to ask you about it tonight," he said, kissing her again. "Let's give the people a thrill and go be glamorous and seen."

"I'm not wearing heels."

"Say the word and I will," he replied, grinning at her.

"No, you're tall enough already."

"Woke up this way," he told her. "I promise a good dinner and an early night in. I'll even go back to my own rooms and sleep alone in the big cold bed if you decree it."

She rested a hand on his chest, head on his shoulder, and he managed to keep quiet and let her think.

"I'd like to go out," she said at last. "Not just to dinner. There's one of those outdoor shopping plazas past the casino – looked fake and dumb but also kind of pretty. We can buy some presents to take home. I just want a nice evening like we could have in Fons-Askaz. Dinner somewhere fashionable. Then back here, and you can stay a while, but you can't sleep the night in my rooms. The staff would know."

He hadn't considered that, and it felt a little bittersweet, but he nodded. "All right. Let me change and see about a car. You find wherever you'd like to eat."

He had seen Alanna smile countless times, at friends and boyfriends and people she didn't even like that much, but when he stood up and kissed her before heading back to his own room, it felt like she offered a completely new smile just for him.

CHAPTER EIGHT

IT WAS PROBABLY just as well they'd had an early night; on Monday morning, things took a sharp turn.

Alanna was at breakfast; she'd woken early, and decided to fortify herself in case Milo still wanted to have a conversation. Instead, before she could text Milo to ask him about their meeting, a woman sat down across from Alanna in the dining room and offered her a slip of paper over her half-eaten pastry.

Alanna saw Will, at the back of the room, start to get up; she gave him a small shake of her head, and he settled back down but narrowed his eyes. She picked up the paper and studied it, glancing back and forth between it and the woman sitting across from her. Handwritten on the paper was a digital path – a route through one of the Palazzo Cavallo's administrative shared drives, presumably to the location of a file.

"I only just have known Milo asked for a full budget," the woman said quietly, in heavily accented English.

"I was beginning to think one didn't exist," Alanna replied in Italian, setting the paper down, and the woman looked relieved.

"It does. We have to have one copy, so the departmental budgets reconcile," she replied. "It's part of my job to keep the master book."

"Why you?" Alanna asked. "I'm sorry, I don't know who you are."

"Because I'm the lowest rung on the ladder, and it's very boring work," she answered, ignoring the implicit question of who she was. "That's an archive," she added, nodding at the paper. "It's accessible to anyone with a login, it's just nobody ever looks for it. I knew someone should see it, but I didn't know who before now. Hard to know, in the Palazzo, who to trust. But everyone trusts the Ansevalis, and we like you. If Milo needed it, I knew you'd have a use for it."

"Thank you," Alanna said. "For the trust and for the information. This will be helpful."

"Just don't get me fired," the woman said with a smile, and left the dining room at a casual stroll. Alanna tucked the paper in her pocket, took a last sip of coffee, and tried to be as casual going back to her rooms.

Laptop open at the table by the window overlooking Athena's enclosure, Alanna followed the path on the slip of paper through five nested folders, some of which were only identified by a series of numbers. Eventually she came to a folder that was full, row upon row, of spreadsheets. Each of these was simply marked with a number.

She opened one – 2020.xlsx – and found that it was the year for the information stored inside. At first blush it did look like a budget, but then she frowned and studied some of the codes. This wasn't a projection, a guess at what would be spent where, or even a statement about what could be spent where.

It was a ledger. It was what *had been* spent. What had been deposited and moved around, too. It was an avalanche of information, compared to the little trickle Milo had been able to source.

It could also be a trap. If one of the council wanted to imply to them that there was nothing wrong with Galia's finances, a fake archive would be the way to do it. She copied the files over to her laptop's hard drive while she considered what to do.

Well, she knew a few things about Galia, enough to do a random audit and see if things that should be in the files were there. If she had at least that much confirmation, she could call Milo and Bruno about it.

The files were dense with information, but the current year's budget was easily sorted; once she worked out some of the codes, she could even find entries paying for her own stay – extra food, musicians, alcohol for the receptions. There was her ball gown, too.

"Yikes," she mumbled, when she saw the price of the gown.

She also knew, in a general sense, when Michaelis had been in Galia last; she opened the year she thought it might have been, as well as the two around it, and combed through the much less detailed numbers in those files. This data would all have been entered from paper records, or imported over from earlier spreadsheet programs if the duke had been particularly progressive about digital archives, which he probably hadn't. The poor clerk who had given this to her might have been the one to build them from paper. In any case, there wasn't much in the way of text, just codes and numbers. There were clearly several receptions in those years, marked by expenditures on food and drink, music and staff, but they weren't broken down by who had visited, and some didn't have exact dates attached.

She considered this, closing the older files. Even if they weren't big fans of computerized bookkeeping, they'd probably begun keeping digital records at least twenty years ago. She counted backwards, to one year after her first year at Institut Alpin, and opened the file. What she was looking for didn't show up under any designation she thought of at first – the name of the school, anything to do with education or scholarship funds. Finally, she just searched "Ansevali", and that turned it up immediately: "Ansevali M" in a notes column.

There were a handful of expense entries tagged with Milo and Ofelia's names. They came from the duke's discretionary fund, not an educational fund, but there were entries in late summer, several years running, that were about the amounts one would pay for a year's tuition at Institut Alpin, or at an elite school in Galia. Perhaps the duke's personal staff had administered some kind of named scholarship fund, so that it wouldn't come out of the allocations for local education.

It probably shouldn't be so exciting, finding one or two particular numbers in column upon column of them, but she'd always enjoyed this kind of detail work. It was why she'd loved being Gregory's right hand at the palace.

Still loved it, she reminded herself. This was temporary. He was waiting for her to come home. Hopefully she could, in another few days.

She took her phone out and sent off a text to Bruno and the Ansevalis, asking if any of them were in the Palazzo and could come to the suite. She was just texting Jerry the same when there was a knock on the door and Jerry's voice on the other side calling in Italian.

"Good morning, Duchessa! Don't behead me for oversleeping."

"Come in," she called in English, and he put his head in the door, grinning at her. "Your breakfast manners are as appalling as your Italian, but your timing's good regardless," she said. Her phone beeped and she consulted the lock screen. "The Ansevalis are on their way."

"Why, what's going on?" he asked, coming inside. He leaned

over her and tipped her chin up to kiss her, albeit briefly. "Also, shouldn't you be getting ready for council? They want you at ten today, don't they? Half past nine now."

"Damn – I'm going to have to cancel," she said, gritting her teeth.

"Send me instead," he suggested, settling next to her on the sofa. "You and I both go to meetings for Gregory, it's not unheard of. And it'll put them in their place, you sending the idiot to deal with them."

"Self-esteem," Alanna sing-songed.

"I was speaking from their point of view, that's others-esteem," he protested.

"Just watch yourself, I'm going to call you on that from now on. Anyway, I'm not sure if they'd let you in – might be a bigger deal than just me canceling. We can ask Milo when he gets here."

"Why do you need to cancel, anyway? Find something juicy?" he asked.

"I think so," she said, gesturing at the laptop screen. He turned from studying her face to look at the screen instead, and then leaned forward to see it better.

"Whoa. Is this…" He touched the trackpad on the laptop, scrolling up and down. "Looks like the ledger they use on the estate back home, only about a million times more complicated."

"You read your estate's ledgers?"

"I do now, have for the last three quarters. Have your grandparents not shown you the documents for your estate?"

"No, they have – they wouldn't give me the birds and the bees but they went through the operating budget with me very thoroughly when I was fourteen. I check in every so often, but mostly Grandfather manages it. It just didn't strike me as something you'd be interested in," she said, derailed from explaining how she got the ledgers by the idea of Jerry, their Jerry, poring over spreadsheets and doing pivot tables.

"Oh, I'm not interested in them, they're mind-numbingly boring," he said, eyes still on the sheet. "It's the worst part of the gig. But one has to make sure the steward's not embezzling and such, and if my mother's not going to do it – and she's not – I might as well. Fortunately our household manager is as honest as he is uninteresting. Ideal man for the – "

He broke off abruptly, head tilting, and was opening his mouth to speak again when there was another knock at the door.

"Come in," she called, and Milo entered, followed by Bruno and Ofelia. "Close the door. Milo, you may need to make an excuse for me to the council this morning."

"I told her she can send me if she wants," Jerry said, highlighting a line in the spreadsheet and continuing to scroll. "Not sure how the council would take that."

"Probably find it welcome; they'd rather deal with a man," Milo replied. "Tell me why, first, if you can?"

"Someone from the finance office just sent me these," Alanna said, removing the laptop from Jerry's grasp and turning it around to show them. Milo sank down into a chair, taking the laptop from her. Ofelia sat in the other chair, and Bruno looked around before dragging one over from the table near the window.

"It's full ledgers going back decades," Alanna said. "Apparently they made it this one poor clerk's job to keep them all – "

"Of course they did," Milo murmured.

"We should have expected that. For years the duke's personal security codes were kept on a flash drive in someone's pocket," Ofelia groaned. Milo was blinking at the sheet, hands moving quickly on the trackpad and keyboard.

"This is everything," he said, astonished. "Payroll, deposits in, expenditures – if someone embezzled, it's probably in here. If someone transferred money to a bank in the Bahamas it might even outright be called 'Bank in the Bahamas' in this notes column. This is madness. It's our own national Panama Papers," he said, looking up at her. "Half the council is implicated here. Maybe more. Is this real?"

"As far as I can tell," Alanna said. "There's real entries, across several years. It looks like I'd expect it to look overall. But I haven't been able to systemically audit it."

"Who gave it to you?" Bruno asked.

"I don't know her name. She just told me where to find it all and left."

"Smart woman."

"I don't think Milo spoke to her when he was trying to get this kind of data – she said she didn't know until just now what you were looking for. I get the sense she's been dying to know who to give it to," Alanna said.

"Bruno," Milo said, and Bruno got up immediately, crouching next to his chair, one arm slung over his shoulders as he studied the screen with him.

"Yes, I see. I don't know if I understand, though," Bruno agreed, when Milo pointed at something. He looked over at Alanna. "I – no offense, I know you're trained in this kind of work, but I'd like to take this to…my people."

Ofelia raised her eyebrows at him, then looked pointedly at Alanna.

"I told Jerry yesterday, about Bruno being in the Guard," Milo said. "Sorry, Ofelia. Didn't have time to brief you."

"Important information to have," Ofelia said sharply.

"It was a very long day," Alanna put in gently.

"There's data here that could ruin any councilmember that's been maintaining power through financial control of the duke," Bruno said. "The Guard of the Horse has access to discreet, thorough forensic accounting. With these files, we might be able to bring down the council. No wonder they wouldn't give them to you, Milo. And some…some clerk just had them all?"

"She told me, everyone trusts the Ansevalis," Alanna said. Bruno's mouth curved upwards and he glanced affectionately at Milo, who didn't appear to notice, still studying the sheet.

"With this, and with Alanna on the throne, Galia could be holding elections in two years. Maybe less," Milo said, looking at Ofelia.

"Does it have to be me?" Alanna asked. "If we have this, can we force them to accept a different heir?"

"Very possibly. But is there anyone you'd trust to serve in your place? You know the potential heirs you've found. Do you know any of them personally?"

"Not well enough that I'd tell them what we in this room know," Alanna admitted.

"I have a question," Jerry said softly. "Two, actually. Promise they're relevant."

"Go ahead," Alanna said.

"Does the Guard of the Horse also have access to a reliable

DNA testing lab?" Jerry asked. "One that can do a rush job discreetly."

Bruno looked perplexed. "Probably," he said. "I can ask. Why?"

"It's relative to the second question. Milo, scroll up – there's a line item highlighted. Can you tell me what it means?"

"Yes, I see – " Milo began, and then his eyes narrowed, mouth thinning.

"That's a relative of yours, isn't it?" Jerry asked. "Not M for Milo or O for Ofelia."

"Milo?" Ofelia asked.

"When I came in, Alanna had a filter on the sheet," Jerry said. "She'd been searching your surname."

"I was trying to confirm the sheet was real. I thought, you both went to school on scholarship from the state…" Alanna gestured at the laptop. "I found the lines for your tuition."

"This one isn't school tuition, though," Milo said. "This is six figures paid out."

"To a relative of ours?" Ofelia asked, perplexed.

"To Mama," Milo said, looking up at her.

"*What?*" Ofelia asked.

"Ansevali C. is Catrina, our mother," Milo said to Jerry. "But this can't be right," he continued, turning his attention back to the laptop. "It's got to be a mistake. She was employed by the Palazzo, it's probably misplaced from the payroll sheet, and it's about what she'd earn if you took a zero away – "

"Your mother was staff here?" Alanna asked, the details beginning to fit together.

"She was one of the duke's personal secretaries. It's how we know so much about palace operations," Ofelia said. "We grew up in the Palazzo, practically. That's how she got the scholarship money, too, she knew who to ask – "

"She asked the duke," Alanna said.

"Yes, probably," Ofelia said dismissively.

"No. Personally," Milo said. "She asked His Grace. The school money's from his discretionary fund."

He opened a different file, studied it, opened another one.

"There's…I think there's no scholarship program," he said. "I'm not seeing anyone else under these codes. I've never spoken to any other

Galian who went to Institut Alpin, but I thought it was just because there's such a stigma against taking charity in Galia – nobody wanted to admit…"

"The duke sent you both to school on his dime," Jerry said. "And he gave your mother some kind of payment."

"Yearly," Milo murmured. "There's at least three – no – at least five yearly payments here."

Ofelia had her hand over her mouth.

"We used to joke that Mama stole a house," Milo said, voice tight. "When we were little she bought a house near the Palazzo – mostly it's apartments around here, but there are a few houses. They aren't cheap. There was no way our mother bought a house, that house, with a nice yard and a good view of the promenade, not for what she made in the Palazzo, with no husband in the picture. When we were young, she joked she stole it. When we got older she used to say she got a lucky break. That's why they call us jumped-up, you know," he continued, bitterness in his voice. "Not just because we went to Institut Alpin and the Galia School for Youth Leadership or because we're good at our jobs. It was because we were a secretary's kids but we always dressed like a duke's kids. Looked nice, good manners, fine house, new car…"

"You're calling our mother – " Ofelia began, and then swallowed. "Milo, Mama didn't take money for sex with the duke."

"That's not what he's saying," Jerry said. "She was taking the money for you two, to give you a good life." Ofelia looked at him. "Ofelia. Do the math. You're the oldest. You're the heir."

She looked away, and Alanna realized that she'd known since Milo mentioned the duke's discretionary fund. She just didn't want to admit it. Alanna wouldn't either, in her position.

"Jerry," Alanna said.

"Yes'm."

"Go to the council. Take Will if you want. Tell them I'm unwell and you're there to stand in for me. You'll need to sell it a little."

"No shortage of selling it," Jerry said.

"Milo, Bruno, you should leave my suite before someone sees you here," she continued. "Call your friends in the Guard, only people you trust. I want a single sheet of paper, two days from now, that I can use to ruin the council. Is that doable?"

"Might be two pages, the way these files look," Bruno said, seemingly torn between amusement and disgust.

"Even better. Can you figure out a way to get a paternity test done?" Alanna asked.

"Sure. I'll see what's available."

"Ofelia," Alanna said, and Ofelia, who had bowed her head, looked up at her. Alanna gestured to the sofa cushion next to her. "You and I are going to stay here and figure something out."

Ofelia chewed her lip, then nodded and got up, coming to the sofa to sit. Alanna put an arm around her shoulders.

"This is a good – " Milo began, and Alanna shot him a look. "But politically – "

"Milo, she's your sister, give her five damn minutes," Jerry said, standing up.

"If he does that he's going to realize she's not the only child of the duke in this room," Bruno said, and Milo went pale. "Milo. Come on. Let's do this somewhere else."

Jerry walked them to the door, Milo cradling Alanna's laptop. She didn't really want to let someone else take her laptop, but she did trust Milo, and anyway she suspected he was in enough shock it would be hard to get it back right now. In any case, they probably wouldn't go exploring on her hard drive, and it wouldn't be a disaster if they did. She didn't have anything dangerous unlocked and there wasn't anything incriminating, though there was a collection of Star Wars fanfic she didn't care to be judged for. Jerry saw Milo and Bruno into the hallway and then leaned back in.

"I don't care if I'm arm-wrestling Brasolin for the fate of Galia, if you need me, you text," he said. "I'll come running."

She nodded. "Text Gregory and Michaelis for me? I'm going to need a call with both of them later."

"Sure. I've got calendar access, I'll book you in," he said, and closed the door behind him. Ofelia, her forehead resting on Alanna's shoulder, shuddered.

"It is good, Milo's right," she said.

"It's not good," Alanna said. "It's helpful. Not the same thing. If you are the duke's child, you can take Galia in hand. If Bruno can come through with evidence to ruin the council, you can do everything you and Milo set out to do. And not to be poetic about it, but there's…something very mythical in the idea of two children of the sitting ruler, without knowing it, growing up to be such staunch defenders of the country he almost ruined. But we don't have to think it's good, Ofelia. I didn't even know the duke and I don't like him. I can't imagine knowing him personally and finding out you're his child."

"We probably should have known," Ofelia murmured, leaning away from her. Alanna kept her arm over her shoulders, but very lightly, ready to let go if need be. "It's not like the pieces weren't there."

"Why would you assume, though? Everyone knows the duke didn't have children. Everyone told you that you were middle class."

"Heh," Ofelia said, rubbing her knuckles against her nose. "Middle class would have been a promotion."

"Well," Alanna said reflectively, "the next time someone calls you a Jumped-Up Ansevali, you can have them imprisoned."

That got a laugh, at least, and Ofelia dug in her pocket for a handkerchief, blotting her eyes, wiping her nose.

"We still don't know, anyway," she said to Alanna. "Jerry's right. We'll need to do a test and it'll need to be unimpeachable."

"Not necessarily. Not at first, anyway," Alanna said. "We can have one done today, if we can get some of the duke's DNA. Think that's possible?"

"His rooms are on the third floor. They've been sealed since he died," Ofelia said. "Bruno can get access. There must be a hairbrush or something similar."

"We'll confirm what we think is going on, here," Alanna said. "Maybe confirm with the Guard of the Horse and then use an independent lab for proof. We have a little time. Even if you aren't, the financial data alone is going to give me what I need to start fixing this. But I think we both know you are."

"Do you suppose the council would accept me? I'm not nobility – it's not like they were married. I have political capital, but not nearly as much as you do just by virtue of being close to the Shivadh king."

"No…but Milo is friends with the king. Old school chums. And you…are close with me," Alanna said. Ofelia looked skeptical. "You could be. I'd like us to be friends, too, you know. Either way, it's in our interests to support you. If you go into the council with the backing of

Askazer-Shivadlakia and enough evidence to ruin them…well. I've never project-managed a coup before, but this could be fun," she said. Ofelia smiled at her. "Want to help me plan it, Your Grace?"

"Lord." Ofelia put the handkerchief away. "Yes, I suppose I'd better."

Outside, under the window, Athena chuffed in the long grass as they hatched their plan.

A lot had to happen, very quickly and very discreetly, that day. Jerry, realizing this on his walk to the council chambers, squared up and took a hit for the team, making himself so obnoxious for the entire duration of the council session that they were too busy being annoyed he wasn't Alanna to wonder why she wasn't there.

By the time he got out he felt he'd crammed an entire week of bad behavior into three hours. He carb-loaded with pasta at lunch in the dining room, flirting with the staff who came and went as he texted the Shivadh palace.

Gregory, of course, generally had full Mondays, and Michaelis was technically retired but functionally a busy man. It wasn't that they didn't want to talk to Alanna, but they had to push things around to make it work, including both of them hating the conference call feature and thus wanting to be in the same place at the same time when they called her. He kept an eye on their conversation, but he'd had at least a firm commitment from them to both be present in some form or other at two o'clock, and the rest was just them wrangling with each other.

Bruno, just after Jerry walked into the council, had texted a group chat that included Milo, Ofelia, Alanna, and himself, plus a number he didn't recognize. He scrolled through it at lunch, but it seemed to be mostly logistics surrounding a rapid DNA test, so Jerry sent a series of gif images showing various talk show hosts announcing "You ARE the father" and otherwise left them alone. Alanna sent a private message thanking him because he'd made Ofelia laugh.

It's what I do, Jerry said. *I'll take that jester job if it's still open, I do better at that than vizier.*

You are helping to mastermind the downfall of a royal government. You've never been more vizier-like, she replied.

Jerry chuckled. *Should have packed my medallion of office.*

You mean the video game character costume medallion you bought at the street market? Alanna asked.

It looks very dramatic, Jerry replied. *Want me to bring you up some lunch?*

We've eaten. Bring me up yourself, though. You should be on the call with Greg and Michaelis.

He sent a thumbs-up and stood; he was almost to the doorway of the dining room when Brasolin entered, and the way he moved made it clear he was there either to see Jerry or prevent him from leaving.

"Consigliere," Jerry said. "Nice to see you again so soon."

"Your Grace," Brasolin replied, and then just stood there.

"Anything I can help you with? I wouldn't try the chicken today, the sauce is a little spicy for my tastes," Jerry said.

"I wanted to inquire after Her Grace. I hope she's not too ill."

"Just a headache. I think she'll be fine."

"I noticed also that Ms. Ansevali has called in sick – perhaps there's something going around," Brasolin said.

"Really? I saw Milo this morning, I hope he's not a carrier," Jerry replied. "You know how these big, badly-ventilated old buildings are – one person gets sick and comes into work, everyone gets sick. I don't think it's a flu, though, not in Alanna's case anyway. She had a rough Sunday," he said, which was completely true.

Brasolin gave him what Jerry could only identify as the stinkiest stink eye of his experience. He supposed the man had been working on it for about fifty years, and it showed. Jerry didn't believe in the Evil Eye but his mother had given him a hamsa ring to protect against such things as a child and in that moment he wished he'd brought it along. He rubbed the signet ring on his finger with his thumb.

"Please convey my wishes for a swift recovery," Brasolin said at last. "We would hate for her to be absent again tomorrow."

Message received, you unpleasant gargoyle, Jerry thought. Out loud, he said, "I'll convey your sentiments to Her Grace."

Upstairs, in Alanna's suite, he announced, "Brasolin knows Ofelia called in sick and he's being very weird about it. We may have to sneak her out later. I volunteer to serve as a diversion while you dress her like an old woman and wheel her downstairs in a chair."

"If I can't sneak out of the Palazzo, I don't deserve to be here," Ofelia replied. She seemed to have rallied, at least, from the shock of the morning.

"That's the spirit. Hey, I was thinking, Count Carlo's marriage bid was for the duchess, not for Alanna; he just wants to be duke," Jerry said. "You should give it some thought. He'd put in the work, and when you overthrow yourself he'd probably fall on a sword for you."

Ofelia sniffed. "I can do better than Carlo."

"Yes, but can you have more fun?" he asked.

"Welcome to your future, where every man wants to marry you off, usually to himself," Alanna said, coming out of the bedroom. "Jerry won't tell you this but he'd be an okay husband if you asked."

"I'm taken," Jerry said with a grin.

"Yes, I saw the photograph from your karaoke adventure," Ofelia replied. Jerry covered his face with one hand.

"Milo's working up an exciting new agenda for the week," Alanna continued. "How'd council go today?"

"Fine," Jerry said, "but I hope his agenda includes you being in council tomorrow, because Brasolin will get even edgier if you aren't."

"Damn, we'll have to go shopping in the afternoon," Alanna said to Ofelia.

"Don't have anything to wear to seize power?" Jerry guessed.

"PR campaign. Ofelia and I are going to be seen out on the town. The more visible she is with me, the better. And technically we are distant cousins, not that anyone knows that, but she's some portion Shivadh, if only by marriage," Alanna said.

Jerry did the family tree in his head, something he actually wasn't that bad at; he lifted his hand to map it out.

"You are Ofelia's paternal great-aunt's granddaughter," he said at last. "Oh, make it daughter of the paternal cousin, that simplifies it. Sort of. Second cousins."

"Handy skill," Ofelia observed.

"Only in very niche situations, but yes," he agreed. "Love any other reason to be useful, though, if you two have any. Milo and Bruno took the boring jobs, at least."

"Bruno's probably standing over a scientist as we speak,

watching the DNA test develop. Milo's working on the blackmail."

"Isn't blackmail if you aren't asking for money," Jerry replied. "Technically, it's coercion."

Both women looked at him.

"Blackmail is when you want money, coercion is when you want *results*," Jerry said.

"Legally speaking, he's correct," Ofelia said, a little perplexedly.

"And how do you know this?" Alanna asked.

"I've known some unfortunate people in my time," Jerry replied. "Never had either done to me personally, but it's on the bucket list. So what's the plan?"

"Working that out now," Alanna said. "Although I will say, if the Galians didn't want drama, they shouldn't have called a Shivadh."

"I can't wait," Jerry said.

All three of their phones went at once; when he looked down he saw a message from Bruno. *Confirmation. Ofelia is daughter. Milo full sibling. Be there in a few with documentation but they agree it wouldn't hold up in court — lab's not impartial.*

"Another puzzle piece falls into place," Jerry said. His alarm went off to mark five minutes to the call with the palace; he'd barely registered it when Alanna's phone rang. She put it on speaker.

"You're early," she said, but she sounded pleased.

"Only me, I'm afraid. Gregory will be here soon. Didn't see the point in waiting," Michaelis replied. "Am I coming through clear?"

"You are, Uncle Mike," Jerry said. "Hear us okay?"

"Yes, Gerald. I should have known you'd be where trouble was."

"I had a question, actually, if we have a few minutes before Gregory gets here," Jerry said. "Do you have the recipe for the pie that hit Brasolin in the face forty years ago?"

Michaelis's laugh was deep, booming down the line. "I believe it was just a pie tin full of whipped cream, actually. Would have been a waste of good fruit if they'd used a real pie."

"No argument here. Also, we need to introduce someone to you," Jerry said.

"Wait, hold on, Gregory's here — " There was a rustle and the sound of voices talking distantly.

"I am indeed here," Gregory said finally. "Sorry for the delay."

"Good timing, actually," Alanna said. "We have some news, and we need some help."

"Of course. What can we do?" Gregory said.

"It turns out the duke had a child," Alanna said. "Two, actually."

"Oddly unsurprising," Michaelis said. "Have you found them?"

"They found us," Alanna continued. "It's Ofelia and Milo."

"The Ansevalis?" Gregory asked, stunned. "Did they know?"

"We didn't," Ofelia said. "We wouldn't be in quite the same mess if we had. Mind you, we'd be in a different, more complicated mess, so there's that, at least."

"Good point," Jerry murmured. "Uncle Mike, that's Ofelia Ansevali. Her Grace, I should say."

"Not to state the obvious, but this is good news, isn't it?" Michaelis asked. "It gets you out of being duchess, Alanna, and brings you home fairly quickly, I'd imagine. From what I've heard of you, Ms. Ansevali, either you or your brother would make a fine ruler."

"Little more complicated than that," Alanna said, while Ofelia looked pleased by the compliment. "Which is why we're calling. Gregory, I don't think we need you to do anything, but we might need documents attesting to our ability to throw some money behind Ofelia."

"I hate to be crass, but I am king and I need to ask, how much money?" Gregory said.

"Nothing that would break us. We might not even need to commit to sending it, just to…"

"Threaten to," Ofelia said. "Perhaps not even that."

"This is sounding more fun all the time. I'm sorry I'm missing it," Michaelis said.

"That's the other part of the plan," Alanna told him. "I have a front row seat for you, if you're willing to run an errand for us."

"You have my full attention," Michaelis said.

It was difficult to maintain a sense of normality, that Monday and the two days following. They'd fixed the day they would go to the council as Thursday: it gave them time to make arrangements, but left Friday for what they hoped would be the work of cleaning up, of putting the word out and sweeping away the dust left behind.

But in the meantime, Alanna still had to attend council on Tuesday, all three hours, and for an hour on Wednesday. There was a luncheon to attend, and a tea, and she had to be seen out with Ofelia. Jerry had to call up Carlo and arrange for another night out, mentioning that he'd be bringing both Alanna and Ofelia along, which meant Carlo had to compose a very careful guest list.

"He's a little bit of an ass, but he does seem to like being helpful," Jerry said, hanging up on a skeptical Carlo. "You might replace his dad with him on the council. He'd at least be better than Senior."

"Not sure he'll want it, once we remove his father," Ofelia said.

"Don't prosecute and you'll be okay. Carlo knows where the payday is," Alanna said. "And it'll keep the old man from retaliating."

"I'm more worried about Riva," Milo said, studying the dossiers that Bruno had brought them. "There's nothing in the ledgers that incriminates him. He might not actually have done anything wrong. But he's still very powerful, and he is going to hate Ofelia taking the throne."

"If he's honest, then he's probably capable of seeing reason. Or at least of knowing when he's beat," Jerry observed.

"Let's hope," Ofelia said.

"Anyway, if we're going out Wednesday evening and committing treason on Thursday morning, I want a curfew," Jerry said. "I need a reason to be back here and in bed no later than two in the morning. Midnight would be better."

"Emergency call from home?" Milo suggested. "Gets both of you out of there at once."

"It does leave Ofelia to the tender mercies of the Bright Young Things," Jerry said.

"I've handled them before. And I'll have to anyway, when you leave," Ofelia pointed out. "Chivalrous of you, Jerry, but not necessary."

"Well, if you change your mind, let me know and I'll start a fight with Carlo. Alanna can hustle you away in the melee," Jerry said.

For all of Jerry's fretting, Alanna found their night out with Carlo and the Bright Young Things sort of fun. None of them were willing to be rude to Ofelia's face, at least with Alanna there, and everyone wanted to be near Alanna. It required Jerry and Carlo to bookend her, and it was fun to be charmed by Carlo while Jerry leaned into her and smelled good and smoldered subtly. And when the call came in from Georgie at midnight, purporting to be from the Shivadh palace, he handled it so completely that she mostly listened to him sell it to Carlo and then let herself be pulled out of the bar.

"Sorry to leave you like this," he yelled over the music. "Little thing but it just can't wait. Carlo, can you look after Ofelia for us? Huge favor to me," he added with a wink. Carlo blinked at him and then nodded, a knowing grin spreading across his face.

Georgie was down the block, and when she saw them come out of the bar, she flashed her lights. Jerry slung an arm over Alanna's shoulders companionably, as if a little tipsy, and then held the door for her, posture straightening as he climbed inside after.

"Someday," he said in her ear, as they zipped back to the Palazzo Cavallo, "when we are not engaging in high adventure in foreign lands, I'll actually get to take you out and kiss you in public and everything."

"Looking forward to it," she replied, twining her right hand in his left. He clicked his signet ring against the City of Gold, scrolling through Photogram.

"PR campaign is working. Ofelia's got her own hashtag," he said. "Also, it's hard to look good in photos taken in dim karaoke bars but you and she are both managing it, duchessa mine."

"Glad we've got our priorities settled," Alanna sighed.

CHAPTER NINE

THURSDAY MORNING, ALANNA arrived at the council chamber with an entourage: not only Milo, who often sat in on council meetings as secretary, but Jerry, who had been there only once, and Ofelia, who hadn't ever been there. She also brought in a handful of sergeants-at-arms: Palazzo security officers who, in this case, had been hand-picked by Bruno as friendly to the cause. The security already in the council chambers looked perplexed at the last minute shift-change, but left easily enough for an unexpected paid day off.

And it meant that Alanna and Ofelia were already there, chatting amiably with each other and surrounded by trusted people, when the council members began arriving. It was almost ten when Riva approached and coughed discreetly.

"Your Grace," he said to Alanna. "We should begin soon. We'll need to clear the chamber."

"I'm afraid there's been a slight change of agenda," Alanna replied. "We'll start on time, but I need to address the council on the question of my succession to the throne."

"Ah, you've made a decision!" Riva looked pleased. "And your…colleagues?" he asked, eyes flicking from Jerry to Ofelia.

"I have some legal needs that Ofelia will be helping with," Alanna said. "Jerry's just here because he's a hanger-on."

Jerry gave Riva a crooked grin. He'd pulled up a chair next to Ofelia's, so that he and Alanna sat on either side of her, although Alanna was at the head of the table, with Ofelia off to the side. "Can't get enough of all these politics," he said.

"Well, we wait on Her Grace's pleasure," Riva said, giving Jerry a dark look, and took his seat down the table. Brasolin, across from him, was reading some brief or other; most of the other consiglieres were chatting or waiting to begin. Alanna confirmed that everyone who was going to arrive had arrived, and then knocked sharply on the table to draw their attention.

"Gentlemen," she said, when they were all looking at her. "I'm afraid I need to interrupt our regular business. I have some happy news for Galia regarding the succession of the duchy."

"I'm sure we're all pleased you've come to a decision, Your Grace," Brasolin said.

"I hope you'll be downright delighted," she replied. Brasolin's eyes narrowed. "In determining whether I should take the throne of Galia, I wanted to make sure there were absolutely no other pretenders who might interfere. I decided that if I was going to make the sacrifice of moving here and ruling, there should be no question of my legitimate claim to the throne. Such diligence is sometimes rewarded – fortunately or unfortunately – and in my case, I discovered someone else had a better claim to the duchy and the throne of Galia than mine."

The men began to murmur among themselves.

"Steady on, Brasolin," Jerry said quietly, much too quiet for him to actually hear. Brasolin wasn't talking or fidgeting like the others, Alanna saw. He was looking at Ofelia.

He knows, she thought. And then, *Wonder just how much he knows, and when he learned it.*

"There have been rumors since I arrived that the duke had a direct heir, a child who could claim the title," she continued, "I've since been able to confirm it. Just this week a DNA test – "

"Your Grace, I'm sorry, could you repeat that?" Riva said.

"She said, *the duke has a child*," Jerry said in Italian, raising his voice. Riva looked like he wanted to murder him. Jerry seemed to be enjoying himself.

"A DNA test was performed this week," she said. "Confirming the duke has two biological children, born and raised here in Galia."

"Two," Riva said skeptically.

"Nonsense," Brasolin added.

"I'm afraid it's true. However, I'm pleased to say that the duke's eldest child is not only qualified to take power in Galia, but I think ideal for the job," Alanna said. "Ofelia Ansevali, therefore, will be invested as Duchess of the Horse this morn – "

The council burst into uproar, a dozen voices shouting at once in Italian. Alanna could see, under the table, that Ofelia's hands were shaking, but her only visible reaction to the yelling was a small smile.

"Absolutely not, this is a coup by the Ansevalis – "

" – can't possibly be true, I won't accept less than an independent lab's test – "

" – the hell is Ofelia Ansevali? Should I know her?"

"You did this, Milo, you ambitious little prick – "

"Gentlemen," Alanna said, and then louder, "Gentlemen!" When that got her nothing, she turned to Jerry. "Would you?"

"Love to," he said, and tucked his tongue behind his teeth. The shrill whistle he blew was loud enough to make her molars hurt, but it did silence them.

Into the silence, there was the sound of a door opening.

"Anticipating turmoil, I had a few extra measures put in place," Alanna said, as an aide entered. He went to Brasolin first, something all of the council aides had a habit of doing, and which Alanna decided it was time to put a stop to.

"I think the person you want to speak to is me," she said loudly. The aide glanced at Brasolin. "He doesn't control who enters this room. Currently, I do. I also control who is employed by the Palazzo. So if you want to have a job in five minutes, you tell me," she added more gently. That got his attention.

"Your Grace, there's an…individual from Askazer-Shivadlakia who says he is here to see the council," he said apologetically. "He's demanding entrance."

"I know. Let him in."

There were quiet murmurs at this, until the aide went to the main entry doors and, with a regretful look, opened them fully.

Alanna had watched a lot of political theater, over the years; the Shivadh palace had a policy that the children in it had free access to almost all proceedings. She and Gregory, and sometimes Jerry, had seen dramas play out on the floor of Parliament, in the grand reception hall, at balls and small parties. So she knew that the vast majority of the time, Michaelis was remarkably unassuming. Gregory referred to the Shivadh royalty as "functionally bureaucrats" and he wasn't far off the mark.

But Michaelis had also spent twenty years learning rule at his father's side and a further forty in politics, and there was a certain switch he could flip – he'd taught Gregory, as well – that changed that.

Even out of the royal blacks, which would have been inappropriate to the situation, Michaelis had a gravitas that could silence a room. He hadn't had much occasion for suits, lately, but he was in one now, neutral brown with an antique gold shirt under a high-collared waistcoat. He walked into the council chamber with his shoulders back, head high, eyes sharp, and mouth set – there was a mixture of solemnity and displeasure on his face that Alanna could recognize as an act, but she doubted anyone else could. He stopped at the foot of the table, hands clasped lightly behind his back.

Next to her, Jerry let out a low whistle.

"Lady Daskaz," Michaelis said. "Thank you for your invitation to attend. Gentlemen," he added, nodding around the table, and then to Ofelia, "Duchessa."

There was another eruption of murmuring at that, but at least it wasn't shouting. Michaelis cleared his throat. Silence fell.

"Welcome to Galia, Your Majesty," Alanna replied. She knew that he preferred *Your Grace*, now that he was retired, but there were enough Graces in this room without adding one more. "We appreciate your presence."

"The pleasure is mine. I understand there's a dispute I may be able to resolve."

Brasolin scowled. "We have no need of washed-up former monarchs – "

"Brasolin, from now on you will speak when spoken to," Alanna said sharply. He opened his mouth. One of the sergeants-at-arms, at a gesture from her, put a hand on his shoulder, and he closed it again.

"We may have words later about that remark, Brasolin," Michaelis added in a gentle tone, like a parent scolding a toddler.

"Your Grace," one of the senior consiglieres said, and the way his eyes drifted it was impossible to tell if he was addressing Alanna or Ofelia. "While I don't necessarily agree with Consigliere Brasolin's assessment of the situation, traditionally we have not, ah, resorted to diplomats of other nations to resolve our own internal disputes."

"I understand your reserve," Ofelia said, and Alanna shot her a smile. "However, Galia was ill-equipped to provide what was needed in this case. His Majesty isn't here to offer diplomatic or political aid, merely data." She turned back to Michaelis, who nodded. "You've brought us some documentation, I believe."

Michaelis unbuttoned his suit jacket, taking an envelope from an inside pocket.

"This is a DNA test," he said. "Performed in Genoa by a lab unaffiliated with Galia or Askazer-Shivadlakia, using anonymous codes for those involved. Would you care…?" he offered it to Ofelia, but she gestured for him to continue. He opened the envelope and took out a few folded sheets of paper. "It concerns, primarily, two individuals, female contributor 8857 and male contributor 8858. On testing, the laboratory confirmed that male contributor 8858 – "

"This is a farce," Riva said. "The lab could be forged, the submissions falsified – "

"I wasn't finished," Michaelis said mildly. The men on either side of Riva subtly leaned away. "Male contributor 8858, whose DNA was collected by the Guard of the Horse from the bathroom in the suite of the Duke of the Horse Tomas of the House of Galia, is confirmed to be the father of female contributor 8857, collected by the Guard of the Horse from Ofelia Ansevali directly. This one," he added, turning to the second page, "identifies male contributor 8859 as the son of male contributor 8858 and full sibling of female contributor 8857. 8859 was collected by the Guard of the Horse from Milo Ansevali directly."

"Now," Alanna said, and every head in the room turned back to her. "You can question whether the results are valid, Consigliere Riva. Have your own performed, if you like. And when they come back valid as well, see how popular you are with the Duchess of the Horse."

Riva was pale, anger in his eyes. "You cannot simply assert a duchy and have done," he said.

"Why not? You did to me," she said. A few of the men blinked. "You looked at a family tree and assumed I was blood of the duchy and wanted the title. I was ideal, after all – a young, foreign woman with no partner, with close ties to someone you need right now – "

"We do not need Askazer-Shivadlakia," Brasolin blurted.

"Our national budget very much says otherwise," Ofelia replied. "Mostly thanks to you, Brasolin."

"I beg your pardon – "

"Gentlemen, I'm circulating a memo to the council," Ofelia

announced, and Milo took a sheaf of papers out of his folio, passing them around the room. As Bruno had predicted, the memo took up two full pages per copy, and a lot of consiglieres turned as white as the paper it was printed on when they saw what it said. "You may review it at your leisure. In the next week or so, we'll discuss which parts may be made public. And which parts may become evidence in criminal court."

"This is blackmail," another man said.

"Coercion, actually," Jerry corrected. The man shot him a poisonous look. "Don't hate the player, you volunteered for this game," Jerry told him. It earned him a quiet chuckle from Michaelis.

"In any case, you can't have it both ways," Alanna said. "You can't believe we are sneaking Shivadh liars when we tell you who Ofelia is, but also ask us to rule your country. Either I'm a double-agent or a duchess. If I'm a double-agent, you can't possibly want me on the throne. If you want me on the throne, then I must be unimpeachable. And if I am, then when I say that I renounce the duchy in favor of the duke's natural heir, you're going to have to eat it."

"Sort of how this works," Jerry added. "Absolute power, invested in a single biological heir. Seems like it backfires sometimes."

"Can't say I support it," Michaelis said.

"You were a king," Riva retorted. "Your son is king even now."

"We were both elected," Michaelis replied. "You should try it. Brilliant for the ego. At least, when you're not getting a pie to the face."

Even Alanna inhaled at the audacity of that, but it had the desired effect. Brasolin stood so quickly his chair was shoved into the sergeant-at-arms still behind him; the man staggered backwards, and only a quick headshake from Ofelia kept him from diving in to tackle Brasolin, whose fists were clenched. Michaelis tilted his head at him as if he were an interesting painting.

"If this man is not removed from the council chamber as a spy and an insurrectionist, you can have my resignation," Brasolin spat. "These insults – "

"Okay," Alanna said. Brasolin stopped mid-rant, turning to stare at her.

"Your resignation, if you please," Ofelia added. She set her copy of the memo on the table, smoothing it out. The first paragraph concerned Brasolin.

His mouth worked silently for a moment. Then, without another word, he turned and left – through a side-door, so he wouldn't have to pass Michaelis, who watched him go.

"Any other resignations immediately pending?" Ofelia asked. Alanna, with a small smile, stood and stepped aside from the chair at the head of the table. Ofelia, nodding at her, rose and took it. Alanna stayed standing, resting an arm on the back of Ofelia's chair.

"I'm not a vengeful person, on the whole," Ofelia said. "I like to think I serve the interests of the duchy. And I do see your point, Consigliere Riva, about unsealed lab results and DNA tests done in private. We will have a proper, detailed, and public test performed at our leisure, which you may supervise yourself if you like. However, that will take place after I am invested as Duchess of the Horse. It's past time someone took the reins of the country properly. In the meantime, Your Majesty, we appreciate you…running this errand for us."

"Always pleased to oblige," Michaelis replied. A few of the men in the room exchanged glances. Alanna could tell what they were thinking: that Ofelia Ansevali had the power to make a former king her errand-boy – to summon a man who hadn't been in Galia for thirty years to bring her a piece of paper. And from there Alanna could see the realization rippling outward.

Ofelia Ansevali was trained just as much as Alanna was to rule, and still connected through some unknown bond to the Shivadh nobility. She could give them everything Alanna could, and more – she was a native Galian, known to the people, but touched with glamor through her association with Alanna and Jerry. She was willing to threaten the council with the memo instead of simply ruining them. She could be expected to play their game, at least to an extent.

And all they had to give up to get her was the illusion of control, which Alanna wouldn't have let them keep in any case.

Ofelia Ansevali had also just driven Alexandros Brasolin out of the council. There was not only a power vacuum where he'd left, but an unspoken threat: *If I can remove Brasolin, I can remove anyone.*

"I'm sure we can arrange for a more transparent test at a later date, as you say," Riva said at last. "However, this does radically alter the political situation of the entire country in ways that I think none of us were prepared to consider. Perhaps a few days to…meditate on this would be advisable."

"I entirely agree," Ofelia said. "The country will need to come to grips with this new situation. Therefore, we will allow for a grace period before the enthroning ceremony. Must find a good caterer, in any case," she added with a smile, and stood. Almost instinctively, so did the men. Ofelia shot Alanna a dry look. Michaelis was not bothering to hide his amusement.

"However, I will not wait for my title," Ofelia continued. "The business of running the country must be taken in hand. I intend to go into the reception chamber and, with legal witnesses, sign the documents that will invest me as duchess. I assume anyone who wishes to remain on my council may attend as witness and sign a brief affirmation of their loyalty to the Duchess of the Horse. Anyone who does not wish to remain on the council is, of course, free to leave. You will not be allowed to take copies of the memo with you; leaving the council removes you from the benefit of its confidential information."

"Your Grace, not to offer advice where it's not asked for," Michaelis said, "but as someone experienced in this sort of thing…"

"Suggestions welcome," Ofelia said.

"Perhaps a pension, for those who wish to resign. In recognition of their service."

Clever old fox, Alanna thought. This hadn't been planned; Michaelis was improvising, but doing an extremely good job of it. *Leave now with a payout, or get cleared out later with nothing if you step out of line.* Most of the consiglieres were already wealthy men, but their wealth was tied up with the state's, and some of them were just grasping old codgers whose pride would be balmed by a bribe.

Ofelia nodded. "We'll put something in place. Alanna, Milo, Gerald?"

She stepped out from behind the council table and walked, without hurry, towards the entry doors; Milo, tucking his folio under his arm, stepped in front to lead the way. Alanna took Jerry's arm, falling in behind, and caught Jerry laughing a little when Michaelis offered Ofelia his elbow as she passed.

"Wonder how many of the consiglieres are going to follow," Jerry murmured to her.

"Don't look back," she replied.

"No fear. Do you suppose if he wanted, Uncle Mike could have invaded and taken the throne?"

"I can hear you," Michaelis said from in front of them. "And yes, looking at those sad bastards? I absolutely could have."

"Be kind," Ofelia said. "A number of them are about to lose their jobs."

"Couldn't happen to a more deserving dozen," Michaelis replied. "Pleasure to meet you in person, by the way, Your Grace."

"Charmed, Your Majesty," Ofelia replied. "I'm a great follower of your podcast. As I've told Alanna, I think you offer a number of useful lessons about rule. Allow me to invite you to lunch after I ruthlessly seize power."

"Gladly. It was a long drive from Genoa."

Alanna leaned into Jerry, who shifted his arm, lowering his hand and pulling out of her grasp so that he could twine their fingers together instead.

"Is it wrong that watching you and Ofelia devastate a room full of appalling old men really got me going?" he whispered in her ear.

"It absolutely is. Also, thank you," she whispered back.

"Are we going home after this?"

"Apparently we're going to lunch. If you're nice you can sit next to me."

"When do we go home?" he asked, and she could hear in his voice a plaintive echo of her own yearning.

"Soon," she said, patting his arm with her free hand. "Maybe as soon as tomorrow. This afternoon I have a job for you."

Late that afternoon, while Alanna and Ofelia were enjoying drinks and pretending to work in Ofelia's office, Jerry arrived with a file box. He set it down with the look of a man bringing home a trophy of war.

"You found something," Alanna observed. "What did you bring us?"

"Varied delights," Jerry said. "You were right. Brasolin pitched the biggest fit imaginable when he found that he was locked out of his office. The Horse…Guard…guy that I talked to said they had to remove him from the building. They say they should have arrested him but you gave orders not to."

"There's no need to be vicious as well as political," Alanna said.

"I would have had him arrested," Ofelia replied.

"Her reign of terror begins," Jerry said. He popped the lid off the box. "The Guard has his computer now, anyway, but as instructed I had a rummage around in his office."

"Jerry's great at finding things people want to hide," Alanna said.

"Comes of my devious mind," Jerry replied. "Behold, highlights of an eighty-year-old career politician's home away from home. This," he said, pulling out a heap of files, "is information he shouldn't have had, according to Bruno."

"Good to know, but I must say, most of us have some of that around here," Ofelia said.

"Yeah, I asked Uncle Mike, he said it's pretty normal for people to end up with stuff that wasn't meant for them, especially after a couple of decades. I haven't read it in detail – you're the lawyer – but it seems harmless enough. That said, if you wanted to arrest him for treason…" he waggled the files.

"It's a point. What else?"

"Very boring pornography," Jerry said, flashing a magazine with a topless woman on the front. "For a man in his position, he had what I'd consider extremely plain tastes. Runs to boobs and blondes."

"Were you looking for the rougher stuff?" Alanna asked. Jerry grinned at her.

"I wasn't looking for porn at work at all, but I guess it's something people do. And lastly, I have a present," he said, taking an envelope out of the bottom of the box. "Which explains why he was absolutely enraged he couldn't get in. This is a duplicate birth certificate for Ofelia Ansevali which lists Tomas, Duke of the House Horse, as her father, with a countersignature by the duke himself. I'm guessing any certificate you've seen leaves that part out," he said to her.

"Our father's name was always blank. Mine and Milo's both," Ofelia said, holding out a hand. Jerry put the envelope in it.

"I've got one for Milo, too," he said sympathetically.

"So Brasolin knew," she mused, opening the envelope and

studying the certificate. "But he didn't want me on the throne."

"You would have been too powerful," Alanna said. "A direct descendant, with a younger brother for social capital – you with legal training, and the knowledge you have of the inner workings of the Palazzo? I was the much better candidate to have my strings pulled by all of them."

"So they thought," Jerry said.

"I wonder how he got it," Ofelia said. "I wonder if the old duke gave it to him, or if he stole it somehow."

"Possibly that's how he got to be so powerful," Jerry said, nodding at the birth certificate. "I'm sure the duke's affairs weren't secret by any means, but there's a difference between chasing the staff and having two children with one. Begging your pardon," he added to Ofelia.

"Perhaps it was ill-gotten dirt, but I imagine not. I think he was keeping them safe for my…father," Ofelia said, as if trying the word out.

"Is there a chance Tomas didn't know about the two of you?" Jerry asked. "Someone else arranged for the payments, maybe?"

"No," Ofelia said. "Money didn't leave his discretionary fund without him knowing. And there was no reason for anyone but him to send Milo to a school for kings or me into a diplomatic career. I think he was grooming us for rule. I think he wanted to put Milo on the throne. The male heir, you know. I wonder when he was planning on telling us," she added, looking down at the birth certificate again.

"Got more than he bargained for," Jerry said. Ofelia frowned at him. "Well, from what I've heard of him, I'd bet he wanted what they all want. That puppet they thought Alanna could be. He set you two up to be his proteges. Doesn't appear to have taken. Ungrateful, I call it," he added in an imitation of Riva at his most pompous. Ofelia snorted.

"Yes, well, I will repay all of this with some brisk housecleaning," she said. "What's the English? Sunlight is the best soap?"

"Something like that," Alanna agreed.

"A year or two to get the books in order and prosecute those who need prosecuting. A propaganda campaign perhaps, and some public opinion polls. As soon as possible, a constitution and a general election," she said. "Parliament and a prime minister. No more dukes for Galia. We don't love our dukes as you love your king."

"Fair," Jerry pronounced. "Don't be surprised when you get elected, though. Galia's got a lot in common with Askazer-Shivadlakia, deep down."

"I'll remember that." Ofelia set the birth certificate on the desk, gently. "If you don't mind, I need to make a few calls, and speak to Milo."

"His birth certificate is under the rest of the porn," Jerry said, pointing into the box.

"He will no doubt appreciate that," Ofelia drawled. Jerry held the door for Alanna, following her out.

"Rough on the poor kids," Jerry said, once they were out of earshot.

"She's your age, you know."

"Yes, but I've lived a debauched life. In noble years I'm nearly fifty," he told her, and she laughed. "Very appropriate age to wed, fifty, especially to a young delight such as yourself."

"You are the grossest," she told him.

"I do my best. We have all afternoon ahead of us, and I got a favor out of Uncle Mike," he said, taking a set of keys out of his pocket – the keys to Michaelis's prized Jaguar.

"A favor, or did you steal them?" she asked.

"He's tied up with Bruno in the archives; he won't miss the Jag if we take it out. I'm only a new version of me, you know, not a completely different person," he said, when he saw her expression. "A quick drive. You should see the vineyard terraces on this side of the mountain."

"Terroir nerd," she told him.

"A man could get used to being called names by you," he replied.

Jerry was well pleased with himself by dinner that evening. He'd gotten to drive the Jag with Alanna on the bench seat next to him, tucked under his arm, and she'd been impressed by both his driving and the vineyards, which gave him a weird sense of gratification. The pretty terraces full of vines weren't even his, but the land had once been his family's, so he allowed himself a little pride in them. The winery nearby poured tastings for Alanna and sold them a few bottles of what she liked, and they made it home in time for a nice dinner that evening.

It was probably wise not to be seen out too much, and Alanna seemed just as happy to stay in, so they had a simple meal – just Alanna at the window, Jerry next to her, and Michaelis across from them, smug at having spent the day irritating every Galian politician he could find and exploring the royal archives with Bruno as his guide.

And then, just as they were finishing up the meal, the best thing in the world happened.

"That's a very pretty ring, Alanna. I don't think I've seen you wear that before," Michaelis said, nodding at her thumb as she finished her glass of wine. "Reminds me of one Eitan gave to Sarah, years ago."

"That's the one," Jerry said. Michaelis looked at him, surprised. Alanna was hiding a smile so hard he could almost hear it. "I got it from Mom before we left for Galia. Looks good on her, doesn't it?"

Michaelis' surprised look turned into a baffled stare, and it was so rare that Jerry got to troll his uncle that he couldn't resist. He gave Michaelis the most innocent face he could, for a beat longer than was comfortable, and then turned to Alanna. "You'll need to get it sized, though. Can't wear it on your thumb forever, it's not proper."

Alanna played into it so beautifully he could have kissed her (would, later). "I thought about that, but it's so intricate – we might need to just have a new one made. That way I could have it done in the traditional silver, and you could get a matched one with the Askaz estate on it, if you liked."

Michaelis gestured between them with his fork, then looked at the fork like it annoyed him and set it down. "If you two are playing some kind of joke on me…"

"No joke," Jerry said casually. "Planning on a long engagement, though. Can't steal Gregory's thunder, after all."

Michaelis was so silent and still that for a second Jerry began to worry he really was having some kind of attack.

"Well," Michaelis managed, then cleared his throat. "Well, I imagine Sarah will be pleased. You know how fond of you she is, Alanna. I can't fathom what your grandmother will say, but I hope I'm there to see her reaction."

"There's that royal will of iron," Jerry said to Alanna. "He wants to give you a hug so badly. It's destroying him that he has to pretend he's not absolutely losing his mind that you're going to marry me."

"You're making that a lot easier," Michaelis told him.

Alanna got up from the table and came around to hug Michaelis from behind while he was still seated, her chin hooked over his shoulder, arms looped across his chest. Jerry watched, pleased, as he squeezed her wrist and then turned to press his forehead to her temple affectionately.

"Not that anyone asked *me*," he added, with a sidelong look at Jerry, "But you have my blessing should you need it."

"We haven't told anyone yet," Alanna said, releasing him and going back to her seat. "It's still very new. We wanted to make sure Galia was stabilized first."

"Wise of you. But we are going home tomorrow. Will you tell Gregory?" he asked. Which Jerry knew was his way of saying *Can I tell Jes?*

"Jes can keep a secret," Alanna said, clearly also reading the question correctly.

"Thank you," Michaelis said, without apology, and took his phone out. About thirty seconds after he sent the text the phone began beeping. He looked down at it. "Jes is very pleased for you, and says congratulations. Noah's going to dust off his horrible wedding Powerpoint."

"I love that thing. Tell him I want it updated with this season's worst," Jerry said.

"You are my nephew, Gerald, and I could not be more pleased with either of you just now, but I cannot bring myself to encourage you," Michaelis said. Jerry noted his smile and basked in the approval regardless. "Besides, Noah's a self-starting young man, he doesn't need to be told."

"That reminds me," Jerry said, getting up to go to his jacket, where it lay across the back of the sofa. "There's still some business to wrap up in Galia, and here's me doing my part."

"What is this?" Alanna asked, studying the bundle of paper he handed her.

"Those are Athena's travel papers," Jerry said. "Last week when you started making calls, I thought I'd do a few too. For two people who live less than twenty minutes apart and work in the same building, we have *wildly* different spheres of influence," he added. "But I used to date the sister of a big Hollywood guy who comes to Italy to make cheap slasher films. Put in a call to him because he knows every movie star who thinks they're an eco-activist for paying carbon credits on their private jets. Several of them could use the PR boost of rescuing an exotic animal."

"Ah. Like Cher and that elephant," Michaelis said. Alanna, distracted, looked at him questioningly. "It was in the news. I do follow current events, even when they're ridiculous. She helped rescue an elephant and got it sent to a park somewhere. You can't read an article about the elephant without her getting dropped in there."

"Big fan of elephants, are you?" Jerry asked.

"Everyone likes elephants," Michaelis said dismissively.

"My point," Jerry said, leaning into Alanna, "Is that a very famous movie star with a slight image problem is going to pay for Athena to be shipped to a tiger rescue in Texas. They weren't accepting new beasties, but they are accepting large sums of money in exchange for taking in one more tiger."

"Unfortunate but true that hard work often fails where good connections succeed," Michaelis said.

"It was hard work too," Jerry protested.

"It looks like it," Alanna said, giving him a reassuring smile. "You're sure this place in Texas is all right?"

"Yep. They're a closed preserve. No tours, no breeding. She'll get to hang out with all the other old lady tigers and dish dirt on the duke," he said.

"So," Alanna said. "Happy endings all around."

Jerry waited, resigned, for her to finish the joke, but before she could, Michaelis did.

"Especially for Jerry," Michaelis murmured, and Alanna erupted into laughter.

CHAPTER TEN

THEY LEFT THE following afternoon for Askazer-Shivadlakia with a mostly quiet send-off, if a little later than planned.

"I had the situation in hand," Michaelis insisted, as staff loaded Jerry and Alanna's luggage into the car Will would be driving back. Georgie was in the other one; Michaelis's Jag, parked nearby, was waiting for him.

"You left the Palazzo on foot, with no security or staff," Milo said. "What did you expect to happen?"

"Absolutely nothing, which is what happens when I do it two, three times a week in Fons-Askaz," Michaelis replied.

"I told him not to!" Georgie yelled from the car.

"I wasn't expecting anyone to recognize me, especially out of uniform, let alone want to talk to me," Michaelis protested.

To say he had been mobbed was probably overstating things, Alanna reflected, but she'd seen images on Photogram of him surrounded by young Galians, looking baffled by all the attention but smiling and chatting with them regardless. They'd had to send Georgie with a car to rescue him. Jes probably hadn't stopped laughing yet.

"Why on earth did you leave the Palazzo alone?" Jerry asked, not looking up from his phone.

"I wanted to see the city. Thought I might find a nice cafe for lunch. Possibly even pick up some postcards. It's what normal people do," Michaelis told him.

"The fact that you think you're normal is endlessly funny to me," Jerry said. "Gregory does that too, I think it's some kind of delusion."

"I beg your pardon, *twelfth Duke of Shivadlakia,*" Michaelis replied.

"Exactly. I'm not in denial that my life is super weird," Jerry replied. "We're burning daylight and I want to go home. Al?"

"Waiting on you, far as I'm aware," Alanna said, and Jerry raised an eyebrow and pointedly climbed into the car. "Are you going back to the lodge, or stopping at the palace first?" she asked Michaelis.

"Best report in to Gregory first, I think," Michaelis said, accepting his keys from a staff valet. "Yourself?"

"I want to see Gregory and Eddie, and I think Jerry's dreading going back to the estate. He's homesick for the people, not the place. We might stay the night in the palace."

"Come to the lodge if you like," he said. "There's room to stay over, and we have plenty of food. Might ask Gregory if he and Theophile want to join us, actually. Celebrate your engagement, if you're planning to announce."

"I think so, at least among friends. But are you sure you don't want Jes and Noah to yourself for a while?"

"I saw them yesterday before I left. You've been gone weeks," he said, and kissed her forehead. "We'll sort it out when we get home."

He jogged off towards the Jag, clearly ready to be on the road, but Alanna didn't get into the car yet; she turned back towards the Palazzo, and saw Ofelia standing on the steps. When she approached, Ofelia smiled.

"Hate to dump a country on you and run, but I think you'll do better with us out of your hair," Alanna said. "How's your first day going?"

"About two-thirds of the council didn't show up this morning. Couple of them sent their sons, including Carlo. Couple of daughters too, which was nice. The wind is blowing change," Ofelia said. "Milo's pleased by it all. You have no idea how much paperwork something like this generates, but he was born for that."

"The next few months probably won't be easy on either of you."

"Well, they'll hardly be more difficult than working for the Duke. Although I'm hoping I can count on the group chat when I need to vent," Ofelia added, holding up her phone.

"Such times we live in," Alanna said. "I'll ask Jerry to do something humorous every few weeks, he enjoys entertaining people."

"I wish you would. And you know you're both always welcome here…as long as it's not in the next six months or so," Ofelia said.

"I can't promise Michaelis won't be back sooner. He really hit it off with Bruno."

"His Grace is always welcome. I imagine if he showed his face in Galia again, a few of the old council might decide to permanently move to Italy." Ofelia closed the gap between them and kissed her on the cheeks. "Travel safe. Thank you. It hasn't been easy on anyone, but at least it's been usefully difficult."

"That's the Shivadh spirit in a nutshell, usefully difficult," Alanna said with a grin. "Call anytime."

When she climbed into the car Jerry scooted over, buckling up the middle seatbelt and crowding her comfortably into a corner, arm over her shoulders. He had his laptop, turned to tablet mode, and that program open again.

"What is this, really?" she asked, poking at it as the car pulled out of the drive. "I've seen you messing with it since we left home. It looks like a logic puzzle, but it's not a video game at all, is it?"

"It's definitely a puzzle," he said, using the stylus to draw a diagonal slash across the screen, zooming it out. "It's a diagram I had our steward build. Digital map of the ducal seat. I am lord of all you survey," he added, rotating it slightly until it made sense – there was the palace, down in the southwestern corner outside the boundaries of his estate. There was the main building, and beyond it the landscape on her ring – hills and terraces, pastures, orchards, and ponds.

"What are you doing with it?" she asked, studying the map.

"Laying out a new land management program. Crop rotation, orchard plantings, stewardship of old orchards we left to run wild. Turns out if you don't prune an olive tree it goes feral, so I've got prunings planned for the really old groves. Might double crop yields on what we have, and we're putting in new crops as well," he said. "Converting a lot of the lawns into growing terrain. But you have to kind of fit everything together – make sure the right plants are in the right zones, check the soil acid levels, that kind of thing. It's not as interesting as an actual video game, admittedly. I won't drone on about it."

"You could," she said. "I mean, I'm not interested in this stuff the way you and Gregory are – "

She broke off, because he'd made a thoughtful noise.

"Never considered it that way," he said. "Gregory and I both being interested in the agriculture. I guess it's true. But that doesn't mean you want to hear it."

"What I was going to say," she said, grasping his left wrist with her right hand, rubbing the City of Gold against his skin, "was that I'm not interested in this the way you are, but I wouldn't mind hearing. You've been hearing me talk about governing Galia for days on end. You talk, I'll rest. I might not hold onto much of what you say but I like the sound of your voice, and you like talking."

He smiled and kissed her. "I do like talking. Do you really like my voice?"

"Of course. Very soothing."

"Then I won't be hurt if you fall asleep, my dear heart," he said. "Would you like the olive groves first, or the apiary? I have plans for new pomegranate trees, and I can show you the fields we're going to open up for next winter's lowland dairy herd grazing. I've also found hardwoods over by the river – there's a lot of prospect there for sustainable exotic woods, although that's very long term. Kind of thing the next generation or two might see better returns on. And I have to watch the runoff, can't disturb Uncle Mike's fishing down at the lake. Best start with the olives," he decided, and she watched him move the diagram around, idly listening, until she drifted off.

Gregory must have seen them coming, or possibly he heard the Jaguar's engine; in any case, when they pulled into the little yard at the kitchen entrance, he was coming out of the kitchen to meet them.

"I'm so glad you're back," he said, enfolding Alanna in a hug. He let go with one arm to grab Jerry by the shoulder, then released her so he could hug Jerry as well.

"Thank you for going with," he said in Jerry's ear.

"It was fun. Let's never do that again," Jerry replied.

"Certainly not," Gregory agreed, leaning back. "Father, I hope you brought me a souvenir."

"Bringing these two back isn't enough of a present for you?" Michaelis asked, gesturing at Jerry and Alanna, but he also tossed Gregory a small box. Gregory caught it, gave Jerry a startled look, and then popped the flap up, opening it. Inside was a small cheap tchotchke – a figurine of a man on a horse, a replica of a statue of a previous Duke of the Horse from one of the local parks.

"It's the Duke of the House Horse," Jerry told Gregory, who laughed.

"I love it. I'll keep it on my desk. Now, come inside and you can tell me all about it," he said, leading them through the kitchen. Simon gave Alanna and Jerry a wave as they passed.

"Missed your cooking, Simon," Jerry called.

"Of course you did!" Simon replied. "Galians will put bacon in anything, the monsters!"

"Eddie's picking up food, he'll meet us at the lodge," Gregory said, leading them into the family dining room. "I'd love to get a full report, but I think the details can wait given I'm already seeing Galian press releases, and I'm sure you're all tired. Perhaps just the basics."

"We do have news to share," Michaelis said, pulling out a chair and settling in. "Gerald, Alanna, would you like to go first?"

Gregory looked at them curiously. Jerry turned to Alanna, only to find she had turned to him. Nobody was going to make this news more interesting than he could, so he squared his shoulders and said, "Your Majesty, I've asked for the hand in marriage of the Lady Alanna Daskaz, prospective Duchess of Askaz, lately of Galia, and she has consented. We are here to request your permission – "

At that point Gregory's jaw dropped and Alanna broke down laughing.

"You two," Gregory said. "You – did you propose?" he asked Jerry. "Did you propose to Alanna? Like…not as a joke?"

"Stop, stop," Alanna squeaked.

"When were you even dating? Because you I love," Gregory said, pointing at Jerry, "but you, I know you're not *insane*," he finished, pointing at Alanna.

"I'm marrying him for his money," Alanna said, voice about an octave above normal.

"And I think she'll be a good and obedient wife," Jerry said. "Tractable. Knows her place."

"Is that the face I made?" Michaelis asked Alanna, indicating Gregory. She nodded. "Lord."

"Father, is this real?" Gregory asked.

"Yes. They told me in Galia. I have no explanations, I'm afraid, but they seem sincere."

"Being away from home offers a lot of clarity," Jerry said, and caught Alanna's hand in his, lifting it so he could kiss her thumb, where the ring sat. "And also I had to pin her down before some trashy Galian count made a play."

"That's – congratulations to both of you," Gregory said. "That certainly blows my plans for asking all about Galia's government and finances out of the water."

"We do actually have a brief for you," Alanna said, seating herself. "And Jerry tells me the dukes have very long engagements so there's plenty of time for that later."

"Well, you know better than I do what I need to know," Gregory said, as Jerry sat next to her. "Tell me everything relevant. I didn't actually expect you two to destabilize the country and then install a new duchess friendly to my administration. I feel like I should give you some kind of bonus."

Alanna did most of the talking, after that. Jerry was aware she'd make a better narrative of it than he would, and she'd be more concise than Michaelis, who like Gregory had a perhaps over-powerful inclination for detail. Gregory listened intently, drinking it all in.

"I think I'll have to appoint an ambassador," he said when they were done. "Certainly send some of our people to offer support to the new duchess. Not you two," he added, because Alanna did look like she was about to yell *not it*. "I'll give Milo a call on Monday and discuss options. I'd like to set up a regular chat with Ofelia."

"I think she'd appreciate that," Michaelis said. "She's a bright young woman and eager to learn the craft."

"He just likes her because she's a fan of the podcast," Jerry said.

"Shows impeccable taste, to my mind," Michaelis replied.

It was a relief when they reached the fishing lodge that evening. Travel was done for the day; they'd given Gregory their report, and Alanna was tired enough not to feel guilty that she wouldn't need to speak with her grandparents until at least tomorrow. Jerry had already had a cordial homecoming phone call with his mother, and didn't sound eager to go back to the ducal seat full of empty rooms and loud dogs. Alanna was now in charge of nothing, for the first time in weeks – for the first time since Gregory had hired her, if she was being honest. It felt wonderful.

All they had to do was settle their bags in one of the upstairs suites (it would be a little warm, but Jerry opened the windows and got a breeze blowing through) and then come downstairs. There, they could peacefully sit at the kitchen bar and watch Eddie take over the old lodge kitchen, press-ganging Noah into service as sous chef. Although he did first spend roughly two minutes yelling loudly and hugging them when Alanna told him they were engaged.

Jes poured the wine while Eddie prepared appetizers; they gave Jerry a raised eyebrow when he gestured for them to skip him, but didn't say anything. A minute or so later, he got up and circled around to slip into the kitchen, deftly avoiding Eddie and Noah at the stove.

"Don't touch the cheese," Eddie ordered, as Jerry opened the refrigerator door.

"I try not to touch anything in here, this fridge is older than the lodge. It was probably here first," Jerry said, taking out a bottle of orange juice. "Mind if I pilfer some?"

"Go ahead," Michaelis said.

"Learn some new cocktail recipes in Galia?" Jes asked.

"Oddly enough, no," Jerry said, coming to the bar, facing Alanna, who passed him his wine glass. "They're all crazy for Eddie's Davzda cocktails. Taught them your new pomegranate soda one, in fact."

"Nice to be a legend in my own time," Eddie said, tending to the sauce that was bubbling on the stove. Jerry filled his glass halfway with juice, sliding it back across the bar. Alanna took it and put it at his place.

"I'm mostly off alcohol these days, you know," Jerry said casually, putting the orange juice away. "Never was a fan of wine."

Alanna beamed at him, but he was hiding his face in the fridge; when he finally did emerge, he caught her eye and nodded before dodging around Eddie to get back to his seat.

"Wine or not," Gregory said, holding up his glass, "a toast to Jerry and Alanna, who managed to overthrow a government and get engaged in under two weeks. I can't fault your efficiency."

"And on that note, prepare for your first course of challah bruschetta alla Theophile," Eddie said, taking a pan of toasted bread slices out of the oven and beginning to plate the food. Jerry slid an arm around Alanna's waist and she pressed her hand over his, twisting his signet ring around his finger.

That night, lying in the slightly undersized guest bed in the breeze-cooled suite, listening to the soft clatter of Michaelis and Jes doing the last of the tidying-away downstairs, Jerry pulled her up against his side, kissed her hair, and said, "I'm going to do my very best not to kick you away in the night, but I'm sometimes a restless sleeper."

"I promise not to take it personally," Alanna said. "You realize this is the first full night we get to spend together? In a guest suite at the fishing lodge, on a bed that I'm going to have replaced as soon as I'm back in the office."

"Better than my place," he said. "A dozen Shivadh Hunthunds yelping around outside and all my ancestors glaring down at us."

"And my apartment would have been desolate, after the last two weeks," she said. "Better to have family around, just for tonight. Very proud of you, by the way."

"For what?" he asked, amused.

"Orange juice at dinner."

"You took it well enough, thought I'd press my luck," he said.

"Gregory didn't blink," she told him. "Nobody did, really. Bet you this time next week Eddie's cooked up a dozen mocktails from what he knows of your tastes."

"I won't say no," he said. He ran his free hand over his face, then up into his hair. "Speaking of."

"Speaking of," she repeated, when he was silent.

"I genuinely don't want to make this your job," he said. "But…if you want to. If you'd like to tell Greg. About the ADHD stuff. Maybe Uncle Mike too? And that it's okay for them to tell people if they want. I don't mind, I just…don't really need to have that conversation." He turned his head to rest his chin against her forehead. "If that's okay. It doesn't have to be. You don't have to, I mean."

She nodded, tapping her fingers against his chest. "Yeah. It's fine. I'll let them know. I won't make a big deal out of it."

"Gregory probably will anyway," he sighed.

"Well, he is Shivadh."

It wasn't Gregory in the end, though. It was Michaelis who, a few days later, caught Jerry as he was leaving breakfast at the palace.

"Do you have time for a walk?" he asked, and Jerry frowned at him, perplexed. "Now or later. I'll be around today."

"I can do now," Jerry said. "Why are we walking?"

Michaelis just tipped his head in the direction of the side entrance, the one that let out near the lake. Jerry followed, neither of them walking particularly quickly, Michaelis ambling and seeming to gather his thoughts.

"I had a word with Alanna," he said, after a while. "Once things calmed down after we returned from Galia. About how things went while you were there."

"Is this the shovel talk?" Jerry asked, and Michaelis frowned.

"The what?"

"It's slang. Is this where you threaten me if I hurt her?"

"Ah. No, Alanna's capable of managing you if anyone is," Michaelis said. "Besides, if I thought you were going to hurt her, I'd strike first."

"That's..." Jerry searched for a word. "Proactive of you."

"I do what I can. No, this is somewhat the opposite, in a way."

"How so?"

Michaelis put his hands in his pockets, frown deepening. "I think, Gerald, I owe you an apology."

"An apology? For what?"

"When you were younger, when your father was still alive – Eitan and I weren't especially close. He was so much older than I was, and we had rather different upbringings, which affected how we raised our own children. I knew you weren't getting the same kind of parenting as Gregory was. But we also knew you had two competent parents, and you were clearly bright and well cared-for. Between the country, and

Gregory, and Alanna after the accident – Miranda and I didn't pay as much attention as we should have."

"I didn't expect any extra attention," Jerry said.

"No, why would you? You were a child, you didn't know to expect it. Doesn't mean you shouldn't have had it," Michaelis said. Jerry considered this, and it struck him that this was a different conversation than the one he'd expected. He stopped walking, struck by it.

"This is about the ADHD," he said.

"Alanna – perhaps rightly – observed that if I had paid more attention, you wouldn't have had to figure it out yourself, alone, at the age of thirty," Michaelis said, stopping as well and turning to face him.

"I asked her to tell you, not give you a damn moral lecture – "

"She feels protective of you. There's nothing bad in that, Gerald. Extremely good quality in a partner, in moderation."

Jerry kicked a rock off the path. "She said she wouldn't make a big deal out of it."

"Then nobody should have told me, an infamous lover of drama," Michaelis said with a smile. "She isn't wrong. If I'd known then what I know now, I would have done things differently. I certainly would have taken more of an interest in your grades at school. Rather than only taking an interest in your mistakes afterward."

"I knew it was because you cared, though. I never thought you…you know, didn't like me or whatever," Jerry said, gesturing large enough that he knew, really, he was flailing.

"Hm." Michaelis regarded him. "That's good. Considering what I do know now, I think you should hear this anyway: I'm sorry we didn't do better for you. And I'm very proud you've done so well regardless."

Jerry felt his face heat, looking away to try and hide it. "Well. Thanks, I guess."

Michaelis, mercifully, let him have the moment; he walked on, turning on a gentle arc back towards the palace, and didn't speak again until Jerry caught up.

"In any case, she mentioned your new interest in agriculture," Michaelis said when Jerry joined him, as if they were picking up where they'd left off on some other conversation. "I thought I should remind you that what resources I have are at your disposal. Politically and as your uncle. I'd like to hear about your work, if you have the time. It sounds like you're experimenting with techniques that Gregory should bring to the agricultural cabinet – "

"*Great for tomatoes,*" Jerry chimed in, and Michaelis chuckled.

"I enjoy the fact that Theophile thinks we don't know that's actually a joke about growing marijuana," he said.

"Uncle Mike!"

"Don't tell him. I'm seeing how long I can stretch the joke before he works it out," Michaelis said. He regarded Jerry sidelong as they walked. "Have you and Alanna thought about how a marriage would impact the estates? Unless one of you gives up a title, you're going to unite them unavoidably. Not necessarily a bad thing, but it could grow complicated, legally speaking. Especially if you have children."

"Was that a hint?" Jerry asked, grinning.

"While I would love nothing more, I'm focusing my efforts on Gregory and Theophile right now," Michaelis replied. "Enjoy the margin Gregory has bought you."

"I usually do. As for the estates, I've been looking at some options for mine. Nothing I've talked to Alanna about yet, but I will eventually, before I do anything. I have to get the new plans in place first. Have to pitch it to my mother, too. But I'm thinking of collectivizing. Incorporating the estate as a holding company and splitting stakes among the staff."

"That would destroy the duchy as we know it," Michaelis said.

"Who cares? The land would still be there, and more useful than it is now. I'd still have my title. Some of the staff have been working there for generations, since before the duchy was even established. The longer I look at it, the more I think it's not mine to own."

"You'd give it all up?" Michaelis asked. "Twelve generations of your people on that land?"

"Yep," Jerry said simply. Michaelis was quiet as they walked.

"You'll have to make sure the workers are protected," he said finally. "Limits on stakeholding. Nobody can own a majority stake or form a bloc majority. But done properly, it would be a great step for the country. And as you say, there's no reason you couldn't keep the title. Or get yourself a new one. Gregory minted one for Theophile."

"I could be Duke of the Horseshit," Jerry said, and Michaelis let out a bark of laughter.

EPILOGUE

THE KINGS OF Askazer-Shivadlakia did not, by preference, work on the weekends. Even Gregory, who liked his work and had a young politician's drive to overachieve, tried to arrange life so that his time was free for his family.

Still, sometimes it was unavoidable. If they were going to push through the bond deal, with Askazer-Shivadlakia and its neighbors helping Galia get back on its feet, he was going to have to make a few sacrifices. Ofelia, at least, tried to be as efficient as possible.

"I know it's a handshake deal," Gregory said that Saturday morning, leaning back in his chair and studying the ceiling, phone on the desk next to him. "Earliest I can get any kind of complete documentation to you will be Wednesday. But if you're ready to push the bond sale on Monday, the cash from the Shivadh government to cover sixty percent of the investment will be there. We're representing four separate smaller nations with that amount, I do expect France to try and pick up some leftovers, and Italy's documented they'll cover whatever we don't. So if I screw this up I'm on the hook with them, too, because they'll be overinvesting. I'm very motivated not to screw it up."

"I think a handshake deal with Askazer-Shivadlakia is sound," Ofelia said over speakerphone. "We appreciate your help too much to waste your time, Gregory. We can open the sale on Monday as planned."

"In that case, congratulations, Your Grace – on Monday afternoon we will be united by something even stronger than marriage or children."

"Cash," Ofelia said, with exaggerated relish. "And I won't keep you – I know how Alanna values your weekend brunches."

Gregory checked the clock. "Ah – thank you. Say hi to Milo and Bruno for me. They should try to get here for a visit before summer ends; we'll take them to the best beaches."

"I'm sure they'll enjoy that. Ciao."

"Ciao, Duchessa," he replied, and hung up the phone, shoving it into his pocket as he hurried down the hall.

He could hear the royal family at brunch long before he reached the dining room. Generally Alanna was one of the more well-behaved brunchers, but Eddie did have a knack for setting her off, and he could hear her lecturing him about some food or other.

"I am not responsible for the fact that every language in this part of the world steals from all the other languages and none of them have more than five words for breakfast pastry," she was saying.

"Croissant, brioche, danish," Jerry began listing. "Cornetto – ooh, baguette – "

"Not a pastry," Michaelis said, voice a low rumble even under Jerry's.

"But you eat it at breakfast," Jerry said.

"We're not talking about bread for breakfast, she specifically said pastry."

"Wait, what's the difference?" Noah asked.

"Between a bread and a pastry?" Eddie said, as Gregory reached the doorway. He leaned against the door jamb, unnoticed for the moment, watching the debate rage.

"This is going to get into the area of 'what is a sandwich' very quickly," Jes said.

Eddie began ticking things off on his fingers, clearly searching his memory for some culinary class in his past. "Fat ratios, amount of gluten, amount of water – texture, but that's really based on the other three – oh, pastries sometimes have fillings."

Odd how the heart could beat a little faster, Gregory thought, just watching someone you loved be pedantic about something.

"So do some breads," Alanna said. She was leaning against Jerry, his arm slung over her shoulders. One of her hands rested on his, twisting his signet ring around on his finger. "Anyway, this is missing the point, I cannot be blamed for the fact that brioche means a different kind of food in every town in Italy."

"They probably do it just to annoy the French," Michaelis said. "Given what we do to annoy the French, I can't fault Italians for that."

"What do we do to annoy the French? All I've ever done is buy their chocolate," Jerry said.

"Institutionally. We're flagrant anglophones right on their border," Michaelis said. "And they're very mad Gregory's cut them out of the formal bond deal with Galia."

"I did it just to annoy them," Gregory said. The reaction was both swift and gratifying; his father looked over and smiled a welcome at him, eyes lighting up, and Alanna and Jerry both waved him into the dining room. Eddie scooted to make room next to himself, and Jes gave him a nod while Noah hovered, wanting to sit on his other side. He helped himself to a scone and a cup of coffee and settled in next to Eddie, bumping him with an elbow affectionately.

"Bonds all stitched up?" Jerry asked, picking at the last of a croissant (possibly a brioche).

"Yes – the wire transfer's set for Monday morning, paperwork to follow, as soon as the bonds are legal," Gregory said. "That reminds me," he added, taking an envelope from his pocket and handing it to Noah. "Thanks for doing the podcast about the Galian infrastructure bonds. It really did help get people on board."

"Whoa," Noah said, unfolding the onionskin sheet inside the envelope. It entitled the bearer to one hundred Galian liry at two percent interest, payable after ten years minimum. "Is this what they actually look like?"

"Technically it has no face value. It's just a souvenir," Gregory said, accepting a brief sideways hug from the boy. "But the digital bond'll be in your name tomorrow, and Ofelia understands the power of an elaborate document."

"Look, there she is," Jerry said, leaning over to point out her portrait in the intricate series of engravings around the border. "There's Milo, nice to see him getting credit for setting it all up. And Gregory, because he brokered it. Ugh, Riva. Suppose they had to put him on there to shut the old man up."

"At least he seems to have accepted Ofelia as his fate," Alanna said.

"Ah, look, there's Athena," Jerry added, indicating the little prowling tiger in one corner. Noah swept crumbs off the table and spread the bond out so he could go over it in detail; Jerry sat back so Michaelis could lean in and explain the terms printed above the engraving to Noah, who was still in a beginner's Italian class. Eddie tugged Gregory gently away so he could wrap his arm around his waist, and Gregory let his whole weight rest on him, relaxing.

"Not bad work for a Saturday," he said to Eddie, watching the others. "And a good reward to come back to."

"Yeah? Not mad I divided the room with questions about brioche?"

"They look like they've recovered," Gregory said. He rested his head against Eddie's, pleased with his little family – happy, safe, mostly sane, all together in one place. "Glad you're here with me."

"Yeah, me too," Eddie agreed. "Second luckiest bastard on the planet, me."

"Oh yeah? Who's the luckiest?"

"You," Eddie said, grinning at him.

"Sure," Gregory agreed, the last of the morning's stress bleeding away. "No argument here."

Annotation & decoration by Gerald
(ben Eitan Dux Shivadlakia)

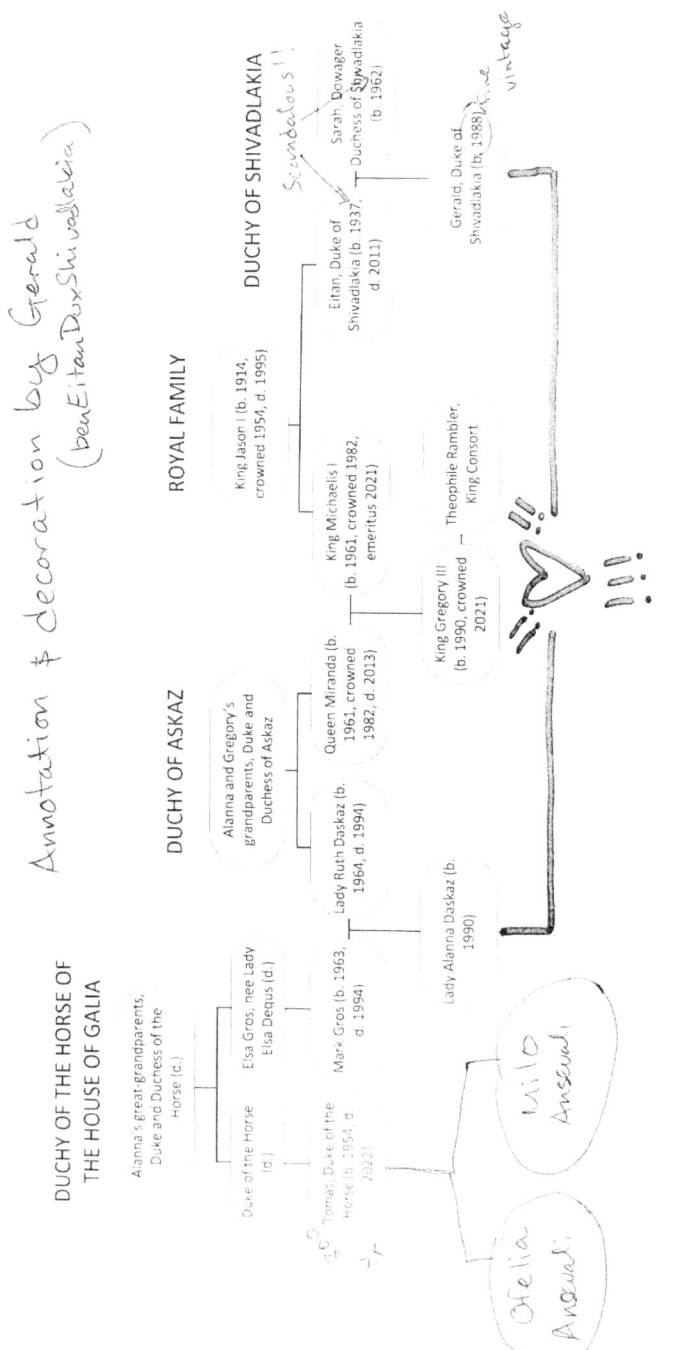

DUCHY OF THE HORSE OF THE HOUSE OF GALIA

Alanna's great-grandparents, Duke and Duchess of the Horse (d.)

- Duke of the Horse (d.)
- Elsa Gros, née Lady Elsa Dequs (d.)
- Mark Gros (b. 1963, d. 1994)
- 9° Tomas, Duke of the Horse (b. 1954, d. 2022) Jr

- Milo Anseul
- Ofelia Anqual

DUCHY OF ASKAZ

Alanna and Gregory's grandparents, Duke and Duchess of Askaz

- Lady Ruth Daskaz (b. 1964, d. 1994)
- Queen Miranda (b. 1961, crowned 1982, d. 2013)
- Lady Alanna Daskaz (b. 1990)

ROYAL FAMILY

- King Jason I (b. 1914, crowned 1954, d. 1995)
- King Michaelis I (b. 1961, crowned 1982, emeritus 2021)
- King Gregory III (b. 1990, crowned 2021) — Theophile Rambier, King Consort

DUCHY OF SHIVADLAKIA

Scandalous!!

- Eitan, Duke of Shivadlakia (b. 1937, d 2011)
- Sarah, Dowager Duchess of Shivadlakia (b. 1962)
- Gerald, Duke of Shivadlakia (b. 1988) the vintage

CONTENT WARNINGS:
This listing is to the best of my ability and made in good faith.

- Brief mentions of parental death (Chapter One); Alanna's parents passed when she was young and the specifics are occasionally referenced.
- Discussion of potential drug misuse (Chapter Five); Alanna discovers Jerry is taking Adderall and confronts him, assuming he's taking it as a party drug. Jerry reveals that it is prescribed medication for previously-undiagnosed ADHD, but he discovered his ADHD while using Ritalin as a party drug.
- Discussion of alcohol misuse (Chapter Five and onwards); Jerry mentions some issues he had with alcohol prior to his diagnosis, his process for easing off use, and whether or not he is considered "sober". Throughout, he entertains himself by pretending his mocktails are actually cocktails to everyone else.
- Discussion of neurodiversity (Chapter Five and onwards); Jerry has chosen to keep his ADHD diagnosis from his family and expresses some attitudes, his and others, surrounding it that aren't entirely healthy. Chapter Six includes a description of what could be considered a sensory overload episode; Chapter Ten has a brief but emotional discussion of parenting issues surrounding neurodiversity, mainly positive in outcome.
- Brief discussion of food issues (Chapter Six); Gregory mentions Jerry used to stop eating when he was homesick at school for brief periods.
- Bullying scene (Chapter Seven); Jerry is angry at Milo and lashes out inappropriately in a way Alanna explicitly describes as bullying towards Milo. He later makes a full apology and it's clear that Milo, while not enjoying it, also knew it wasn't really about him, so there is no lasting trauma.
- Surprise paternity reveal (Chapter Eight); the reveal of a parent's identity leads to uncomfortable feelings for various parties.